FORTUNE'S PROMISE

SUE JOHNSON

TOADSTONE PRESS

© Sue Johnson 2017

Sue Johnson has asserted her rights under the Copyright, Design and Patents Act, 1988, to be identified as the author of this work.

First published by Endeavour Press Ltd in 2017.

This edition published by Toadstone Press 2019.
ISBN: 978-1-912869-09-1

FORTUNE'S PROMISE

SUE JOHNSON

Prologue

December 1811

The night was painted silver. Lucinda Beckford, leaving home to attend her first ball, gazed at the frost-sparkled road lit by the glow of the full moon as the carriage made its way to The Grange.

Lucinda was dressed in blue muslin that echoed the colour of her eyes. The gown was trimmed with silver and the same ribbon had been woven through her dark hair. A fizzy feeling of excitement danced in Lucinda's stomach and she smiled at her father, sitting on the opposite side of the carriage.

"It's good to see you smile, my dear," he said. "I hope tonight will be the first of many such happy occasions."

The clip-clop of the horses' hooves echoed into the darkness as the carriage turned into the narrow lane that led to The Grange. They found themselves in a line of carriages and Lucinda hugged herself with excitement as she saw the magical-looking house drawing closer. Candlelight shone from every window, echoing the colour of the moonlight, and Lucinda felt as if she was entering an enchanted palace.

The Midwinter Ball, held every year by local lawyer Ambrose Leitch, was done so with the aim of banishing the gloom of winter.

Ambrose was a rich man and no expense was spared to make the Ball a spectacular occasion. Hot-house flowers graced every alcove, adding their perfume to the mixture already crowding the ballroom. A group of musicians played lively dance tunes and the dancers whirled around the floor under the watchful eye of their chaperones.

On the supper table pyramids of glace fruits, looking as if they'd been painted by moonlight, stood alongside other delicacies on silver-rimmed plates, with the piece de resistance being a spectacular cake decorated with the sort of flowers Lucinda could imagine being in a fairy-tale garden.

Servants moved amongst the guests offering delicious looking drinks in sugar-frosted glasses.

Many people said the event was as successful as a London season where finding marriage partners were concerned.

When she arrived, Lucinda had waited with a group of other girls, all dressed in a sugared almond assortment of colours, waiting to greet her host.

Standing next to Ambrose Leitch at the foot of the curved wooden staircase was a young man with dark brown hair and eyes the colour of Madeira wine.

"My new clerk Reuben Turner," said Ambrose. "He has newly arrived in Marchington from London."

Lucinda, glancing at Reuben over her fan, suddenly knew what people meant when they talked about love at first sight. It was as if an invisible thread bound them together and all she needed to do was wait.

They danced together twice and then she found herself next to him at supper. The spark between them was obvious to everyone in the room. A group of chaperones were heard to say that there'd be a wedding before the year was out.

"The gardens look like fairyland don't they," Reuben said when he saw Lucinda gazing at the magical landscape illuminated by flaming torches.

She'd smiled at him, wanting to say that she hoped his attention wasn't part of the enchantment, but not wanting to seem too forward.

"Promise you won't disappear in a puff of smoke when midnight strikes?" he asked.

"I was going to ask the same question," she said, casting her eyes down demurely.

When they'd said farewell at the end of the ball, Lucinda was sure this was the beginning of something special. She'd lain in her bedroom in Orchard House watching the same stars that had hung over The Grange gardens, feeling too excited to sleep, reliving every look, every touch and every word they had shared.

She was not disappointed. Further invitations ensured that she and Reuben saw a lot of each other at dinners, local dances and in church. As many people in Marchington observed, they only had eyes for each other. As was also observed, Lucinda's mother had been barely seventeen when she'd set her sights on Josiah Beckford and married him, despite opposition from her guardian. Contrary to expectation, it had been a happy union until Caroline had died from childbed fever following the birth of her seventh child three years previously.

It followed that Lucinda was likely to be just as decisive where choosing a marriage partner was concerned, and the whispers around the town said that it wouldn't be long before an engagement was announced.

However, public opinion didn't stay long in their favour when Lucinda was seen talking to Reuben unchaperoned outside the milliner's shop in Marchington. Widow Parker, the owner of the shop lost no time in calling on Josiah Beckford to discuss his daughter's conduct.

"I'm calling on you out of Christian charity," she said, sitting primly on the edge of an upright chair. "Motherless girls like Lucinda need guidance in matters of romance." She lowered her voice for dramatic effect. "There are rumours of a possible elopement."

Lucinda, eavesdropping on the conversation through the loose floorboard in one of the guest bedrooms that she and her brother John had discovered one wet day when they were playing indoors, fumed silently until Widow Parker had departed in a flurry of stale peppermint and mothballs.

Lucinda stormed downstairs and confronted her father. "How dare that woman say such things about me, father? Why did you not stand up for me? Reuben and I were not planning to elope! That wasn't true."

"A woman's reputation is the most important thing she possesses, Lucinda," Josiah said. "There was nothing I could say."

Reuben had promptly proposed as soon as he heard of the rumours circulating, but Josiah Beckford had counselled delay, repeating the old adage 'marry in haste, repent at leisure.'

"If I sanction your marriage now, then people are going to think there is some substance behind Widow Parker's accusations of improper conduct."

"They can think what they like, father. I don't care," said Lucinda.

"Well, I do. I'll not stand by and force my daughter into a hole-in-the corner marriage. If you both still feel the same six months hence, then I'll give my whole-hearted approval to the match." Josiah's face was stern.

"Six months…," wailed Lucinda.

"Is no time at all," said Josiah briskly. "I have discussed the matter with Ambrose Leitch and he agrees with me. Reuben is to work in London for a while dealing with the affairs of a widow."

"He might meet somebody else…,"

"If he does, then it proves my point that it was worth waiting to see if his intentions were truly honourable."

Lucinda had flounced up to her room and flung herself on her bed in an agony of despair.

There had been time only for the briefest of farewells before Reuben caught the Mail Coach from *The King's Head.* They'd stood awkwardly in Josiah's study, Lucinda feeling close to tears and Reuben looking pale and nervous. "I'll come back to you, Lucinda," were his last words to her before he hurried out of the door.

Chapter 1

July 1812

Lucinda had counted the weeks until Reuben was expected to return. She'd applied herself to collecting china and linen for her bottom drawer and planning what she would wear for her wedding day. In her quiet moments, she went over everything he'd said to her, examining every glance and brief conversation, every touch of his hand during the dances they'd shared and when he'd led her into supper.

She took to loitering around Ambrose's office in the main street, walking slowly on her way to the grocery shop or to pay the bill at the butcher's in the hope that she could accidentally bump into him and then casually ask for news.

She sensed that on these occasions he took pity on her and fed her titbits of information about Reuben. On one occasion he showed her a letter Reuben had sent reporting on his progress in which he asked for his best wishes to be passed on to Lucinda. She hugged these words close to her, counting the days now until he returned. Then, just as she was almost at the point of watching the arrival of every Mail Coach from London, she heard a rumour – something that caused a spiral of fear to rise inside her.

"I wonder if Miss Beckford's been told the news yet?"

Lucinda was looking at ribbons in the milliner's shop, hoping that her friend Hannah might be able to squeeze a few spare minutes to talk to her. She begrudged buying from Widow Parker – the woman who had spread the initial rumours – but there was no other shop in Marchington that sold ribbon.

The speaker was Ambrose Leitch's housekeeper – a thin, rat-like woman who was always on the look-out for gossip. She was talking to Widow Parker, her close companion, who nudged her and nodded in Lucinda's direction.

Lucinda left the shop immediately, the bell giving a sharp 'ping.' She hurried across to Ambrose Leitch's office – all thoughts of modesty and propriety gone. She waited by his desk for five agonising minutes while he read a document, signed and sanded it and gave it to one of the clerks for folding and sealing.

Eventually he looked up.

Lucinda bobbed a curtsey. "Please sir, can you tell me what news I'm supposed to have heard?"

He rose to his feet, gave a polite bow. "I'm sorry, Miss Beckford, but I'm unable to speak with you at this moment. I have an appointment to attend. I will call on your father within the hour."

He hurried past her, a distracted look on his plump face.

Lucinda emerged onto the street, her anxious feelings making her legs feel heavy as lead.

She was thankful to see her friend Hannah, escaped from Widow Parker's shop on an errand.

"What's the matter, Lucinda? Your face is white as milk."

"What is this news that I'm supposed to have heard?" Lucinda caught her breath. "Oh Hannah, you don't think he could've married someone else?"

"I'm sure that's not so, Lucinda." Hannah's freckled face was creased with concern. "It may just be that he's been delayed by further work. There can be no doubt of his true feelings for you."

"So why is Mr Leitch intending to call on my father? Why would he not tell me anything?"

For once, Hannah had no answer. They hugged each other and Lucinda headed home to wait.

"You'd be best to take your feelings out on that lump of bread dough," said Mrs Parsons, the cook. "Like a cat on hot bricks you are, Miss Lucinda!"

Lucinda had arrived home feeling unable to settle to even the simplest task, and passed the long slow minutes waiting for the arrival of Ambrose Leitch by prowling around the house like an animal in a cage.

Lucinda did indeed find that her feelings were soothed by kneading the dough, but then it occurred to her that if she remained in the kitchen which was at the back of the house, she may miss the arrival of Ambrose Leitch. She washed her hands and went upstairs to tidy herself in preparation for his visit.

*

As soon as Ambrose Leitch arrived, Lucinda hurried downstairs to find that Ambrose and Josiah were ensconced in the study and the door was firmly closed. She was obviously not being invited to the meeting.

When she was a child, Lucinda had had free access to this room, sitting under her father's desk while he worked and listening to the sounds of the household around her, absorbing the smells of tobacco, leather and beeswax polish that she associated with his room. When she was very small he would sit her on his lap and she could listen to the ticking of his half-hunter watch on its silver chain.

Since she'd grown up, and particularly following the death of her mother, she'd tended to go in there only to help with any letters that needed writing. She still loved the study best of any room in the house, apart from her own room, because it represented happiness and security.

Lucinda was not deterred by the closed door. She crept up the stairs, so as not to disturb Mrs Parsons and Tilly the maid, who were preparing the evening meal amongst a lot of clashing of pots and pans. Even so, she was careful to avoid treading on the third stair from the top that creaked. From the sounds above her, she could tell that her brother John had escaped from his duties in the brewery and was busy painting in one of the attic rooms occupied by servants in the days when the family had more of them. The smell of paint and turpentine drifted down the stairs and Lucinda could understand why Tilly, who slept in one of the other attic rooms, complained.

Lucinda headed into the guest room, where six months previously she'd eavesdropped on her father's conversation with Widow Parker. She closed the bedroom door, hurried across the room and lifted the rug and the loose floorboard underneath and was able, by half lying on the floor in what would be seen in polite society as a most undignified position, to see down into her father's study. The view of the room was patchy - the top of Ambrose Leitch's neat grey wig and her father's unruly dark hair threaded with silver, seated either side of the familiar conker brown desk, the corner of a picture frame, a scrap of the brown and orange rag rug in front of the fireplace.

The words were clear and what she heard chilled her heart.

"I trust your daughter won't be too distressed at this news." Ambrose Leitch's voice was smooth as cream from a pitcher.

Josiah waved the suggestion away as if swatting a fly. "It's my guess she's already forgotten him. I'm only thankful the marriage didn't take place. Seventeen is too young to be a widow."

Lucinda wished she could wind the clock back to the minutes before she came up the stairs. It was true indeed that eavesdroppers never heard any good of themselves. She put the floorboard and rug back in place and sat on the bed, hoping that if she stayed still she'd keep Reuben safe.

She startled Tilly who'd come upstairs with a pile of freshly laundered sheets for the linen cupboard in that room. "Good heavens Miss Lucinda, you startled me. What be you doing there sitting like a ghost? Are you ill, Miss? Can I fetch you anything?"

Lucinda shook her head. "I need to speak to my father."

"Mr Leitch has just left, Miss."

Lucinda hurried downstairs on legs that felt like she was recovering from a fever. Her heartbeat thudded in her ears and she felt as if she were about to lose her balance.

"Lucinda – whatever is the matter?" Josiah asked, clearly startled at the way she burst into his study.

She hesitated, not wanting her father to know she'd been eavesdropping.

"I want to know when Reuben's coming back."

Her father drew in a deep breath.

"Father?"

"I'm sorry to be the bearer of bad tidings, Lucinda, but Ambrose brought word that Reuben was taken ill of a fever in London and died last Tuesday."

"His funeral…" Lucinda's throat felt raw.

"Has already taken place," said Josiah. "The nature of the illness dictated that this was necessary. Ambrose attended and has collected his personal effects from his lodging house."

Lucinda stood, feeling numb, as if she was in the middle of a bad dream.

"There will be plenty of other young men falling at your feet, Lucinda," said her father gently. "Don't waste your young life in mourning somebody who was not worthy of you."

Lucinda got to her feet, feeling as if all she wanted to do was go to sleep and stay there for a hundred years.

"Young men can fall at my feet as much as they like, father. I shall never marry."

Chapter 2

July 1812

On the outskirts of Salamanca on the Peninsula, the sun was setting in a spectacular colour-wash of red, orange and gold as army physician Adam Lennox washed the blood from his hands after yet another futile attempt to save a soldier's life. The young man in question had wanted nothing more than to go home to his sweetheart.

"Lucy will be waiting for me," he said dreamily, turning eyes the colour of violets towards Adam. His lips were dry and cracked and his skin burned with fever.

Adam had nodded, pressing the young man's hand to reassure him, knowing as he did so that there was no prospect of the soldier living beyond the next few minutes. The young man's right leg had been blown away and too long a time had elapsed before a medical orderly could reach him. The stump was ragged, with shreds of torn flesh already caked in dust and black with flies.

The sun burned down on a terracotta landscape where every drop of water was precious. The air smelled of blood and hot metal and echoed with the screams and cries of injured men.

Even now, battle hardened, Adam still found it hard to accept the damage one man could inflict on another. He'd thought following the army would help take his mind off the unending grief he felt inside – but situations such as this only made it worse.

"We're to be married…," the voice had faded to a whisper, the words disjointed and the soldier's violet-coloured eyes less bright.

A lump caught in Adam's throat. Those eyes reminded him of another death two years before, when eyes like violets had looked at him equally trustingly – and there had been nothing he could do to save her life either. They had belonged to Amelia, the woman he'd loved above all others and would have gladly given his life for.

Amelia had died two years ago, just as the morning sun spread a pink and gold glow across the sky. She had been tricked into marrying his cousin Giles, who had then abused her, taken her fortune and discarded her.

When Adam had returned from visiting a sick friend in London to the news that Amelia was to marry his cousin and not him, he'd been devastated. His immediate thought was to leave England and he got as far as packing his saddlebags. However, he quickly realised that Giles was up to his usual unpleasant tricks and that Amelia might need him more than ever. He prayed daily that she would find the courage to leave Giles and come to him. Fear and remorse had kept Amelia silent for too long, and by the time she did rebel she wasn't strong enough to escape. Giles had her committed to the asylum and had incriminated Adam in the plot.

Adam had found her, consigned to a filthy room in an asylum out in the country, crammed in with several other wretches at various stages of insanity. By then it was too late to do more than have her moved into a private room and a bed with clean sheets. He'd sat with her all night, hoping for a miracle, but she'd died in his arms as dawn broke on the saddest day of his life.

"I'll always love you, Adam," were the last words she spoke.

He'd sat there for hours holding her in his arms, until the Superintendent had informed him that Giles, as next of kin, was on his way. With a final kiss on her cold lips, Adam had left her, riding out into a morning that had lost its brightness.

That was why he'd fled England to offer his services to the army, in the hope that he'd find the bullet that would release him from this life.

As he closed the eyes of the young soldier, he felt a stab of envy, knowing he would willingly have changed places with him in order to be reunited with Amelia.

The only thing keeping him focused towards the future was the knowledge that one day he would return to

England, confront his cousin Giles, and avenge Amelia's memory.

He turned away as the orderlies dealt with the body. He'd not stayed for Amelia's funeral because he knew if he'd had to witness Giles acting the part of the grieving widower, he would have killed him with his bare hands.

Adam headed towards his tent, giving curt nods to those who acknowledged him. He didn't want to engage in conversation with anybody about the progress of the war or anything else. His heart was too full of sorrow.

The colours of the sky were fading like the dying embers of a fire, and darkness was closing in. The whine of the stray bullet when it came was like the answer to a prayer.

Chapter 3

February 1813

Giles Milburn was well used to his father's subterfuges. It was typical of him to take to his bed at a time when Giles needed his help – his money, to be more precise. For Giles was down on his luck again. Only the thought of being sent to prison had sent him back to beg his father for help.

When he arrived at Foxton Lodge, he charmed the maidservant into letting him in and asked for his father to be informed that he had arrived. He hadn't expected to be welcomed with open arms, but neither had he expected to be left waiting in the cheerless parlour.

The fire was unlit and the room, with windows on two sides of it giving views of the dreary February shrubbery, was icy cold.

By the time his father's manservant, Digby, arrived Giles was simmering with frustration.

"Your father is indisposed," said Digby, flicking at an invisible speck on a chair with the white cloth he always carried.

Giles was well used to the way the man always managed to make him feel like he'd crawled out from under a stone.

"I must speak to him." Giles tried to keep his voice level and not sound desperate.

"He has been expecting you to call." Digby looked down his long nose at Giles. He did not move.

"Then tell him I'm here, man." Giles was fast losing patience but knew he needed to keep Digby on his side or he would end up with nothing.

"Very good, Mr Giles, I will see what I can do."

Giles listened to Digby's slow footsteps heading along the hall and then resumed his pacing around the room.

His father was notorious for not heating rooms that he wasn't using, even on a raw February day such as this. Giles was sure this was what had contributed to his mother Maria's early death from consumption. A portrait

13

of her hung over the fireplace. Giles moved closer to look at it. Her hair was dark, held back from her face by tortoiseshell combs, and her eyes were as dark as the sherry wine his father imported from Spain and the Canary Islands. He wondered what she'd think of the current battles taking place across her native country.

Maria Milburn was rumoured to have been a Spanish dancer, although nobody would dare to say it to her face. It was also rumoured that William Milburn had acquired her when he was on one of his voyages to Spain and the Canary Islands to buy sherry and Madeira wine. It was whispered that one of the merchants, unable to settle his debts, had offered his daughter in part payment – and William, noticing the passionate gleam in Maria's dark eyes, had gladly accepted.

Despite the difference in backgrounds, their union had been happy. Maria had adapted well to life in England and had enjoyed having a house of her own instead of having to share a small overcrowded one with her large family. She'd been quick to learn English, although she never lost her Spanish accent, and had presented William with two live children – and three who had not survived beyond infancy.

An icy blast came down the chimney and Giles moved away to the window where the curtains stirred slightly in the draught. A white mist hung over the countryside carrying a chill that ate into the bones. He could do with a hot drink or a bowl of broth to warm him but so far no refreshment had been offered. He was tempted to help himself from the meagre amount of brandy left in the decanter on the sideboard, but knew Digby would notice if he did. Hunger and cold gnawed at his insides and made his anxiety for the future worse. He was down to his last few shillings and desperately needed a change of fortune.

He looked at the shabby furnishings in the room that had once been his mother's pride and joy. His father had refused to change anything after she died so the yellow and cream chair covers and curtains were threadbare and in need of loving care. Giles wondered what his sister Georgiana did with her time, apart from tormenting the grooms. She certainly didn't appear to do much around the house.

The terrace and shrubbery outside the French windows looked hostile and unfriendly, very much like the atmosphere inside the house. Skeletal black trees loomed out of the mist. The long-case clock in the hall chimed the hour and Digby appeared like a gloomy spectre.

"The master will see you now. Please do not tire him too much. He is awaiting his physician."

Giles followed Digby up the stairs to the room on the first floor that had been the scene of several interviews with his father. The other doors opening off the corridor were closed.

On entering his father's room, he was surrounded by the smell of roast beef and spiced wine. The old termagant was obviously not too ill to eat – and it was patently obvious that Giles wasn't to be offered any of the feast.

His father was sitting up in bed, a fur-lined cloak around his shoulders. Even from this position he looked formidable, and Giles was reduced to feeling like a child again. He remembered the first time his father had taken to his bed – when Giles had been sent home from school for some misdemeanour or other. His mother had wept hysterically, saying that his father would surely die, they would all end up in the workhouse and it would be Giles' fault.

Since that time, he'd had a fear of poverty. He'd once walked past a workhouse and had seen the lines of paupers filing into the church on Sunday morning. He'd never forgotten the air of defeat that surrounded them. A young woman had looked at him, thrown him a beseeching look. He'd turned away. Now he was close to the same position himself, he wondered if there would be anyone to help him.

"You've been a great disappointment to me, Giles." The voice issuing from the gloomy depths of the bed was surprisingly strong. "But that is nothing new. I really hoped that when you married, despite tricking your cousin Adam in the cruellest way imaginable, that you'd married for love." He paused, taking a mouthful from a silver goblet by his bed. "It seemed that even then you were motivated by greed and were happy to ruin a beautiful young woman and break your cousin's heart."

Giles stared stonily at the red and gold pattern on the carpet. He'd wondered how long it would be before Adam was mentioned. Ever since he'd been foisted on their family at the age of seven, he'd lost no time in worming his way into his father's affections.

Giles let his father's voice wash over him like ice water as he remembered the winter's evening that Adam arrived. His father had gone to fetch the newly-orphaned boy from London. They'd arrived late. Adam was white-faced with cold and distress and wrapped in his uncle's cloak. Giles and his sister Georgiana had watched jealously through the banisters as Adam was sat by the fire and fed warm bread and milk sprinkled with nutmeg. Then he was carried up to bed in the nursery that had previously been the private domain of Giles and Georgiana.

Georgiana had hated being ejected from the bed next to Giles and placed in the small room that had once been occupied by the nursery maid. She and Giles had sworn to make the newcomer's life so miserable that he'd run away.

"Well, have you nothing to say for yourself, Giles?"

Giles was jerked abruptly back to the present. He had no idea what his father had been saying. He cleared his throat, desperately thinking of something to say that would strike the right balance.

"I thought not," said his father. "Well, let me tell you this. From now on I will no longer be responsible for your gambling debts, your unsavoury activities and your bad reputation. You are now eight and twenty – of an age to be living a responsible life. You have one year to redeem yourself. If after that time you still give me reason for concern or disappointment, then you will be written out of my will and your name will be struck from the family Bible."

Giles was too stunned to speak.

"That will be all, Giles. Here are fifty guineas to help you on your way. Digby will see you out."

He handed Giles a bag of coins, careful not to touch his fingers as he did so. The he rang the bell for Digby who arrived so quickly he must have been listening outside the door. He escorted Giles back to the stables – a sneer on his face.

"I bid you good day, sir," said Digby with a curt bow. "I trust you will have a safe journey wherever you are going."

It was obvious he didn't care where that might be.

*

Giles' sister Georgiana appeared in the stable yard while he was waiting for the groom to saddle Black Boy. Her dark green dress was inappropriately low cut for the time of day and looked creased. Her face was flushed and there was straw in her hair. She had appeared from the direction of the hayloft.

Giles looked at her with a mixture of distaste and admiration. "You look like a trollop."

"Don't call me names! I've heard tell you're not averse to a trollop or two. We all know how Sally Meadows got her baby…,"

A ringing slap from Giles that echoed round the stable yard had her reeling backwards against the wall.

Georgiana pressed her hand to her reddened cheek. "I was speaking no more than the truth. I hate you Giles, and I'll get even with you for this." Tears sparkled in her dark eyes but did not fall. "Adam would never have treated me so cruelly."

Giles glowered at her as he swung up into Black Boy's saddle. "I never want to hear his name again. I pray he's been despatched by one of Bonaparte's soldiers by now."

17

"You're jealous of him. You always were because Papa likes him better than you." Georgiana's expression was defiant.

"Enough – and the Devil take all of you." Giles turned his horse towards the gates at the end of the drive and thundered off.

*

Georgiana watched as her brother and his horse were swallowed up into the murkiness of the day, the hoofbeats muffled by the fog that covered the landscape. She stamped her foot with frustration. She'd wanted desperately to go with Giles – anywhere would be better than here as regards seeing something of the world. However, her brother's treatment of her prevented her from begging him to take her with him.

Her cheek stung in the ice-cold air and she knew they'd given the servants enough to gossip about for the next six months at least.

She retreated to the hayloft above the stables, tears of frustration pouring down her face. She and Giles used to play here as children and ever since then, it was where Georgiana went to think things over.

She climbed the rickety wooden ladder and at last found somewhere she felt safe to unleash the torrent of emotion inside her over the way Giles had treated her. She bit down on her clenched fists to stop the howls of frustration and anger being heard by the servants.

*

Oliver Gray, newly employed at Foxton Lodge and asleep in the hayloft after a night of nursing a horse with colic, awoke to find the woman of his dreams beside him. He sat up, tossing aside the thin blanket he'd wrapped himself in. He was aware of wild black hair, dishevelled attire and he wasn't sure if she was vagrant or gypsy.

"Hush, sweet, you are not meant to be here," he whispered.

As the tears and the other signs of distress didn't stop, he lay down beside her and wrapped his arms round her as he would a distressed animal. Her knuckles were raw and bleeding, the cream lace mittens she was wearing were torn to ribbons.

He wrapped his arms round tighter. She relaxed, leaned her head back against his shoulder. Her hair smelled of exotic spices. She closed her eyes and her long lashes were dark curves on her cheeks. Oliver rocked her as he would a child, certain that she must be a gypsy woman. No lady would have permitted such liberties. He turned her in his arms and touched his lips to hers.

The tears subsided and she responded to the gentle touch of his lips with a passion that surprised him.

*

To his horror he heard footsteps enter the stables below and someone rattled the ladder leading to the hayloft.

"Oliver – you awake yet?" shouted a gruff voice. "Come and look at Strawberry. She's off her feet again."

The girl sprang backwards towards the darkest corner of the hayloft, a look of alarm in her dark eyes. He put his finger to his lips.

Oliver stuffed his shirt into his breeches, pulled on his threadbare jacket and headed for the ladder.

*

As soon as she was able to escape, Georgiana climbed down from the hayloft and made her way back to her own bedroom. She lay on her bed in a state of blissful contemplation. Oliver. She said the name over and over. There she was mourning the departure of her brother when all the time the man of her dreams was here at Foxton Lodge.

She hadn't meant to be so free with him, but a strange kind of force had rippled between them and she was carried away by its magic. She hugged the secret of him to her. He could be her rebellion – the one thing her father wouldn't expect of her.

Despite what Giles thought of her, she hadn't behaved improperly before. In fact, she had a very hazy idea as to what led to the creation of children. She'd seen dogs mating of course, and the mares being put with the stallion, but this didn't seem the same as the magical feelings she'd experienced with Oliver in the hayloft. Had they done enough to create a child? Georgiana shuddered with fear at the thought, but it didn't put her off her idea. She thought of one person who would know the answers to her questions.

*

The following day Georgiana wrapped herself in an old cloak, picked up her reticule and headed towards Sandford Leaze – the rough moorland where Old Ginny lived. Georgiana hadn't been there for years – not since she was a child and she'd accompanied her mother. The common was a lonely, desolate place and most people stayed away, frightened by tales of witchcraft and sorcery. She was keen to get there and back before it grew dark.

As she trudged over the rough ground, wary as she passed little copses where charcoal burners worked, she hoped that Old Ginny was still alive. She didn't allow herself to consider what she would do if she'd died.

Nobody knew what age Old Ginny was. She'd lived in her tiny hut for as long as anyone could remember, fuelling its fire from wood found in the local copse and foraging for the herbs she used in the hedgerows. She was the one many people went to for a variety of health problems rather than consult the local physician.

Maria Milburn had consulted Old Ginny following the still-birth of her first-born child. The potion she was given obviously worked its magic because she gave birth to Giles the following year. It was to Old Ginny that Georgiana was taken when her monthlies began and caused her untold agony. Georgiana remembered the wrinkled old woman with the filthy hands and the vile stink of the hut she lived in. On that occasion she'd been questioned before being given a revolting herbal concoction to be taken every day for a month. Again, that worked and Georgiana had no further trouble.

This time as she headed towards the hut with its thin spiral of grey smoke, Georgiana wondered if Old Ginny could work her magic again.

She knocked on the door and awaited entry. Old Ginny answered quickly, as if she'd been expecting her. "Come your ways in," she said.

Georgiana stepped into the gloomy interior where a log fire spat and crackled. Orange sparks danced amongst the chokingly thick smoke. Old Ginny sat on a wooden box beside it and threw a sprinkle of what looked like salt onto the fire. The flames glowed green, blue and silver.

"You've come about a matter of the heart." Old Ginny's sloe black eyes were half closed, her claw like hands, ingrained with dirt, rested in her lap.

Georgiana said nothing.

"Your money first, then I'll examine you."

Georgiana shivered with distaste, but handed Old Ginny some coins which the old woman tested with her few remaining teeth before tucking them into the layers of clothes she wore.

She motioned Georgiana into the raised platform next to the fire that served as a bed, covered with grubby fragments of blanket and eiderdown. Georgiana lay down, recoiling from the smell of unwashed clothes and bodies. She didn't watch as the lower half of her body was poked and prodded, the old woman talking to herself and cackling as she did so.

"Methinks thee's still a maiden. Nobody's been a riding of thee – mind but you're ripe for the picking. It don't hurt to be careful."

She chuckled to herself as she hobbled back towards the fire and opened a wooden box, extracting two large handfuls of something yellow. "Tansy and ginger – to get rid of unwanted childer. Be sure to put some in boiled water and drink it three times a day – if you forget to use the sponge." She took a dried up looking object from another box and gave it to Georgiana. "Be sure to wear this next time you're with your lover. Soak it in vinegar first."

"Wear it? Where do I put it?"

"In your love nest. Where d'you think?" cackled the old woman. "Now be off with you."

Georgiana was thankful to be out of the foul-smelling hut. She gathered her cloak around herself and hurried home on shaky legs, the lower parts of her body still feeling the cold bony fingers of the old woman.

*

Georgiana wasn't the sort of person to dwell on unpleasant things for long. Memories of the strange events of the afternoon resurfaced and her body glowed as she thought of the touch of Oliver's fingers. They'd glided lightly over her skin, the pressure building until her senses were on fire and it felt as if she was spiralling away to a place beyond the stars.

She'd been so shocked after the event that she hadn't thought beyond the possibility of being with child and the unwelcome consequences. Now that she'd visited Old Ginny and been reassured, she wanted to repeat the experience as soon as she could. Reason told her that gently brought up young women didn't behave in such a way – but she was not that sort of person. She'd often heard the chaperones whisper behind their fans about her mother Maria – a poor merchant's daughter sold to Sir William for a handful of coins.

"If you are determined, you can do anything," Maria had told Georgiana.

It was this side of her make-up that came to the fore as she threw a shawl round her shoulders and headed for the stables.

She heard Oliver in Strawberry's stall talking to the horse as he worked. She stood by the ladder to the hayloft waiting until he'd finished, hoping he still wanted her as much as she wanted him. The sponge that Old Ginny had given her was in place and she hoped she didn't reek of vinegar.

He turned the corner and came face to face with her.

"Forgive me, Miss, you startled me." His face was deathly pale and he wouldn't look at her.

Georgiana didn't move.

"If you'll excuse me, Miss?" Oliver headed for the hayloft ladder.

"Wait," she said.

He stood, looking like a mouse being eyed up by a cat.

"Oliver," she said, "you like your work here?"

He nodded.

"You wish to continue working here?"

"I do, Miss."

"Do you find me beautiful?" She moved closer to him so he could not help but breathe in her musky scent.

He closed his eyes. "I did not realise who you were, Miss."

"That's obvious." Georgiana was amazed at how much she could sound like her father when the occasion demanded.

"I'll pack my things."

"You'll do no such thing."

"Miss?"

"If you wish to continue in your employment here, you will not speak of what happens between us. Do you understand?"

He nodded.

"Good." She moved towards him.

*

A plan formed in Georgiana's mind about how she could get even with Giles. She went downstairs to the desk in her father's study, found a sheet of paper and began a letter to her cousin Adam. It took her a long time because she hadn't paid much attention to her lessons, but when she'd finished a smile of satisfaction curved across her flushed face.

Chapter 4

Giles paused to check his bearings. He'd been riding for three hours and the day was closing in. The white mist covering the landscape hadn't lifted and echoed his feelings of emptiness and uncertainty.

He'd seen very few other travellers – but that was understandable on such a day. He did think about the danger of highwaymen but even they would have to be desperate to venture out in such weather. He felt the comforting weight of the fifty guineas his father had given him inside his shirt and prayed for fortune to deal him a lucky hand as it had on many occasions in the past.

He was on a ridge surrounded by ghostly looking trees. The mist swirled eerily, giving the impression that the trees were moving towards him. Giles shook himself. He was tired, hungry and disorientated. Every so often the mist lifted like a veil and he glimpsed fragments of a town below him – a line of buildings on each side of a road following the ribbon-like winding of the valley below. He had no idea what town it was. He'd been so lost in his own thoughts and frustrations he'd not paid attention to where he was going. He hoped the place had an inn where he could at least spend the night, get water and food for Black Boy, and plan what to do next.

He needed to move on and quickly. He didn't like this place on the hill. It conjured up the memory of a particularly nasty governess they'd had who took delight in telling the children scary stories before bed. He was thinking about one of these when he saw a cloaked figure moving towards him. For an instant, the old nursery fears returned. His uneasiness was picked up by Black Boy, who reared up in alarm.

Giles saw it was a young girl, obviously in a hurry. "Young woman, can you tell me what town that is in the valley, and is there an inn?"

The girl turned frightened grey eyes on him, babbled something incoherent about the fog being unlucky and about maidens being turned into trees by the Devil. Then she raced off down the steep slope that led to the town below.

With a gesture of irritation, Giles followed, finding a less steep pathway to guide Black Boy down.

It took some time to make the descent because the pathway was slippery and treacherous and he'd had to dismount and lead a reluctant Black Boy. When he reached the main street of the town he was relieved to see that there were two inns. *The King's Head*, a coaching inn, looked a little more salubrious than *The Merry Maiden*. The thought crossed his mind that unless his luck changed dramatically there may come a time when he would have to be less particular.

It was late on a Sunday afternoon, the weather too inclement for people to be out walking or socialising, and too early for evensong. The church clock struck four. Daylight had already faded, bringing the chill of frost with the gathering darkness.

"What is the name of this town?" Giles asked a young boy hurrying past on some errand or other.

"This be Marchington," said the boy, looking at Giles as if he were mad.

Giles was on his way across the street when his attention was caught by two young women, their voices like birdsong or music on the still air. The one had tendrils of fair hair escaping from her straw bonnet, but it was the dark haired girl that claimed Giles' attention. There was something about the contrast between the glimpse of raven hair and sapphire blue eyes that stirred his lustful feelings.

They were interrupted by the breathless arrival of the young girl Giles had seen up on the hill. Her cloak was muddy at the hem and she appeared distraught.

Giles shrank back into the shadows, anxious not to draw attention to himself. He waited until they'd all gone and then headed towards the shelter of *The King's Head*, determined to find out more about the mysterious lady who had so aroused his passions.

*

Lucinda Beckford and her friend Hannah Marshall had just returned from a visit to old Betsy Triggs, the person who'd been responsible for looking after Lucinda and her brother John when they were children. It was Betsy who had been responsible for seeing many of the inhabitants of Marchington into the world and out of it. She had been especially kind to Lucinda and Hannah when they'd lost their mothers, and they were repaying her for this now that she was old and ill.

Hannah had made her a woollen shawl and Lucinda had taken a basket of food and kindling, for which the old woman had been extremely grateful.

"You're like your mother, Miss Lucinda – headstrong but with a heart of gold. You'll make a lovely wife for somebody afore too long, just like Miss Hannah here."

Hannah blushed at the compliment but Lucinda's eyes flashed blue fire. "I shall never marry."

"I mind your mother said that once upon a time, until she laid eyes on your father and then she fell at his feet on purpose and cast her spell on him." Betsy chuckled at the memory. "Your Ma was determined, Miss Lucinda, even though her Aunt tried to talk her out of it. You'll be the same when you meet the right man."

"That will never happen," said Lucinda, the colour rising in her cheeks. "My chance of happiness died with Reuben Turner in London."

"There are many strange things in heaven and earth," said Betsy. "The Lord gives as well as taking away. I be thankful to you both for calling on me. It's taken my mind off the bad omens everyone is talking about – especially with that mist a haunting of us."

"People don't still believe that tale about the nine maidens do they?" asked Hannah.

There was an old legend that said if there was fog on Longdon Hill on the day after the February full moon then the Devil would come to Marchington and carry away a young maiden to add to the ones that were said to have been changed into trees. The nine trees on the summit were once said to have been maidens who were caught dancing on the Sabbath and had been turned into trees. Indeed, the atmosphere there was so eerie even on a summer's day that many local people walked the long way round the hill in order to avoid being anywhere near the circle of trees.

"I believe even the Rector himself refuses to ride over Longdon Hill," said Lucinda with a wicked grin, her good humour restored.

The church clock struck four.

"I must go," said Hannah. "Widow Parker has some work she wishes me to finish this evening and she's none too pleased about supplying extra candles."

"For all her talk of religion she's as keen on making money as the next person," agreed Betsy. "It's not right, now you'll soon have a husband to think of."

"We're saving what we can towards our own little business," said Hannah with a smile as she pulled on her cloak.

She told Lucinda all about Charlie's plans for their future as they walked back towards the market cross.

"Knowing Charlie, it'll be something to do with horses…,"

Lucinda was about to say how pleased she was that Hannah had at last found happiness, when she was almost flattened by Tilly, who was racing along the street in a most undignified manner.

"Miss Lucinda," she sobbed, flinging herself at Lucinda and nearly knocking her over, "I just seen the Devil up on Longdon Hill. His eyes was burning like coals and he were sitting on a black horse. He asked me what place this was. I been a good girl, Miss Lucinda…."

"Don't be such a goose, Tilly. If it was the Devil, he'd surely know where he was. You shouldn't believe the old superstitions."

Hannah said a brief farewell and hurried on to Widow Parker's shop, leaving Lucinda to reassure Tilly.

"Stop shaking so, Tilly. Of course the Devil isn't following you. Why did you go across Longdon Hill in the first place if it scares you so much – and today of all days?"

"If you please, Miss Lucinda, I stayed longer with my mother and the little ones with her not being well, and then I got worried about being late so I took the quickest way. I never thought it'd end up like this." Her voice ended in a wail.

"Come along, there's nothing to be worried about now. Let's go home and get warm by the fire."

Lucinda spoke the last words as much as to reassure herself as Tilly. She'd noticed a dark haired man leading a wild looking black horse towards the stables of *The King's Head*. As they passed, with Tilly jabbering away about her little brothers and sisters, the man stopped and stared at Lucinda.

Lucinda had been used to appraising glances from men of all ages, but there was something unsettling about this man's penetrating gaze. She shivered and hurried on, feeling uneasy until she and Tilly had reached Orchard House, gone inside and shut the front door behind them.

*

Giles Milburn lay on his bed in *The King's Head* feeling content that things were indeed working out to his advantage. The room was adequate and the sheets clean. He'd already partaken of roast beef and potatoes and a glass of claret in the panelled dining room. He'd spoken to the landlord and had ascertained that Miss Lucinda Beckford was the only daughter of Josiah Beckford, owner of the Marchington Brewery. She was unmarried and likely to be in possession of a legacy from her mother when she turned one and twenty.

"I heard tell she doesn't wish to marry," said the landlord after Giles had persuaded him to sit and drink with him, "on account of the death of someone she had hopes of marrying." He divulged many more secrets about the family that Giles tidied away for future use.

He smiled to himself. Before too long he would make Lucinda Beckford an offer of marriage she could not refuse.

Chapter 5

Adam floated between life and death.

In the heat of fever, he wondered if this was what purgatory was like – unremitting heat and thirst and no prospect of relief. He called out for Amelia in his delirium, remembered cool hands placing a damp cloth on his forehead, hearing a voice he didn't recognise saying Amelia wasn't there. Adam knew she wouldn't be there in that space between the worlds but he wondered how long it would be before he was allowed into the gardens of Paradise to be with her.

During his quieter moments, he was just aware of pain – in his head and in his right leg. The pain was made worse by the hands that pulled at dressings, probed his heated flesh. Now and again faces loomed close to him, he was propped up and given sips of water that cooled his dry lips but within minutes he was in the same condition as before.

The faces varied and the voices rose and fell. He caught snatches of conversation, tried to make sense of them but drifted away before he had a chance to do so.

"Don't give much for his chances…,"

"Nearly died in the night…,"

"It's not his time to go yet…,"

He was aware of being put on a cart and jolted for hours on end. The sun burned overhead like a golden eye that missed nothing. He blacked out with the pain and when he was next aware of anything, the temperature had cooled and he was in the belly of a ship, rocked by its motion. A young soldier with a head wound covered in a dirty bandage was sitting nearby.

"You 'ad us fair worried, sir. Thought you was a gonner more than once."

He helped Adam to sip some water.

"Can you take a little broth, sir? It'll help to build your strength."

"Where's the gate to Paradise?" asked Adam.

"Well, it ain't here, that's for sure," said the soldier, "but I for one am glad we're headed for England."

As Adam's condition improved, he lay in his hammock watching the rise and fall of the grey waves and wondering what he was going to do with the rest of his life. He drifted in and out of sleep and most of his dreams were of the last time he'd seen Amelia – the texture of her hair like spun gold on the white pillow, the violet colour of her eyes and the dreadful marble coldness of her lips when he kissed her for the last time.

When he'd recovered a little, he spent time on the deck relishing the salt spray and the lash of the wind. As the white cliffs of Dover loomed nearer, he felt a longing to be far away from England. Maybe when his wound had healed, he'd consider going to the colonies. He'd heard they had need of physicians for the new towns that were being created.

There was no doubt of his skill as a healer. The other physicians attached to the army had commented on the good recovery rate of the people in his care. They'd made fun of him because of his habit of washing instruments and his hands between patients, despite the scarcity of water on the battlefield. It was something he had learned from a Moorish doctor to whom he'd spoken soon after arriving in Spain.

Back in England, Adam was taken to a large house in the Kent countryside that was owned by one of the army colonels he'd served alongside. Two wounded officers were also taken there and they spent their days regaining their strength and being fed and fussed over by the colonel's servants.

The two officers played cards and spoke of nothing but the progress of the war, fretting about how soon they could re-join the regiment. They tried to interest Adam in their games, but soon gave up the attempt, obviously considering him dull company.

Adam gazed out of the windows at the snow swirling from a sky the dull yellow of a faded bruise. The whiteness blanketed everything and he knew he was trapped here until it melted away. He turned to his medical books for comfort and planned his departure from England.

*

Two days before he was due to take a ship for America, he received two letters. One was written on thick cream paper, the address written neatly in black ink, whereas the other looked tattered round the edges and reeked of cheap perfume.

The first was from a wealthy widow whom he had first met in Bath three years previously. She'd heard he was now back in England and in danger of leaving again. Before he made a final decision, she had an offer to put to him.

"*I know there have been unfortunate rumours, but I am guided by the good opinion of a friend in London who was successfully healed by you.*

I should like to offer to be your patroness providing you remain in this fair country of ours. My terms include the offer of a house of your own and the introduction to some of the local gentry in south Worcestershire in exchange for you calling on me regularly and accompanying me to Bath when required so that I may take the waters there.

Please contact me as soon as you are able to let me know if these terms are acceptable.

I am, sir, your obedient servant
Sophia Beeching

Adam put the letter on one side, determined to write back and say that whilst he was grateful for the offer, he had made other plans for his future.

He picked up the other letter. The paper was just as thick, but the writing was uneven and full of blots and smudges.

It was from his cousin Georgiana. She had never bothered much with her lessons despite having a succession of governesses. The letter was poorly spelt and full of crossings out.

"Deer Adam,

I am sorry to heer you were hert. I hope yore bad leg is soon better. Giles has treeted me very badly and I crave yore help …"

Adam tossed the letter to one side. He'd been enticed in the past to be a peace-maker in the endless quarrels between Georgiana and Giles. Every time it had ended up with him coming off worse and he had no intention of being put in that position again.

The memory had not faded of how Georgiana had treated him when he'd first gone to live with his uncle and aunt. His parents had died in an accident when the carriage they were travelling in had turned over and they were both killed. Something had spooked the horses, they'd run scared. Adam had been thrown clear and ended up with only minor injuries.

He was the only surviving child, his brother and sister having died when they were babies.

When Adam thought back to that time all he could remember was people speaking in low voices, black clothes and a feeling of emptiness inside. The only bright spot that stood out like a candle flame in the darkness was his uncle arriving in order to take the young Adam home with him. He'd gathered him up and made sure his meagre belongings were collected together and had said how much he was like his dear Mama.

Adam had relaxed in the foetid warmth of the coach as it jolted and swayed, feeling thankful that he would be safe now. How wrong he was. He was woken from sleep on that first morning by young Georgiana pulling his hair and asking: "Doesn't this make you want to cry?"

Adam had done his best not to do so, but it was when she'd started chanting about "Your mother's dead. She's in the ground. Your father's dead…," he'd not been able to help himself.

*

Life was so unpleasant for Adam, he decided he would run away. He saved some food from breakfast, packed his belongings into a bundle and left the nursery at a time when the children were meant to be having their afternoon rest.

Their governess was dozing in her chair as he made good his escape, down the back stairs and out of the servants' entrance at the bottom.

Within minutes, he was heading towards the gates and the crossroads beyond. There was an open stretch of road with no bushes to shelter behind, just before he reached the imposing-looking wrought iron gates flanked by stone lions. Adam heard a horse approaching along the road outside and stopped, hoping that it would carry on past.

Luck wasn't on his side that day. To Adam's horror, his uncle rode towards him on his grey hunter. The possessions Adam was carrying told their own story.

His uncle dismounted and they walked back to the house in silence. When they reached the stable yard, one of the grooms came to tend to the horse. Adam and his uncle went indoors with the boy fearing he was about to be beaten for his actions.

"Why were you running away from us Adam?" asked his uncle when they were inside his study.

Adam stood, marking out the pattern on the Turkish rug with the toe of his boot, not knowing what to say.

"Well, Adam, what have you to say?"

"I don't belong here, sir."

"Don't belong! My dear child – you're the image of my beloved sister and if you don't belong in this house I don't know who does."

Adam stood still, saying nothing.

His uncle narrowed his eyes. "My son and daughter haven't welcomed you – is that it?"

There was a pause when the sound of the long-case clock in the hall beyond seemed abnormally loud.

"There is no need for you to say anything, Adam. The matter will be dealt with."

The matter was indeed dealt with and Adam ended up in a room of his own which afforded him a measure of privacy.

*

Adam put the letters to one side. He reflected how strange it was that they'd arrived so close to his planned departure. One more day and he would have been gone – embarked on a ship for Boston – and may never have read them.

The letter from Georgiana and its intrusive scent aroused the feelings of frustration and anger he felt against Giles. He remembered what his uncle had said on the occasion he'd tried to run away. "*Nothing was ever solved that way, boy.*"

He felt guilty that he'd not written to his uncle as often as he should have done, especially now that he was ill.

"*Since the quarrel with Giles, father has not left his room,*" Georgiana had written.

Adam knew he couldn't keep running away. He'd escaped to the Peninsula thinking to immerse himself in work and blot out his feelings of anger, loss and sorrow. It hadn't worked. He needed to avenge Amelia's death in some way, and confront Giles in order to heal himself. He wouldn't achieve that by embarking for the colonies.

He'd been tempted to take that course of action because of being discredited by Giles, and because his signature had been forged on the papers that had consigned Amelia to that terrible place where he'd found her.

Adam sat lost in his thoughts for so long that the sky had darkened and the crescent moon showed like a curve of silver against indigo velvet. He got to his feet, lit candles, found pen and paper and wrote two letters – one to his uncle to say he would call on him as soon as he possibly could, and the other to his patroness accepting her kind offer of help.

Chapter 6

The weather continued to be bitingly cold with snow flurries and brooding cloud pulled low over the hills like a blanket. Lucinda's sense of unease continued – mainly because her father showed signs of reverting to his previous habit of gambling. For the last two nights he'd come back a little the worst for drink and had stumbled his way up to bed. Lucinda hoped he'd exercise caution and not bet more money than he could afford.

His skill and daring at card games as a young man was legendary. While her mother was alive, this habit had been tamed but now in the depths of winter he seemed to be recovering from the paralysing grief he'd suffered at her death and returning to his previous haunts.

Caroline Montgomery had almost refused to marry the young Josiah Beckford when he gambled everything on the turn of a card in order to win her a sapphire and diamond ring that was rumoured to have been made for Marie Antoinette.

She was horrified that he could be so irresponsible as to risk Orchard House and the brewery on the turn of a card.

"I nearly changed my mind about marrying your father for fear that he'd make me homeless once we were married," Caroline had once told Lucinda. "I threatened not to wear the ring, feeling it may have bewitched him."

Josiah had talked her round, promising that as long as she lived he would never gamble again. She forgave him and the ring was the one Caroline was wearing in the portrait Josiah commissioned just after their marriage. Caroline was dressed in her wedding gown of cream sprigged muslin with a pink rose between her long-fingered hands, and the ring flashed blue fire matching the eyes that were so much like Lucinda's.

Lucinda had the ring now, worn on a thin gold chain round her neck and hidden in the bodice of her gown. It was her dearest possession.

She watched as her father pulled on his riding cape and called for his horse to be saddled. There was an air of excitement about him that worried her.

"You will be careful, father?"

"Nonsense, Lucinda, of course I will. What harm could possibly come to me. I'm dining with Sir James Torrance and we will have a hand or two of cards."

Sir James Torrance was the local magistrate and had a reputation for turning a blind eye to situations if offered the right price. On the last occasion he'd dined with them, he'd squeezed Lucinda's arm as if testing bread for freshness and pinched her cheek playfully, saying she'd be a tasty armful for a lucky young man. His sour faced wife had glared at Lucinda as if she'd provoked the exchange.

*

Mrs Parsons smoothed her apron over her fat curves. The kitchen smelled of the beef stew and dumplings she was cooking for the evening meal – plain fare for some households but a favourite of Mr Josiah's. She was upset that he wouldn't be here to eat it, only Miss Lucinda and Mr John who never took much notice of what was put in front of him, his head being too full of his paintings and other airy fairy nonsense.

Caroline Beckford had once said that her children had the wrong attributes. John, the elder of her two surviving children, was imaginative and dreamy and was never happier than when he was sketching something – a flower, a tree or a person. It was expected that he'd take over the business when his father died, but as he'd never shown much interest or aptitude, then heaven knew what sort of job he'd make of it.

Caroline and Betsy, the nurse maid, had spent many occasions rescuing the young Lucinda from Josiah's office where she'd wander in and settle comfortably in her little 'house' under his desk.

"Maybe you should take Lucinda on as your apprentice," Caroline had said on the occasion when that young lady had shown her ability to add a column of figures with far less difficulty than John demonstrated.

Since Caroline died, John had paid lip service to his role in the business, getting up at a reasonable hour and walking over to the brewery and checking the progress of the work. However, something would always spark his imagination and by the time his father appeared, John would be sitting in a corner sketching with a piece of charcoal, earning the disapproval of his parent.

"If the right opportunity came, I'd go to London and try out my fortune painting portraits for the nobility," John told Lucinda after they had finished dinner and were sitting together in the parlour.

Lucinda, who had already experienced the loss of Reuben in London, had burst into tears and begged him not to go.

"I couldn't bear the thought of losing you too," she said.

"You would not do that. Reuben was just unlucky." He hesitated. "You were unlucky to have lost the person you loved almost as soon as you'd found them." He dried her tears. "But Lucinda, we only have one life and if you believe what the Bible tells us then we should make the most of it. I intend to do this with my painting – whatever jibes father throws at me."

"You're a man. You have more choice in life." Lucinda was aware she sounded sour as vinegar.

John went upstairs shortly afterwards and she sat in the candlelight thinking of the years stretching ahead of her like a lonely road. Lucinda gazed at the portrait of her mother on the parlour wall and it seemed as if the eyes had a gleam in them as if she was holding onto a secret. '*Just wait,*' they seemed to be saying.

Lucinda went upstairs to her room. She felt on edge, worrying about what her father was doing. She hoped he'd exercise caution and not gamble too much on the turn of a card. She lay down on the bed covering herself with the eiderdown. Although she hadn't intended to go to sleep, she fell into a fitful doze. She dreamed that she was hurrying along a road and could hear footsteps following her, getting closer. She was too frightened to turn round and see who her pursuer was. The road stretched on into the distance and she couldn't see any way of escape.

She was aroused from the depths of this dream by a loud and frantic knocking on the front door. She was unsure at first if this was part of the dream but then she heard the voices of Mrs Parsons and Tilly downstairs. She heard them call her name.

Lucinda got up, a sense of foreboding in her heart.

She went along the corridor and knocked on John's door. He didn't answer. She pushed the door open. His bed was empty, which meant that he'd probably fallen asleep over his work upstairs. She climbed the narrow flight of stairs. The smell of paint and turpentine got stronger as she did so. She knocked on the door, could hear loud snores issuing from the other side, but John didn't answer. The door was locked.

The knocking from downstairs was getting louder, the voices on the other side of the front door more insistent.

"Let them in, Mrs Parsons," shouted Lucinda. "It's father."

She hurried downstairs, aware that her hair was probably like a bird's nest.

"You can't be too sure, as it isn't footpads," said Mrs Parsons who was brandishing an iron doorstop in one hand and a brass candlestick in the other.

"For pity's sake, put that down, you'll hurt someone," said Lucinda.

Mrs Parsons and Tilly hovered behind her, both in their night clothes. Mrs Parsons' hair was tied in rags and she was wearing a voluminous white night cap that looked like you could boil a pudding for twenty people in it.

Mrs Parsons put the door stop on the hall table but kept hold of the lighted candle. "You can't be any too sure these days that folks is honest. No sense all of us being murdered in our beds."

"We ain't in bed now," whispered Tilly, then "Ow," as Mrs Parsons cuffed her on the ear.

The knocking on the other side of the door came again.

"It's my father," repeated Lucinda pushing past them, undoing the bolts and opening the door. A blast of ice-cold air rushed in, causing the candle flames to flicker wildly.

Josiah stood on the doorstep, supported by a man on each side. He looked pale and his right arm was hanging awkwardly. They all smelled of alcohol and Josiah and one of the men who Lucinda recognised as a lawyer from the neighbouring town looked unsteady on their feet. She instantly recognised the third man.

"You'd better bring him in," said Lucinda. "Then tell me what has happened."

From the shadows outside the door she could hear the stamping of a horse's hooves.

She led the way to the parlour and the three men followed, leaving damp footprints on the flagstones in the hall.

Mrs Parsons and Tilly hastened to light the oil lamps and bring more candles. Josiah gave a hiss of pain as they lowered him down onto the sofa and covered him with a rug.

"Tilly, you must go for the doctor," Lucinda instructed. "Tell him he must come immediately."

Tilly began to whimper. "Miss Lucinda, I be afraid of the dark." Then she looked at the tall man in the dark blue riding coat and began to hurry towards the door. "You've let the Devil in, Miss Lucinda. That's the man I saw up on Longdon Hill the day after the February full moon."

"Don't be a fool, girl, or you'll be taken back to the workhouse where we got you from." Mrs Parsons pushed Tilly towards the door. "Do as you're bid and no more nonsense."

Lucinda agreed with Tilly. If it wasn't for basic good manners she'd want this man with the insolent expression out of the house. She didn't like the way his eyes raked down her body as if he was undressing her with his eyes, one garment at a time. She shivered.

"You at least should remember your manners, Lucinda," said Josiah. "Isn't there some refreshment you could offer these gentlemen?"

"All in good time, father," said Lucinda. "Will one of you gentlemen please tell me how this accident occurred?"

"Later, Lucinda," said Josiah, his face ashen with pain.

"He has Mr Milburn to thank for not being killed," said Lawyer Craycombe. "One of the horses went out of control and would've trampled him had it not been for his quick thinking."

Lucinda stole a quick look at Giles Milburn. Something in his demeanour made her feel uneasy. She knew without doubt that had her mother been alive, he wouldn't be sitting in their parlour.

*

Giles sat feasting his eyes on Lucinda Beckford, hoping the doctor would take his time. He liked the sight of her aroused with passion and the way her sapphire eyes flashed. His idea of doing something to one of the horses under the guise of going outside for some fresh air was a good one. He'd administered a dose of pepper to its rectum, something he'd learned from another unscrupulous gambler, and the trick had worked perfectly.

He'd heard about Lucinda's disappointment in love but he was confident that once they were married she'd soon forget about what had gone before. She had the look of a woman who was made for passion.

*

The doctor arrived, wearing his breeches over his nightshirt and looking a little dishevelled, with Tilly hovering nervously in his wake. When she noticed Giles was still there, she hurried, head downwards towards the safety of the kitchen.

"Well Josiah, what have we here?"

He examined Josiah, pronounced the arm broken and asked Lucinda to assist him with setting the bone.

"I'm sure these gentlemen may be excused now," he said.

Mrs Parsons showed Lawyer Craycombe and Giles Milburn out of the house and retired gratefully to her bed.

*

Out in the chill of the February night, Giles bade farewell to Mr Craycombe and headed back to *The King's Head*. He felt a bubble of excitement as he knew his plan was beginning to work. Before many months had gone by, Lucinda Beckford would be his and he would be raised back up in his father's favour.

Chapter 7

The doctor returned the following morning. He bled Josiah, leaving him feeling weak and frustrated. He prescribed rest and good food and wine.

Lucinda made sure Josiah was settled by the fire in the parlour with a glass of mulled port and brandy and some honey cake. Tilly was instructed to listen for the bell in case there was anything he wanted.

Lucinda put on her boots and huddled into her cloak as she prepared to leave the house to run some errands. She was less than pleased to see Giles Milburn approach the house as she was leaving it. His glance swept her body and she felt a sense of revulsion. It was all she could do not to shudder. Only the suspicion that he might take this as a sign of her pleasure kept her body from betraying her thoughts.

She sketched the briefest of curtseys. "I am sure my father will be pleased to see you," she said pointedly. "However, please do not tire him. He is far from well."

*

When Lucinda returned at midday, she was irritated to see that Giles Milburn was still there, ensconced at a make-shift table on the other side of Josiah's study as if he belonged there. She was thankful when he made his excuses and left, despite Josiah's entreaties that he should stay.

"Why was he here, father?" Lucinda demanded as soon as the door had closed on the unwelcome guest.

"I needed help with my correspondence, he writes a fair hand," said Josiah, his face flushed in defiance as it used to when Caroline caught him doing something of which she didn't approve.

"John or I could have done that for you, father. You had only to ask. The doctor said that you should rest."

"Rest," said Josiah. "There'll be time to rest when I'm in my coffin."

Lucinda felt agitated. It was typical of her father to avoid the subject.

"Why did you ask Mr Milburn for help, father. I would have been happy to write letters to your dictation."

"John was busy with his pretty pictures. You had errands to run."

"As you can see, father, I have now returned. I am sure there was no matter that was so urgent that it could not have waited an hour or two."

"Enough," said Josiah. "I am head of this household and if I elect to engage help, then that is my affair."

"Then do not expect me to make him welcome if he calls again, father. I do not trust him."

Lucinda went upstairs to put away her bonnet and cloak, feeling a sense of unease.

*

Within a fortnight, Giles was an established fixture at Orchard House. He'd arrive every morning, bowing politely to Lucinda, his face smug. She always made a point of going out as soon as he arrived, leaving instructions with Mrs Parsons to attend to anything her father needed.

Hannah understood how Lucinda felt. She had called round to see Lucinda with some dresses that a customer had donated 'for use by the poor.' She wondered if they would be of any use to the brewery workers' children. Lucinda made tea and cut slices of gingerbread and they sat in the parlour with a view of the garden. The room had originally been decorated under Caroline's direction and was done in soft greens and pinks, echoed by her favourite roses in the shrubbery outside.

Giles had thankfully gone and Josiah had retired upstairs for a rest. The accident had taken more out of him than he'd realised.

"I can imagine you must feel hurt, Lucinda. After all, you could do just as good a job as Mr Milburn."

"It annoys me intensely that he can walk into our home as if he has a right to be there. Father seems completely taken in by him. I can't remember him being duped so soundly since the time he bought Mama some lace handkerchiefs from a pedlar who called at the door."

"What was wrong with them?" asked Hannah.

"They looked well enough on the surface – and the pedlar woman was clean and tidy – but he neglected to open them out. When Mama did so, they had all gone into holes. She was able to use some of the lace and she did laugh about it, but she told him he should have a care not to take things at face value."

Hannah laughed.

"Oh, Hannah, what can I do to make Papa see sense?"

"What does John say?"

"John!!" Lucinda's frustration showed in the way her eyes flashed and she began pacing the room. "All he's interested in is his latest portrait – and his plans to move to London and paint the portraits of anyone who will pay a decent price."

"He has great talent, Lucinda."

Lucinda shrugged. "He does, but it doesn't help with matters at the moment. He and father barely speak."

"Maybe it's time they talked to each other," suggested Hannah as she got up to leave.

"I'll try," said Lucinda.

*

She was unable to broach the subject that day because John announced that he wouldn't be dining with them that evening – he'd been invited to dinner with the local banker to discuss a commission for painting a portrait of his daughter on her marriage.

Lucinda and her father dined alone, struggling to make conversation, the air between them heavy with unspoken secrets.

When her father announced his intention of going out that evening, Lucinda was concerned.

"Is it a good idea, father? You are not yet recovered from your accident and should be resting."

"Stuff and nonsense," said Josiah. "I shall only be walking as far as *The King's Head*. It will do me good to have a change of environment."

"Will Mr Milburn be there?" The feel of his name in her mouth made Lucinda feel ill.

45

"What if he is?" asked Josiah. "He's been more help over the last fortnight than my own son."

"That's unfair, father. John would have helped if you'd asked him."

"I should not have to ask."

*

Josiah departed for *The King's Head* and Lucinda fidgeted around the house, finally going up to bed and lying awake until she heard him fumbling with the lock. It then sounded as if two sets of footsteps stumbled upstairs and she thought she heard Giles Milburn's voice. One set of footsteps went back down the stairs and the front door slammed.

The following day Josiah was pale and subdued and Lucinda wanted to send for the doctor again.

"Not a bit of good doing that," said Josiah. "He'll only bleed me again."

He didn't meet Lucinda's eyes when he said this.

*

Lucinda decided it was time to enlist John's help. She went up to his room and hammered on the door until he opened it.

"Steady on, Lucinda. I didn't get to sleep many hours ago." He blinked at her owlishly. His dressing robe was splashed with blue and yellow paint and the air in his room was thick with the smell of it.

"John, we need to do something about father before Giles Milburn takes him over completely."

"Not many weeks ago you were complaining because father had no interest in life. Now he appears to have rediscovered a zest for it, and that's wrong as well. I'll never understand women as long as I live." He smiled, blue eyes dancing, trying to make a joke of the situation.

"John, this is serious. I don't like the way Giles Milburn is usurping your place in the business. It should be you or me writing letters to father's dictation – not …him."

John considered this, his head on one side like a blackbird examining a worm.

"Father always complains about my handwriting – and I expect he feels you have more than enough to do with the running of the house."

"That's exactly what he said – but he should know that I have always taken an interest in the business even if you have not."

Lucinda turned on her heel and headed towards the stairs, frustration with the male members of her family boiling inside her.

*

Lucinda didn't have time to dwell on the situation with Giles Milburn because the day of Hannah's wedding to Charlie Marshall was fast approaching. The wedding was to take place on the first Friday in April at the little Saxon church where Hannah and Lucinda's mothers were buried. John was to give her away and Lucinda was acting as her bridesmaid.

Widow Parker had given Hannah the afternoon off by way of a honeymoon, provided she was back at work bright and early the next morning.

"I trust you appreciate my generosity in not stopping your pay for the afternoon." Hannah did a perfect interpretation of Widow Parker's vinegary tones.

*

On the Sunday before the wedding, the banns were called for the final time. Hannah nudged Lucinda excitedly as they sat together in the cold church. After the service, they came back to Orchard House and sorted through Lucinda's gowns so that Hannah could borrow one to wear for the wedding.

"Who does that woman think she is?" demanded Lucinda, pulling a pink sprigged muslin gown from a wooden chest that she knew would look better on Hannah than it ever had on her. "The least she could do would be to give you the whole day off for your wedding."

"She has been generous in renting us the cottage next door," said Hannah, who always tried to see the best in people.

"Generous, my foot!" said Lucinda hotly. "She's only trying to keep you where you'll be most use to her."

"Charlie says we'll have the last laugh," said Hannah. "Hopefully it won't be long before he can set up his own little business."

Lucinda busied herself with searching for reticules and shoes in another trunk so that Hannah didn't notice the tears in her eyes. She'd imagined the two of them planning the clothes for her wedding. Her heart ached to think that this would never happen now.

*

On Friday morning, Lucinda stood behind Hannah in the church, her heart feeling raw as she heard the couple exchange their vows. Then they went back to Orchard House for glasses of ale and slices of gingerbread before the couple went hand in hand to their cottage. The landlord of *The King's Head* had offered them refreshments at the inn, but Widow Parker had forbidden this saying she didn't wish anyone in her employ to be seen in a public house.

The landlord had chuckled at this and had sent a flagon of cider to the cottage by way of a wedding present instead.

*

Giles Milburn, observing the small party emerging from the church, felt a frisson of excitement as he stared at Lucinda Beckford in the blue muslin gown and bonnet that exactly matched her sapphire eyes.

Never before had a woman excited him so much. Never before had he been forced to wait so long before getting what he wanted. The fact that she would be extremely wealthy in a few years' time was an unexpected bonus.

He hoped that before very long he and Lucinda would be celebrating their own wedding day.

He certainly hadn't felt this level of arousal when he married Amelia. In truth, the main reason for that attraction had been the prospect of upsetting his cousin Adam.

*

Old Betsy who'd come to the wedding had caused tears enough by declaring that Hannah and Lucinda looked as pretty as a picture. "Your dear mothers would be very proud of you girls," she said. "You're a credit to them."

She'd come back to Orchard House for a glass of ale, catching sight of Giles on the way. "Which is more than you could say of the likes of him," she continued, mouth cramped with distaste, age and deafness keeping her voice loud as a town crier's. "It'll be a good thing for Marchington when that creature departs. 'Tis said he's a bad influence on your father."

"Do you think there was any truth in what she said about Giles Milburn?" asked John when they were on their way home from taking Betsy back to her cottage.

"I'm sure there was," said Lucinda. "Things haven't been right since he arrived in Marchington and I wish he'd go back to where he came from."

As Lucinda and John walked back to Orchard House they recovered some of their earlier closeness. They reminisced about their escapades as children and the times they'd egged each other on to steal sugar cubes or jam tarts from the pantry.

They both pulled a face when they noticed Giles Milburn's hat on the hall table when they arrived back.

"It's a wonder father hasn't started charging him rent," said John.

Lucinda grinned at him, feeling that at least John was on her side now. She felt a surge of relief that things might get better from now on.

Then their father's study door opened and Giles strutted out like a peacock making a great display of himself.

He headed towards the garden door, no doubt heading for the necessary house – but not before Lucinda had seen what he had obviously intended her to notice.

"John – did you see?" she said, not caring if Giles heard or not. "He's wearing father's watch."

"Are you sure you didn't drink one glass of ale too many, just like old Betsy?" asked John. "Are you sure you are not mistaken?"

Lucinda shook her head. Her cheeks burned with indignation and outrage. How could her father give away something so precious? Before John could stop her she headed towards the study door and went in.

"Father, how could you hand your watch over to that odious man?"

Josiah didn't look up from his ledger, but his cheeks flushed.

"Father, have you been gambling again? Mother gave you that watch as a wedding present – you cannot have forgotten her so completely as to be so careless with it. John was to have inherited that if anything happened to you – now we may never see it again."

Josiah's usually florid face flushed a shade darker. "I will do with my belongings as I wish, Lucinda," he said, looking up from his ledger at last. "And you would do well to remember that. Giles won the watch fair and square – and that is the end of the matter."

Giles came back into the room, sweeping Lucinda a formal bow, and sat down in his chair in the corner as if nothing had happened. The silver watch case gleamed softly against his green silk waistcoat in the remaining shreds of daylight filtering in through the window.

Lucinda remembered how, as a child, she used to clamber onto Josiah's lap and snuggle against his chest and listen to the comforting tick of the watch that was like a heartbeat.

"As you wish, father," she said and turned on her heel and left the room, shutting the door behind her.

John was waiting for her in the hall.

"You should know by now Lucinda that you and father are too much alike. Neither of you will stand being lectured and neither of you will admit you're wrong."

"But Mama gave him the watch on their wedding day – I didn't think he would ever part with it."

"It won't bring her back to him."

"I know that," snapped Lucinda. "I might have known you'd not see it as important, or even notice that it's one more thing that creature has taken from us."

She stormed up the stairs, shut the door of her bedroom and threw herself on the bed in a storm of frustrated tears.

Giles, noticing the raised voices between brother and sister in the hallway, could guess the reason for the upset. He couldn't for the life of him see why Lucinda was so upset about a mere watch. Granted, there were sentimental attachments – he'd noticed how reluctant Josiah had been to hand it over – but the object wasn't going to leave the family, was it? His eldest son – Josiah's grandson – would inherit the watch eventually.

Chapter 8

June 1813

Georgiana hugged herself with excitement as she sneaked down the back stairs to the place where she'd arranged to meet Oliver and smuggle him up to her room. She was unaware of the watcher standing heron-like in the shadowy passage-way that led to the housekeeper's room and the kitchen.

Oliver was ready and waiting nervously in the darkest corner of the stable yard. Georgiana's heart swelled with excitement when she saw him. She took him by the hand and led him back the way she'd come, whispering that they'd need to be as quiet as mice so as not to alert anyone to their plan.

Georgiana had chosen a time when the servants had finished their duties. A chink of light under the door to the servants' hall and the mouth-watering smell of stew indicated they were enjoying a late supper accompanied by somebody playing a tune on the fiddle. The door to the Butler's Pantry, Digby's domain, was firmly closed.

Georgiana led Oliver up the winding staircase and along a maze of corridors. She opened the door to her bedchamber and beckoned him in, closing it behind them with an excited shiver. She'd left a few candles burning, contrasting with the silvery glow of the moonlight flooding through the window. The bed with its ivory silk coverlet looked like part of the moonbeams.

The room smelled of the orange blossom perfume Georgiana's mother had always favoured.

They kissed for a long time, whispering endearments to each other. Then Oliver lifted her in his arms and carried her over to the bed. At they began to shed their clothes like unwanted skins, it felt as if they were the only people in a magical world.

Their paradise did not last long. With a sense of alarm, they both heard the clamour of footsteps in the corridor outside. They lay still, like rabbits caught in the beam of a powerful lantern.

The door burst open, swinging back on its hinges with a crash.

Georgiana's father stood there in his fur-edged dressing robe, holding a candlestick in one hand and brandishing a club with the other. Digby stood behind him, his face when Georgiana caught sight of it a supercilious mask of satisfaction when he saw the state she was in.

"What is the meaning of this – this outrage?" spluttered her father, his face crimson with fury. "Cover yourself at once, daughter. You should be horsewhipped through the streets for this abomination…,"

Digby and the footman busied themselves with bundling Oliver out of the room.

Feeling sick with shock, Georgiana could hear Oliver being dragged down the stairs. She gathered her dressing robe around her and attempted to follow them.

"Please don't hurt him. It's my fault that he's here. We love each other."

"Love!" spat her father. "You were behaving like animals."

"Please, father. Let me go to him."

"Do not move from this room." William Milburn's face was suffused with anger. His neck-cloth appeared too tight and he was having trouble breathing. He struck out at her with his club, catching her on the side of the head. She fell sideways onto the bed and he rained blows down onto her partly-clothed flesh.

Georgiana fought back, using a pillow to fend him off, pushing herself upright so that she was poised ready to spring at him.

To her surprise, he made a strange gurgling sound in his throat and fell backwards. He lay still, his bloodshot eyes glaring at her accusingly.

Digby and the footman returned. The footman wiped a smear of blood from his hand. Georgiana shuddered, wondering what they'd done to Oliver.

"Where is he? What have you done with him?" Georgiana clung to Digby's sleeve.

He shook her off as if she was a troublesome fly. All his attention was focused on his master.

The groom was sent to fetch the doctor and Digby and the footman carried William to his room. He was unable to speak coherently but his meaning was clearly interpreted. Georgiana was to blame for what had happened and she was not to move from her room.

*

Georgiana's attempts to reach the stables that night were blocked by Digby, who was following his master's instructions to the letter and had locked her in. Her first chance to escape came when the maid came with her breakfast. Georgiana didn't feel like eating anything but it was easy enough to hoodwink her way past the young girl and make her way down the stairs and out to the stables.

She bullied the stable lad into telling her what had happened. The straw in the hayloft was blood-stained and all Oliver's possessions were gone.

"His face were a mess," the lad said.

Georgiana winced at the thought. Her own bruises showed black this morning and she ached all over.

"Where have they taken him?"

The lad shrugged. "Far enough to cause no more trouble here. Mr Digby were all for calling the magistrate at first. Then he thought better of it – not wanting to bring the family's name into disrepute."

"Which direction did they travel?"

"I'm sorry miss. I don't know."

Digby appeared in the stable yard looking unusually dishevelled and out of sorts. "I expected to find you here." He looked down his nose at Georgiana. "I am sure it will be of no consequence to you, but your father has just passed away."

"He can't have." Georgiana stared at the butler in disbelief, before she fainted for the first time in her life.

Chapter 9

June 1813

It was midsummer before Adam felt sufficiently recovered to make the long journey to visit his uncle.

The springtime had gone by in a hazy dream of green and white that felt like a cool draught of water after the heat and dust of the Peninsula. The air was filled with the scent of wild roses, elderflower and hay. Butterflies drifted lazily amongst the hedgerow flowers and Adam slowed his horse to a walking pace, allowing it to rest.

It was late morning and he was on familiar territory, recognising the fields he used to wander alone in order to keep out of Giles' way. He passed the turning to the church and the scattering of farm-workers cottages and looked forward to the welcome he'd receive from his uncle. He'd written to tell him of his proposed visit and had received an enthusiastic response.

*

The ornamental wrought iron gates were open. The sight of a black funeral carriage drawn by four black horses moving slowly towards him along the driveway from the house shocked Adam out of his reverie. A crowd followed on foot dressed in black.

Adam recognised the butler, Digby, at the front of the line of servants and asked him whose funeral it was.

"Why, it's the master's, Doctor Adam. I thought that's why you'd returned. We did try to send word to you." Digby's usual superior expression wasn't in evidence today. His voice cracked with emotion and his eyes were red.

"I didn't know." Adam felt as if his tongue was sticking to the roof of his mouth. He was inappropriately dressed for a funeral, but this was no time to worry about such things. He tethered his horse in the shade of a tree and followed the butler to the carriage behind the hearse in which sat his cousin Georgiana, swathed in black from head to foot and weeping copiously.

From the brusque way that Digby addressed Georgiana, Adam had the feeling there was more to tell about his uncle's death.

"Oh Adam, I'm so glad you're back." She flung herself at him and he recoiled from the smell of alcohol, her sickly violet perfume and the musky scent of her skin.

"Try to act with some dignity," he said stiffly, pushing her back onto her side of the carriage.

She sniffed noisily and began shredding the lace on her damp handkerchief.

The funeral cortege wound its way out of the drive and back the way Adam had just come towards the small country church. They filed in to the chilly atmosphere inside, the smell of lilies and musty hymn books.

After the service and the burial in the churchyard, they returned to the house for refreshments that nobody seemed in the mood for. Giles was conspicuous by his absence and Adam was thankful for this.

"I didn't know where to find him," sniffed Georgiana to Adam. "And even if I had, I do not think he would've come. He and father parted on bad terms. I've never seen father so angry. Then Giles called me…," she gave way to tears again, her face red and blotchy and her eyes bloodshot.

*

They gathered in the drawing room for the reading of the will and Adam noticed how shabby the house looked compared to when he was last here. They sat like statues, Adam's blue and silver waistcoat the only brightness in the room. The lawyer, a desiccated man with creaking bones and pale hands like fragments of ice read the will in a flat, expressionless voice. It was as if he breathed out dust with the words. A tortoiseshell butterfly beat its wings against the glass and Adam wished that he too could be free. From the sound of it, his uncle's fortunes had been declining for years. The estate would need to be sold in order to pay the outstanding debts.

*

"What will happen to me?" a tearful Georgiana asked Adam when the last of the mourners had gone.

Adam had agreed to stay in order to go through some paperwork with the lawyer the following morning, and to study the contents of a letter that his uncle had left him.

"I have no idea, Georgiana. You may have to seek work as a governess or seamstress."

She shuddered. "I couldn't."

Adam lost patience with her and retired to what had once been his uncle's study. The room was decorated in shades of brown, caramel and cream. It was lined with books and housed his uncle's large polished oak desk with its three drawers on each side. The desk was by the window which was hung with cream brocade curtains.

Adam sat in his uncle's brown leather chair, feeling as if he was a child misbehaving. The surface of the desk housed his ink stand, blotter, pens, paper and his unopened correspondence. Many of these looked to be from creditors and Adam resolved to do as much as he could to help with these before he left Foxton Grange. He asked Digby to bring candles and then asked him in confidence what had happened to cause his uncle's demise.

The butler stood clearing his throat for so long that Adam felt like slapping him on the back.

"Spit it out man, it cannot be anything I've not heard of before."

Digby looked as if he was about to have a fit, turning pale, then puce.

"Well?" Adam was tired and the pain in his knee was excruciating.

"It was Miss Georgiana, sir." The butler looked awkwardly towards the door as if someone might be listening.

Adam caught the faint emphasis on the word 'Miss.'

"Pray continue, Digby."

"Mr Milburn had retired early for the night. However, he was awakened a few hours later by strange noises.

Being of a disposition that feared fires breaking out, he roused myself and the servants and directed us towards the parlour. Hearing further noise and suspecting burglars instead of fire, he called us back and went in search of the culprits. The footman and I were close behind but Mr Milburn was the one that found them…in Miss Georgiana's bedchamber, sir."

"Found whom? " Adam demanded.

"Why Miss Georgiana and … one of the grooms, sir." Digby's voice sounded as if he was swallowing thorns. "He's been dismissed, of course, without a character. But in the rumpus, nobody noticed Mr Milburn had collapsed. By the time the doctor was summoned, he was dead."

"Thank you Digby, that will be all," said Adam.

The butler made his exit, looking pale with relief.

Adam turned his attention to the papers in front of him. He noticed a letter that had arrived since his uncle's death. He recognised his cousin Giles' handwriting on the thick cream paper.

He broke the seal, spread it out and began to read. It was full of Giles' usual cockiness, stating that despite the limited help his father had given him in his hour of need, he was now making good progress and was planning to remarry.

"I have not yet asked the young woman in question," he wrote, "but I have no doubt that she will accept."

Adam slapped the desk hard when he read this, causing the candle flames to flicker. The sheer audacity of his cousin infuriated him.

He got up from the brown leather chair and paced to the window, looking out at the shrubbery beyond and the way the moths flitted ghost-like around the bushes in the fading evening light.

There was no question that the young woman who had aroused Giles' interest was in great danger, whether or not she reciprocated his feelings. He remembered the bruises on Amelia's body, many of them yellow and faded, bearing witness to months of abusive treatment.

Adam had no idea who the young woman was, but his mind was focused on the idea that if no proposal had as yet been made, then maybe he could urge her to accept him instead. Adam had no wish to marry. He was certain he could never feel for anybody the depth of love he'd felt for Amelia. However, he felt that he could atone for her death by protecting another woman.

Giles was obviously unaware of his father's death, so Adam could at least present himself in Marchington with the intention of giving him the news and seeing what the situation was.

He set off after his appointment with the lawyer. He did not speak to Georgiana before he left Foxton Lodge and refused to feel guilty about this. He tucked Giles' letter into his pocket and headed towards Marchington.

Chapter 10

On arriving in the main street of Marchington the following afternoon, it was obvious that there was some kind of celebration in progress.

He hadn't realised that the town was so close to where his new patroness lived, and planned to call on her when he'd dealt with matters here.

He saw a single street that ran through the middle of the town edged with shops that were closed today. He could see that brightly coloured tents had been set up in a field above the town and barrel organ music and a hubbub of voices floated down towards him. The street was quiet, apart from a group of men talking outside *The King's Head.*

Adam got stiffly out of the saddle, wincing as he tried to straighten his damaged knee, and spoke to the men.

"'Tis the Midsummer Fair," they said, looking at him as if he were a simpleton for not knowing such a thing. "'Tis the place to go for a jug of ale or to find a pretty maid."

Adam was just thinking that a cool drink of some sort was just what he needed. He had no idea where to find his cousin, but decided to stable his horse at *The King's Head* and make some enquiries.

He quickly gained the impression from the surly twist of the landlord's mouth – as if he was eating a crab apple – that his cousin was not popular here. Adam was thankful to have a different surname. He accepted the landlord's offer of a glass of ale and a plate of bread and cold meat before beginning his search for his cousin. The landlord fussed around him, setting a place for him in the coffee room. Adam was grateful for the peace and quiet. Apart from two ladies awaiting the arrival of the Mail Coach, there was nobody else in there.

Later, as Adam stepped out into the street, he saw his cousin ahead of him. The usual feeling of revulsion swept over him, together with the urge to get revenge for the way he'd treated Amelia. The injustice of every situation that had happened since childhood swelled up like a river in flood and almost knocked him off balance. He stood for a moment, until the tide of anger had settled to a feeling that bubbled inside his chest like an overheated cooking pot.

He followed his cousin towards a narrow pathway that led past the graveyard and the church. The noise of the barrel organ was getting louder and the smell of roasting meat drifted on the warm air, mingling with the scent of hay and roses. Giles had disappeared from view but Adam soon discovered that the path got narrower after it passed the graveyard and church, and curved steadily upwards until it reached the fair field.

The noise was becoming deafening now – a wild patchwork of voices and music. The ground under Adam's feet was dry and cracked and the air within the confines of the green tunnel in which he now found himself was hot and sweltering. People were coming past him, squeezing by in the narrow space, some of them smelling and acting the worst for drink. One family came past with a gaggle of tired-looking children. The ruddy-faced woman held a little girl in her arms, who was trailing a cloth doll by its yellow woollen hair. The older children were finishing the remains of twists of toffee, their faces and clothes sticky.

Adam emerged from the green tunnel into the fair field that was framed by hazy blue sky. He felt overwhelmed for a few minutes by noise and colour. The stalls around the edge were decorated with coloured flags and appeared to be selling all manner of items – trinkets, ribbons, cakes, sweetmeats. The stallholders shouted their wares, each trying to outdo the others. A large tent selling ale appeared to be attracting the attention of many of the men. There were games and sideshows and Adam guessed that the occasion must be the highlight of the year for the local people.

He was just pondering where to find his cousin amongst this haystack of people when he turned and found himself face to face with him.

"What the devil are you doing here?" Giles sounded hostile. "How did you find me? Has my father sent you to check up on me?"

"I need to speak to you about an important matter." Adam was aware he sounded clipped and sharp but his emotions were raw with the experiences he'd had since arriving back in England. Even so, this was hardly the time and place to inform his cousin of the latest events.

"I thought you were still playing soldiers," said Giles. "In fact, I'd hoped to have seen the last of you…,"

He broke off as two young women approached – one dark, the other fair. They'd come up the same pathway as Adam had followed moments before, and had been laughing together, the sound like music or birdsong. The dark haired one froze when she saw them. Adam noticed the naked hostility in her sapphire blue eyes.

Giles' demeanour changed. He bowed to the two young women, a smile on his face. His eyes gleamed like a dog sighting a bowl of food. Adam was familiar with the look.

"Mrs Marshall, Miss Beckford, may I introduce my cousin, Adam Lennox, who is lately returned from the Peninsula."

The two women bobbed curtseys. Adam bowed.

"Do please excuse us, gentlemen," said the dark haired one. "My brother is waiting for us and we should not detain him."

They bobbed curtseys again and moved gracefully across the field towards the brightly coloured stalls.

"Do I take it that Miss Beckford is the young woman you intend to marry? May I say that she doesn't look too anxious to spend long in your company?"

Giles grew red with anger. "What do you know of this? Has my father been gossiping like some village scold? Damn him to Hell if he has."

"I was sorting my uncle's affairs when I found your letter. I have the unhappy news that he has passed away."

"Trust you to be there at the opportune moment." Giles sounded bitter.

"I arrived on the day of his funeral. I am sorry to break the news in this way, but matters are more serious than you may imagine."

They were drawing curious glances – two well-dressed young men having a barely civil conversation on a day when most people present were concentrating on having fun. The lively barrel organ music was at odds with the mood of their discussion. Young girls roaming round with baskets of cakes, sweetmeats and trinkets held off from approaching them even though they each looked as if they could easily buy the entire contents of their baskets. The one man with the face flushed with ill-temper was well-known to some of them – the other was a total stranger.

Adam guided Giles into the shade of some trees. A few horses had been tethered there and were stamping their hooves and twitching their tails to keep the flies away.

"Your father has left nothing," said Adam. "He has left instructions for the house and its contents, apart from a few bequests, to be sold at auction. Anything that is left once the creditors have been paid is to be shared between the two of us."

"No doubt at your instigation. Nothing's gone right since the day you were foisted onto us."

"I have repaid the affection my uncle gave me in full measure."

"Once I'm married, there'll be no need to make a slave of myself." Giles looked smug.

"If Miss Beckford is the object of your interest, then she does not appear to reciprocate your feelings."

"She will have no choice in the matter."

Chapter 11

"Odious man!" said Lucinda. "I hope John and your husband don't keep us waiting. I have no wish for those two gentlemen to bear us company."

"I haven't seen his cousin before," said Hannah.

"My only hope is that he doesn't also decide to occupy my father's study."

"Is your father fully recovered?"

"Yes – long since. However, Mr Milburn still presents himself every morning."

Hannah sensed that Lucinda's mood was darkening and sought to distract her. They had now proceeded to the far side of the field but could still see Giles Milburn and his cousin engaged in what looked like a heated conversation under an oak tree.

Hannah pointed to Orchard House, looking like a square white doll's house from the fair field. The brewery lay just beyond it and the river curved beyond that into the distance, glinting silver in the midsummer sunshine. "Look – Tilly's busy."

They watched as Tilly, looking no bigger than a peg doll from this distance, hung something large and red on the washing line.

"What on earth is she hanging on the line – and where has it come from? I don't recognise it," said Lucinda shading her eyes and looking into the distance. "And why is she still working? She and Mrs Parsons have been given the afternoon off to attend the fair."

"I have no doubt you'll solve the mystery when you get home," said Hannah, thankful that Lucinda had been diverted from the problem of Giles Milburn for a short time.

*

John and Charlie were in high spirits when they met up with Lucinda and Hannah a few minutes later. They'd already visited the stall that sold ale and Charlie had won a pink glass heart on a velvet ribbon for Hannah on the hoop-la stall.

She giggled as he tied it round her neck.

"If I had my way it'd be diamonds, sweetheart."

"Diamonds!" said Hannah. "Just listen to him! I'd much prefer a cottage that wasn't owned by Widow Parker."

They circulated round the fair, laughing at the crowd gathered around 'The Doctor' with his covered wagon full of bottles of little pink pills that were supposed to cure a huge variety of complaints from gout to consumption, as well as being able to restore energy and life to even the most flagging of spirits.

"Behold this young woman, ladies and gentlemen," yelled The Doctor who was dressed in a striped waistcoat and high-crowned beaver hat. He pulled a pale, exhausted-looking girl from the inside of the wagon. She was wearing a white dress and bonnet, both trimmed with blue ribbon. There were dark circles under her eyes and sores around her mouth.

"See how quickly she recovers a healthy vigour after swallowing one of my Vital Life pills."

He held up the tiny pill. The girl took it from him and swallowed it with a drink of what looked like lemonade. Then she retreated behind the cream canvas flaps of the wagon.

"We will now wait two minutes," said The Doctor holding up a large silver watch. The crowd waited with an air of hushed anticipation.

"I've seen this trick before," whispered Charlie. "There's two of them…,"

"Hush, he'll hear you," said Hannah holding back a fit of giggles.

"Be patient, ladies and gentlemen," said The Doctor. "In a few seconds from now you will see the amazing results of my miracle pills."

He tapped on the floor of the wagon and the flaps opened. A transformed version of the girl emerged. She was wearing the same white dress but had removed the bonnet. Her glossy dark hair spilled over her shoulders and her cheeks looked pink, her eyes bright. The sores round her mouth were gone.

"What further proof is needed, ladies and gentlemen?" asked The Doctor. "Now who is going to be the first to buy a bottle?"

"How do we know you ain't got two women in there?" demanded a man who'd heard Charlie's comment. "Open up them flaps so's we can see right through."

The people at the back surged forward – some wanting to buy some of the miracle pills, others wanting to see if there were indeed two women in the wagon.

Lucinda, Hannah, Charlie and John watched as The Doctor managed to simultaneously take money in exchange for bottles of pills and guard the back of the wagon. The girl with the flowing dark hair was holding the reins of the two piebald horses and keeping a watchful eye on the crowd.

With a triumphant cry, someone broke through The Doctor's defences and pulled open the canvas flaps. The Doctor soon regained control but not before a number of people had seen the first girl, now scantily dressed, huddled on a makeshift bed.

"I had a feeling he wouldn't stay too long," said Charlie as The Doctor's wagon carved a pathway through a group of soldiers from the nearby barracks, many of whom had pretty girls on their arms.

Charlie told them another story, gleaned from one of the patrons at *The King's Head*, of how sailors were travelling out from Bristol to pressgang unsuspecting young men into the navy. "Just imagine waking up with a sore head to find you're away at sea with no choice in the matter," he said. "The man I spoke to said he had a lucky escape from them. He pretended he was drunk and needed to go to the necessary house. He suspected they'd follow him and be waiting when he came out, so he hid round the corner and when they came looking for him, he pushed them inside and barred the door. With a bit of luck, they're still in there."

"The Militia's just as bad," said John. "The recruiting sergeant stopped me the other day. Asked me if I'd like to join them for a drink." He shuddered. "I've heard what happens when you do that. You end up with a head that feels as if a tribe of goblins are hammering inside it, a silver coin in your pocket and a tale that you've enlisted voluntarily. Everyone knows they're paid handsomely for each recruit they trick."

*

The afternoon got hotter, the field dustier. Stall holders kept up a playful banter, imploring people to try their wares – elderflower wine, spiced biscuits, cinder toffee.

On one section of the field a riotous tug of war was going on between a group of young men from Marchington and a group from the nearby village of Aldington. The squire of Marchington who'd been chosen to referee, was having a hard job to keep order as the supporters of both groups got more enthusiastic.

The local butcher had donated a flitch of bacon to provide additional entertainment at the fair. It was attached to the top of a greasy pole and the local men had great fun trying to squirm their way up to claim the prize. The area was surrounded by a group of men, women and children all shouting encouragement and advice to the next man making the attempt.

"Not that it'll be worth having, being stuck out there for hours in this heat," said Hannah. "Their clothes'll take some washing, too."

Lucinda couldn't help noticing Giles Milburn and his cousin and the way their conversation, even from a distance, was obviously not a friendly one. Giles looked fit to burst and it seemed at one point as if he would actually strike his cousin. In the finish, it was Adam who walked away and Giles who skulked in the shade of the trees, looking the image of the Devil that Tilly had imagined him to be back in February.

She turned away and tried to focus on enjoying the day but a cloud kept covering the sun and she couldn't let go of her unsettled feelings.

John did his best to lighten her mood. They were drinking lemonade and eating honey cakes in the shade of a tree – although Hannah didn't have much appetite for hers - and looking down towards their house again. The red fabric – of which John also denied any knowledge – was still visible, but it was the pear tree outside Lucinda's bedroom window that had sparked his memory.

"Do you remember when you used to climb down that tree and come out with me at night, Lucinda?" he asked.

"Lucinda – you didn't ever do such a thing?" Hannah passed the rest of her cake to Charlie who wolfed it down.

"It was before Mama died," said Lucinda, "and I didn't know John went out sketching at night until he came back once to find the garden door locked. My bedroom window was open and he climbed up the pear tree and in through the window. Imagine how scared I felt when I awoke and saw him."

"And you threatened to tell Mama if I didn't take you with me the next time."

Lucinda smiled. "You did say that it was no use my complaining if I hurt myself."

"Weren't you scared?" asked Hannah.

"I was more scared of Mama finding out, especially the time when some men chased us down near the riverbank.

"Did they catch you?" asked Charlie.

"No," said John, "they'd drunk rather a lot of ale and so we managed to escape. We were lucky though – they tore Lucinda's jacket and it put her off coming out with me for at least a week."

"So why did you stop?"

"Mama became ill and died…," Lucinda's voice faltered. "It didn't seem right after that."

Chapter 12

Giles didn't know who he felt more anger towards – his father for dying before he'd given him a chance to redeem himself, or his cousin for arriving back in his life in such an irritating fashion.

Giles had imagined the scene of reconciliation with his father on the occasion of presenting Lucinda as his new bride. Death had robbed him of this chance – and he hated Adam for bringing him the unwelcome news.

The sight of Lucinda Beckford in the blue muslin gown she'd worn to her friend's wedding was the one thing that kept him focused on a more stable future. Adam's unexpected appearance made him all the more certain that now was the time to put his plans into action.

Giles left the fair field, following the narrow path shaded by trees and bushes that led back down to the town. The sounds of the barrel organ faded slightly and the air around him smelled of wild roses and elderflower. His clothes felt as if they were sticking to him and his sense of urgency to gain what was due to him increased with every step.

When he arrived back in Marchington, he headed down the quiet main street towards *The Merry Maiden*. When he pushed open the door, the air was thick with the smell of smoke, old cooking and unwashed bodies. The smell was so overpowering, Giles nearly walked out again, but he'd been reliably informed that the person he needed to speak to was to be found here, so he persevered.

The low ceilinged room had oak beams and was divided into sections for greater privacy. A soldier and his doxy were making use of one of them, totally ignored by a trio who were the worst for drink and arguing over a game of dice.

"Keep the noise down, damn you," shouted a voice from another cubicle.

Giles could tell from the sleeve clothed in Stroud red cloth that he'd found the person he needed to speak to.

He ordered a jug of ale from the slatternly looking serving woman who sketched a curtsey that was so slight as to be an insult, and pulled open the curtain that had been drawn across.

There followed a conversation in low tones. Money changed hands and Giles stepped out of *The Merry Maiden* into the late afternoon sunshine. He took deep breaths of clear air and allowed a smile of satisfaction to spread across his face.

*

A short time later, he was back up at the fair field. Some of the stallholders were packing away their goods into baskets. Hoarse voices kept shouting their wares, hoping for late customers. Giles was pleased to see that Lucinda, John and their two companions were still there. They'd just finished watching the Mummers Play and were laughing at the antics of the actors as they tried to coax a few coppers from the crowds.

Hannah Marshall looked tired and was leaning on her husband's arm. He and John had just been sharing a joke and were both convulsed with laughter. Their faces were like stopped clocks when they caught sight of him. Lucinda turned her face away from him.

"Gentlemen. Ladies," said Giles, giving them a formal bow.

John and Charlie pulled themselves together and bowed. Lucinda and her friend bobbed the briefest of curtsies. The group went to move on past him. Giles moved in front of them. "Gentlemen, the day is not yet over. Will you not allow me to treat you to a glass of ale?" He looked at John. "It is long overdue that we should let bygones be bygones."

Charlie needed no encouragement, despite Hannah and Lucinda signalling frantically at him not to go. "Come on John," he said. "One tankard cannot do much harm, surely?"

"I really should be…,"

"Come along man, it's time we looked to the future. I'm sure the ladies will spare you for a short time." Giles tried to sound hearty and encouraging.

Hannah looked agitated. "Charlie, you've had more than enough already."

"Tush! Get yourself back home dearest, before Widow Parker comes looking for you." Charlie grinned at her.

The clock struck five. "I'll be late," said Hannah.

"One drink and then I'll be home, sweetheart," said Charlie, squeezing her hands.

Giles stood, trying to be patient, as they made their farewells. He was so close to achieving his aim that he didn't want to spoil things by appearing over-eager.

Chapter 13

"I don't like it," said Lucinda. "Why is Giles Milburn extending the olive branch all of a sudden?"

"I wish Charlie hadn't gone," said Hannah. "I fear that he'll come home drunk and then Widow Parker will throw us out of our cottage. Then where will we be?"

Lucinda noticed how tired Hannah looked and did her best to reassure her friend. "My Mama always said that men had no sense. I'm sure they'll be back in no time, as soon as they realise what an obnoxious person Giles Milburn is."

The two young women embraced when they reached Widow Parker's shop. Hannah opened the door and hurried inside. Lucinda carried on along the street to the turning that led towards Orchard House. The streets were still quiet – a few soldiers reeled out of *The Merry Maiden*, arms entwined, and some small boys raced down the main street, stopping when they saw a cart coming the other way.

Lucinda was thankful for a slight breeze that ruffled the ribbons of her bonnet and carried the scent of roses and fresh hay. However, nothing could quell the turmoil that twisted inside her. Her head ached from the fairground noise and the heat and all she wanted was to lie down in a darkened room with a drink of cool water.

The gravel of the driveway crunched under her boots and the trees that edged it made moving shadows that she could remember frightened her when she was a child. It was then that old Betsy's tales of witches and goblins came to life again, and she could see them in the patterns made by the leaves.

She'd been so drawn to her memories of childhood and being tucked in a warm bed, drowsy and ready for sleep, that when a figure stepped out in front of her from the side of the house, she couldn't help a scream of fright escaping from her.

"Forgive me, Miss Beckford, I did not wish to startle you." Adam Lennox looked genuinely contrite.

"Why are you here?" Lucinda's heart thudded in her chest.

"I need to speak with you."

"To me – but … I have no chaperone."

Adam Lennox waved away her concerns. "I need to speak to you on a matter of extreme importance. Perhaps your maid would remain within earshot?"

"She has been given the afternoon off."

Lucinda turned away.

"I don't wish you to be frightened, Miss Beckford, but I do believe you to be in the greatest danger."

At that point, Tilly returned from running an errand, her bonnet in disarray and her face flushed.

"Tilly," said Lucinda, "Mr Lennox has something he wishes to speak to me about. Will you please accompany us on a tour of the garden?"

Tilly's eyes were like saucers in her round pale face. She bobbed a curtsey.

They proceeded round the side of the house to where there was a terrace and a shrubbery, Tilly remaining a discreet distance away. Adam Lennox made several attempts to begin what he wanted to say to her, each one beginning with "Miss Beckford" – and then a clearing of his throat.

"What is you wish to say, sir?" Lucinda felt a surge of impatience.

"You are no doubt aware of my cousin Giles' interest in you?"

"I am sorry if this may cause you offence, sir, but I have no interest whatsoever in Mr Milburn."

"You have not in the least offended me Miss Beckford. However, please be aware that my cousin has a habit of getting whatever he sets his mind to by fair means or foul."

"I have no idea what you mean, sir." Lucinda was aware her colour was rising.

"I do not wish to embarrass you." Adam's voice was gentle. "My desire is to protect you from further harm."

"How do you intend to do that, sir?" Lucinda's voice was sharp-edged.

Mrs Parsons had come to the back door and was shouting for Tilly.

"Tilly, please remain where you are a moment longer," said Lucinda.

Tilly hovered from foot to foot, an expression on her face like a cornered fox.

"Miss Beckford, if I may speak plainly," said Adam, "I would like you to do me the honour of becoming my wife. I freely admit that this is not a love match for me any more than it is for you, but I can offer you safety and security and a home of your own."

Mrs Parsons' voice was getting more raucous. "Tilly, hurry up wherever you are – and bring some extra parsley for the sauce."

Lucinda glanced round. Tilly looked as if she was about to race for the shelter of the kitchen. If she ran off and Lucinda was seen in the company of Adam Lennox without a chaperone, then her reputation would be in tatters and she may be forced to marry him whether she wished to or not.

"One moment, Tilly…," said Lucinda moving swiftly and catching hold of the girl by her sleeve.

She turned back to Adam Lennox. "I thank you for your kind offer, but I am not yet so desperate that I must seek refuge in a loveless marriage. Rest assured that your cousin will receive the same response should he be foolhardy enough to ask for my hand. I have no wish to marry – ever."

Lucinda turned on her heel and headed towards the garden door, slamming it behind her. Through the small window she saw Tilly scamper towards the herb garden for the parsley. Adam Lennox stood for a few moments as if he expected her to reappear. Lucinda closed her eyes, willing the thumping of her heart to slow down. When she opened them again he'd gone.

*

Lucinda stood for a few moments looking out at the garden – the flitter of butterflies and bees amongst the flowers and the way the sun made patterns on the pathways. She remembered games of hide and seek played in this garden, and how they sometimes strayed into the kitchen garden beyond. This was where, earlier, Lucinda had seen Tilly hanging something on the line set amongst rosemary and lavender bushes so that the clothes and sheets absorbed the smell as they dried. The red item – whatever it was – had already been taken in.

As she went through the garden room – the place that smelled of dried earth and fresh herbs where her mother used to arrange flowers and where the gardener left the vegetables for Mrs Parsons – she overheard Tilly and the cook talking in the kitchen.

"There are some strange things happening with this family an' no mistake," said Mrs Parsons. "They'd never have happened when Miss Lucinda's mother was alive."

"I ain't never seen that gentleman before, so why was he speaking of marriage to Miss Lucinda?" whispered Tilly.

"You hush your mouth, girl. It's not for the likes of us to know about such things. When you've finished those pots, go and finish making the bed for Mr Milburn. That old red counterpane we found in the attic will be aired by now. It's good enough for the likes of him."

Lucinda's senses were alerted. Why was a bed being made up for Giles Milburn? What had her father agreed to now?

Chapter 14

Lucinda did no more than pick at her evening meal, earning a torrent of muttering from Mrs Parsons as she cleared the plates away.

"Could've given us the rest of the day off for all the notice that's been taken of our hard work."

Lucinda's mouth was dry and it felt as if a block of stone had been placed in her throat, making it impossible for her to swallow anything. She'd taken small bites of cold beef and pickles but, no matter how well she chewed them, the food felt like briars in her mouth. Her head still ached and it was difficult to focus her eyes.

She went up to her room, pulling herself up on the banisters as if she was an old woman. She put on her white nightgown, thankful to feel cool cotton against her skin. It was hot and sticky with a feeling of vibration in the air like an approaching storm, making her skin feel prickly. Lucinda got up and opened the window, allowing the smell of fresh hay to drift in through the window.

She closed her eyes and tried to focus on pleasant images like flowers and butterflies. However, unsettling images from the day kept intruding, whirling around her like a merry-go-round until she felt sick and giddy.

The most unsettling question of all was why would a man like Adam Lennox propose marriage to a woman he had never met? It did not make sense.

She lay awake waiting for John to come home so that she could ask him what Giles Milburn had spoken of, and why their father may have asked him to stay at Orchard House. She lay still, willing the nausea to pass, until the sky darkened from blue to indigo covered in brooding dark cloud. There was no moon and the atmosphere in her room, even with the window open, was stifling.

She dozed fitfully, waking to the sound of her window banging to and fro. For a split-second she thought it was John trying to get back indoors, but then realised the wind had risen and the window catch had loosened and was likely to break if she didn't close it.

Having closed it and settled down again, the branches of the pear tree carried on tapping against the window like bony fingers and it was a long time before she got any rest.

When she woke again, feeling gritty-eyed and exhausted from the series of strange dreams she'd had, dreams where she was stuck in a river that she couldn't get out of, and Giles Milburn was standing on the bank offering to throw her a rope providing she agreed to be his wife.

The words of refusal that Lucinda threw back at him became stones that hit the surface of the water with a series of loud splashes that echoed through her head. She opened her eyes. Early morning sunlight was slicing through the leaves of the pear tree, making patterns on the wooden floor of her room. The sound came again – small stones hitting the window. Lucinda sat up so quickly that the room spun. She hurried to the window. Hannah stood there, another handful of ammunition ready to throw. She turned a tear-stained face up to Lucinda.

"Wait there," said Lucinda, "I'll come down."

She poured yesterday's cold water into her basin and splashed some onto her face, dragged her brush through her long dark hair and bundled it into a knot on the back of her head. She got dressed and put on her boots. Then she hurried down the stairs, careful to avoid the third one from the top that creaked and headed towards the garden door.

"What is it?" she asked Hannah, drawing the weeping girl into the garden room.

"It's Charlie – and your John, the army's got them now. The boy from *The Merry Maiden* came to tell me."

"How could that happen?"

"I told him not to go drinking with that Giles Milburn. I knew it would end badly if he did so." Hannah burst into a fresh flood of tears.

Lucinda could hear Mrs Parsons waking up in the little bedroom she occupied just off the kitchen. When Lucinda's mother was alive, it was grandly named 'the butler's pantry' and was used as a place to store and clean the silver. As Mrs Parsons grew older and began to complain about the cold attic bedrooms and her 'rheumatics' as she called them, it was decided to move her into this room.

Lucinda knew that the waking up routine could take some time – she and John had often made fun of it, although of course not in Mrs Parson's hearing. It began with yawning and stretching and then with Mrs Parsons saying her morning prayers out loud. This done, she would then use the chamber pot, which was an equally noisy action.

"Have you eaten anything?" she asked Hannah.

"I couldn't. I felt sick."

Lucinda ventured into the kitchen and cut two slices of bread from the loaf, buttered them and put them on two plates. She poured two cups of milk and, putting everything on a tray, carried it back into the garden room. There was less chance of being disturbed there.

"Now, tell me from the beginning what happened," she said when they were settled side by side at the table where the gardener sorted the vegetables.

Hannah took tiny bites of her bread and butter. "Charlie didn't come back like he said he would. I didn't think much about it – men do get carried away when they have a tankard in their hands. It was only when I'd finished the work Widow Parker set for me that I heard the church clock strike ten and got worried – but what could I do. I didn't want to look like a scold…,"

"What did you do?"

"I waited till first light this morning and then I went to *The King's Head*. Sometimes if he's had one too many he sleeps there in the straw rather than be caught by Widow Parker, she bein' Methody and all. He wasn't there and then the potboy from *The Merry Maiden* came and found me and told me about Charlie and your John bein' taken away by the Militia last night." She burst into a fresh torrent of weeping. "Lucinda, what can we do? I may never see him again."

"It's not hard to imagine who is behind this." Lucinda's eyes flashed blue fire. "There must be a way to release them."

"What can we do?"

"They were taken last night you say?" Lucinda felt as if a lump of stone had settled where her heart was.

Hannah nodded. "The potboy said they were marched along in the middle of a group of soldiers – all of them the worse for drink."

"They cannot fully be taken into the army unless they've sworn an oath before a magistrate. If they weren't taken until last night and today is Sunday, it is unlikely they will do so until tomorrow. If we are quick then we can pay the fine and they will be released."

"Who can we ask to help us?" asked Hannah.

"We must go ourselves to the barracks and speak to the commanding officer," said Lucinda with more confidence than she felt, "and we should go now before any suspicions are aroused. I have a little money, let us hope it is enough."

She hurried upstairs, collected her reticule, took the precious sovereigns from her sewing box, wrapped them in a handkerchief and put them in the bag. She heard somebody moving around in what had been the guest room and stiffened. She didn't want to come face to face with Giles Milburn at this hour of the morning, or to have him ask where she was off to so early in the day – as if he didn't know already.

Lucinda did wonder whether she should wake her father and tell him what had happened, but decided that it was highly likely that he'd summon Giles and place the matter in his hands and then no help would be forthcoming.

When she got downstairs, Hannah had cleared the plates and cups into the kitchen and was casting wary glances towards Mrs Parsons' room where there were sounds of increased activity.

Hearing a light tread on the back staircase, Lucinda knew that Tilly was on her way down. It was best that they should move before anyone knew what they were up to. She and Hannah went out of the garden door, closing it gently behind them, round the side of the house and onto the gravel path, walking carefully so as not to make too much noise. They didn't speak until they reached the main street at the top of the drive for fear of their voices carrying on the sultry morning air.

They walked until they reached the crossroads. Lucinda had never liked this place. It had a strange atmosphere and it was said that many years ago, witches used to be hanged here. They took the right hand turn towards Pendlebury Barracks. This was a lane that meandered along, with woodland on one side rising towards Longdon Hill and fields of green-gold unripe corn on the other. It was bordered by hedges fragrant with elderflower and wild roses and the trees formed an arch over the road, making it dark in places even when it should be full daylight.

The fragments of sky they could see were a glowering yellow colour. Lucinda marched along, determined to confront this problem and make some sense of it. Hannah was lagging behind, her face was pale, her eyes red-rimmed, and she'd made frequent entries to the bushes at the side of the road. Lucinda could hear her dry retching and wished she'd had the sense to bring some water for them.

"What is it, Hannah? Are you ill?"

"Oh, Lucinda! I never got the chance to tell Charlie. I was going to tell him last night after the fair. I'm going to have a baby."

Lucinda didn't know whether to be glad or sorry for Hannah in their present predicament.

"For some reason, Giles Milburn wants John and Charlie out of the way." Lucinda had a puzzled frown between her dark eyebrows.

"If only I'd done more to stop Charlie from going, then maybe your John would've stayed away too."

"What's done is done, Hannah. We have to do all we can to get them released." Lucinda softened the comment by giving Hannah a hug. However, a memory stirred of Giles Milburn's face as John and Charlie went with him. He'd looked triumphant, and Lucinda didn't feel as certain as she sounded that their quest would be successful.

*

They trudged on. Lucinda's clothes were sticking to her and her mouth felt as dry as if she'd been eating crab apples. Their boots and the hems of their gowns were coated in white dust from the road.

"We look more like camp followers than a respectable wife and sister," said Lucinda as they reached the imposing entrance to *Pendlebury Barracks*.

Nevertheless, the sentry on the gate responded to Lucinda's imperious tone and escorted them to the commanding officer's quarters. As they followed his straight red back, Lucinda and Hannah gazed across the dusty parade square where soldiers were obeying the commands of the drill sergeant or loading supplies and baggage onto wagons.

The commanding officer, a tall silver-haired man with a bristling moustache ushered them into his room and invited them to sit.

"There is nothing I can do to release these men from their obligation," he said when he had heard their story. "They have been passed as fit for service by the army surgeon and Sir James Torrance, the magistrate, was here last night and has authorised their applications."

"Applications!" exclaimed Lucinda. "They were tricked."

Sir James Torrance was one of the circle of men her father and Giles Milburn played cards with. Lucinda was more sure than ever that this situation was all Giles' doing.

Hannah laid a hand on Lucinda's sleeve.

"What Miss Beckford means is that her brother and my husband did not intend to join the army." Hannah's voice trembled. "Charlie and I have only been married a few months."

"Then we will do our utmost to return him safely to you," he said – a glint of sympathy in his grey eyes, "but for now they are both in the Militia, having sworn an oath in front of a magistrate, and as such must obey the orders given."

"May we speak to them?" asked Lucinda.

The commanding officer barked a question to the orderly waiting outside the door.

"They've already gone, sir."

"I'm sorry ladies, but your brother and husband are now bound for Bristol and the docks where they will be embarked for Spain. There is nothing more I can do for you."

*

"So what can we do now?" asked Hannah as they left the barracks and headed back towards Marchington.

"I don't know, but we won't just meekly accept the situation as Giles Milburn no doubt expects us to. I just wonder what other nasty little tricks he has up his sleeve." Lucinda slashed at a patch of nettles with her reticule. "How can they have sworn an oath already – there has hardly been time."

*

Adam Lennox, on his way to visit his patroness before she departed to take the waters at Bath, was startled to see Lucinda Beckford and the friend she'd been with at the Midsummer Fair trudging along the lane towards Marchington. Their boots and skirts were coated in dust and they looked distressed and footsore. He stopped, although both ladies looked as pleased to see him as if they'd spotted a viper on the path next to them.

"Ladies, what brings you out so early on a Sunday morning?"

"I'm sure you must have had communication with your cousin and are fully aware of our situation." Lucinda Beckford's voice held an edge of steel.

"On the contrary, I have not spoken with my cousin since I had the pleasure of meeting you two ladies at the Midsummer Fair yesterday."

Adam was tired and wanted no more than a cool wash and a good breakfast. He had spent a long night assisting the local doctor with a brewery worker who was severely injured when he fell off the greasy pole having won the flitch of bacon at the fair.

"Much good it's done us," his wife grumbled. "I told him not to go up there with a belly full of ale – but would he listen?"

As Hannah had surmised, the flitch was rancid from being out in the hot sun and despite the best efforts of both doctors, they couldn't say how long it would take the man to recover.

Adam was therefore in no mood for parrying words with a young woman who appeared to be accusing him of goodness only knew what. Part of him felt relieved she hadn't accepted his proposal of marriage if she was likely to be so shrewish. Maybe Giles would meet his match.

He tried again. "Can I be of any assistance to you ladies? Forgive me for the observation, but you appear to be a little distressed."

"We certainly are distressed, and you are no doubt well aware of the reasons why."

The look Miss Beckford gave him would have stopped a dragon at five hundred paces.

"I am afraid I have no idea of what you are speaking of. If there is anything I can help you with, I would be only too happy to oblige. If not, I bid you ladies good day." He raised his hat to them and then urged his horse forward. It was obvious from their brief curtsies and downcast faces that he was not going to be made privy to whatever was going on.

*

"Lucinda, that wasn't fair, he looks kind, I'm sure he would've helped us." Hannah watched Adam disappear from sight round a bend in the lane.

"He's Giles' cousin isn't he? I'm sure they're both cut from the same cloth – and I'm equally sure Adam Lennox knows exactly what's going on. What other reason would there be for him being so close to the barracks at this time on a Sunday morning?"

"I still can't believe he'd have anything to do with it."

They stopped to rest in the shade of a tree, finding a handful of wild strawberries that freshened their dry mouths.

"My feet ache something cruel," said Hannah," but I don't dare take my boots off. I may not get them back on again."

"Hannah, I can hear something." They'd reached a junction in the road – a wide road that led to Bristol had joined the narrow lane back to Marchington.

Lucinda clambered up onto a grassy bank to take a better look.

"Soldiers, Hannah. They're stopped just around the bend. You don't think …,"

"They cannot stop us from asking, can they?" Hannah forgot about her tired feet and hurried ahead of Lucinda.

Two lines of raw recruits waited under guard at the side of the road while three red-coated soldiers struggled to repair a broken wheel.

"Be quick, lads," urged the sergeant. "We don't have much time."

Work stopped when Lucinda and Hannah approached the ragged lines of men.

"Can I be of assistance, ladies?" asked the sentry on guard duty. "This is no place for you – unless you feel inclined to accompany us to Spain."

"We are not camp followers," said Lucinda icily, ignoring Hannah's urgent tug at her sleeve.

She knew Hannah would follow Charlie to the ends of the earth, but given her condition, she hoped she would not embark on such a dangerous adventure.

"No offence was meant ladies," said the sergeant, breaking away from the problems with the wheel. "We are on our way to Bristol in order to catch the evening tide."

"You have John Beckford and Charles Marshall amongst your new recruits," said Lucinda. She'd just caught sight of Charlie. "I wonder if we might speak with them since no opportunity was given for any farewell."

"I swear I never meant this to happen," said Charlie holding both Hannah's hands in his. Tears glistened in his blue eyes. "If I'd seen so much as a glimpse of a red coat I'd never have gone inside *the Merry Maiden*. There were just the three of us in the taproom – me, John and Mr Milburn. He brought us glasses of ale and was on about wanting bygones to be bygones and all the rest of it."

"He encouraged us to drain our glasses but he barely touched his own." John looked pale and there was a bruise on his cheek. "Then as soon as we'd done so, we noticed the coin at the bottom – the old trick. The drill sergeant stepped out from behind a curtain and within minutes he'd called up some of his men and we were dragged away. This morning, we demanded to see the Commanding Officer and be set free, but he claimed he had witnesses to say we'd enlisted of our own free will – as well as authorisation from the magistrate."

"I've never regretted anything in my life as much as going into that ale house," said Charlie. "I gave my last penny to the potboy to carry a message to you, Hannah."

There was a rumble as the cart got moving again.

"Form ranks," bawled the sergeant.

Charlie kissed Hannah long and deep, ignoring the cat-calls of the other men.

"Let me come with you, Charlie," she begged, tears streaming down her face, not wanting to let him go. She reached up and whispered something in his ear and he hugged her close for an instant, and laid a protective hand on her belly.

"Promise me you'll do nothing so foolhardy," he said stroking her cheek. "It's no life for a woman. If you need help, go to my mother in Lower Warren. She's not the easiest of women but she'd not turn you or her grandchild away."

John hugged Lucinda. "Look after yourself, Lucinda."

Lucinda was about to chide him for being so foolhardy as to go off with Giles, but instead she hugged him back and whispered: "Keep yourself safe."

"Get fell in there," barked the sergeant. "Stand aside please ladies."

"I'll find a way of helping you," Lucinda promised the two men.

She put her arms round Hannah and they watched the ragged lines of men move slowly down the dusty road. Then the storm that had threatened for the last few hours broke. Raindrops as large as pennies fell, laying the dust briefly before turning the lane back to Marchington into a mud bath.

"I must speak to my father," said Lucinda. "Although no doubt by now Giles Milburn will have convinced him it was all John's idea."

By the time they reached Marchington they were soaked to the skin and the bottoms of their skirts were heavy with mud.

"We look like street urchins," said Lucinda. "Come home with me and get dry. Then we can speak to my father."

Hannah shook her head. "Widow Parker's going to have plenty to say about me appearing like this on the Sabbath." She did an impression of that lady: "*It is disrespectful to Our Lord to appear in such a fashion.*" She grimaced. "But despite all her religious talk, she'll still expect me to work today – and I'll get little sympathy when she hears about Charlie. All she'll care about is the rent being paid."

They hugged each other and promised to meet the next day. Lucinda hurried towards Orchard House, eager to speak to her father as soon as possible. She hoped she'd be able to do so without Giles Milburn witnessing her distress.

However, even before she reached the driveway, she could hear an unfamiliar commotion. A strange assortment of boxes and baggage was piled outside Orchard House and Lucinda could hear raised voices.

With a feeling of trepidation, she headed towards the open front door.

Chapter 15

It was after the funeral, when Georgiana caught sight of the letter from Giles that Adam had left briefly unattended in her father's study, that a plan began to hatch in her mind.

Her father had left her without any financial provision, and the prospect of having no home and having to earn her living as a governess or seamstress did not fill Georgiana with happiness.

While Adam was talking to the lawyer and arranging the sale of the house, she had laboriously read the contents of Giles's letter.

A smile spread across her face like melted butter when she realised that her brother had a comfortable situation and would no doubt be in need of a housekeeper. She copied the address for future reference. The future may not be as bleak as she first thought.

*

Lack of money had been a problem on the journey but she'd solved that by seducing a gentleman at one of the inns and enticing him up to her room. She'd plied him with brandy, trying not to gag at the sour smell of his linen or recoil from the touch of his ice-cold hands. When he fell asleep, she stole his money and his pocket watch and made her escape.

She'd also taken as much merchandise from the house from under the noses of the lawyers as she could. She'd sold items of jewellery, some miniature paintings and some hand-made lace. Georgiana was proud of her growing business skills – on all levels.

There were times when she felt guilty. She could hear her father's voice in her head saying how disappointed he was in her. Georgiana learned to ignore the voice. She'd stayed buried in the countryside and acted like the dutiful daughter for most of her life and it had got her nowhere. Her brief dalliance with Oliver had shown her how much more enjoyable life was if she was able to carve out her own destiny.

She hired the best carriage she could find to take her on the last part of her journey to Marchington, arriving first thing on a stormy Sunday morning. It was the first time she'd seen her brother lost for words.

"There is not room for you here, Georgiana," he spluttered. His brown eyes looked hard as bullets and she nearly crumpled at their coldness.

"I think you'll find there is," she said. "If not I shall find Miss Beckford and tell her exactly what happened to Amelia, your wife, and how you had her committed to the asylum. Adam told me about it."

Adam hadn't really spoken to Georgiana about what had happened. She'd eavesdropped on a few conversations and had created her own story. She could see from her brother's face that she was close to the truth.

"I forbid you to discuss my private life with our cousin Adam." Giles spat the words at her.

"You are in no position to forbid me to do anything, brother dear," she said sweetly.

Georgiana looked around the bit of the house she could see. The décor and furnishings were not entirely to her taste, but she was sure this could be remedied in due course. The position, so close to the town centre, was good and from the look of the servants, she was sure of an easy life.

She knew exactly what her brother planned to do next, and Georgiana didn't envy Lucinda Beckford one bit.

Chapter 16

The first sight that greeted Lucinda was Tilly wielding the feather duster as if she wanted to harm somebody with it. Sunday was usually her day off and her mother relied on her going home to help with her collection of young brothers and sisters.

"Another morning like this and I'll be looking for a new situation," she muttered darkly as she swished at the skirting board with the feather duster. "Lawks, Miss Lucinda, what in the world's happened to you? You looks as though you've been dragged through a hedge backwards."

"I must speak to my father urgently," said Lucinda, the battle to obtain justice for John and Charlie triumphing over her need for dry clothes and something to eat. "What's happened, Tilly? Why are you here and not with your mother and the little ones? What is all that baggage doing outside?"

Tilly scowled. "It's all on account of Madam Georgiana or whatever her name is. Mr Giles has got a face like thunder and he's in Mr Josiah's study and says they're not to be disturbed. On a Sunday an' all! I've never heard the like of it."

A bellow of rage from the kitchen and a loud clattering of pots indicated that Mrs Parsons was out of sorts, too.

"I'd best go and see what she wants." Tilly scuttled off before she could explain the situation any further.

The parlour and dining room were crammed with more boxes and baggage, some of them spilling their contents onto the polished wooden floor. Lucinda caught sight of feminine garments trimmed with red ribbons and black lace. A stale musky scent filled the room, overriding the usual smell of beeswax polish.

Whoever Georgiana was, Lucinda had no doubt she was here because of Giles Milburn, and she was heartily sick of the entire family. She hoped she was a former sweetheart who would deflect his interest away from her.

Some of Lucinda's mother's books and precious ornaments had been removed from what had once been Caroline's bedroom and were stacked haphazardly in the hall and dining room. A rose patterned vase from her dressing table had fallen and was chipped. The portrait of Caroline wearing her sapphire and diamond ring, painted shortly after her marriage to Josiah, was propped against the wall, its glass cracked where it had been set down carelessly.

Lucinda snatched it up intending to take it to her room in order to protect it from further damage. At that point a woman with wild black hair wearing a purple silk dress and feathered black bonnet swept down the stairs carrying Caroline Beckford's ebony sewing box.

Her bold dark eyes took in Lucinda's dishevelled appearance.

"Where do you think you're going with that picture? The frame's worth a lot of money." The woman's voice was as harsh as that of an African grey parrot Lucinda had once seen in a travelling show.

"This is my mother's portrait. I am taking it to my room for safe-keeping. Who are you – and on whose authority are you disrupting my home?"

"Oh, it's *your* home is it?" The woman pushed her face close to Lucinda's. "Well, let me tell you, my brother has just appointed me as housekeeper. My name is Georgiana Milburn and I'm very pleased to make your acquaintance." The smile she gave Lucinda was as sickly as the violet perfume she was wearing.

Lucinda didn't waste time going upstairs to change. She headed down the hallway towards her father's study, her wet boots squelching on the flagstones.

"You're not to go in there," said Georgiana. "They are discussing matters of importance that don't concern you."

Lucinda ignored her, tapped on the door and barged in without waiting for a reply. Her father and Giles had obviously been in the middle of a heated discussion and they stopped abruptly with her sudden arrival.

"Lucinda, my dear, what in the world has happened to you? Why are you in this state of disrepair?"

"I am sure Mr Milburn will be able to furnish you with answers, father. Who is that woman outside and on whose authority is she turning the house upside down and upsetting the servants?"

Josiah flapped his hands as if swatting away a fly. "I'm sure matters are not as bad as you make out, Lucinda," he said. "Please leave us for a while, we have important matters to discuss."

Lucinda could feel her emotions boiling inside her. Images tumbled inside her head – Hannah's sad face, the sight of John and Charlie trapped in a situation neither of them wanted, the cracked glass on her beloved mother's portrait.

"Your son has been forcibly conscripted into the army, father. Mr Milburn is to blame for this. I am sure that there is nothing you are discussing that can be of any greater significance than this."

Josiah's face bleached of colour and Lucinda thought he was going to faint or have a seizure. "Lucinda, you are sounding most unlike yourself. I suggest you go to your room until you can behave in a more civil manner to a guest in our house. If you do not calm yourself I will ask the doctor to administer a draught of laudanum. For your information, Giles has informed me of the whole sorry situation. He has done his utmost to get your brother and Charles Marshall released but without success."

Lucinda felt like a firework that was about to explode. She glanced at Giles Milburn. Apart from a slight rise in colour, his face was as bland as ever, making her want to slap him. "Hannah Marshall and I have been to the barracks this morning. We met Charlie and John on the way back and they informed us that Mr Milburn had arranged the whole situation. I am sorry, father, that you do not see fit to support your own son."

Lucinda bobbed the briefest of curtsies and left the room, almost toppling an eavesdropping Georgiana into the hall table. She hurried up to her room and shut the door, leaning against it as she let the waves of anger and tempestuous tears flood from her. No matter what Giles did, her father was unlikely to challenge him and Lucinda wondered what sort of hold he had over him that could have led to their present situation.

Lucinda listened for her father's footsteps on the stairs. When she had temper tantrums as a child, her father would come to her room and talk to her quietly, informing her that she could come downstairs when she was ready to apologise. She heard nothing and she didn't know whether to be glad or sorry.

She caught sight of herself in the cheval mirror. Her boots and the bottom six inches of her gown were rimed with mud. Her face was streaked with dirt and tears and her hair had escaped from most of its pins and was full of tangles.

She peeled off her wet clothes and left them in a heap on the floor for Tilly to take down to the scullery ready for the next wash day. She rubbed herself hard with the towel on her wash stand. She changed into the yellow sprigged muslin dress that was her least favourite and lay down on her bed, covering herself with her shawl. Her head ached and her limbs felt heavy and all she wanted to do was fall into a dreamless sleep.

Lucinda was roused from a fitful slumber later that afternoon by the sounds of raised voices downstairs. She got to her feet, splashed some cold water from the ewer on her face and headed downstairs. Mrs Parsons the cook was on the point of having one of her 'turns.'

"Nobody told me afore now that I was to cook for eight people tonight. Lord knows how they think a piece of meat that's big enough for four is going to stretch to that many. I'm sure some folks thinks it can be magicked. Serve 'em right if I was to hand in my notice." The remarks were punctuated by a loud clattering of pots and pans. Mrs Parsons glared at the retreating figure of Georgiana. "I've never been spoke to like that in all the years I've worked for this family."

Her fat cheeks burned as she picked up her bowl of batter and began to beat it again, muttering recipes like a wizard reciting a spell. "Potato and onion soup, roast beef, syllabub, the best china and glassware. Never heard such a fuss in all me born days."

"I never heard of anyone moving house on a Sunday," said Tilly, who was busy peeling potatoes.

"You mind your manners, girl, criticising your betters like that." Mrs Parsons recovered herself as she noticed Lucinda watching them.

"What's going on, Mrs Parsons?" Lucinda asked.

"Something as they're hatching in Mr Josiah's study," she said. "All I know is they've invited the rector and his wife and the lawyer and his wife and I've no idea how I'm going to be ready in time. Especially with Miss Georgiana or whatever her name is coming in every five minutes with new instructions."

The smell of food was making Lucinda feel ill. She headed out of the garden door. The rain had stopped and the scent of mint and lavender combined with damp earth. It was still warm out there as she headed out towards the rose garden that had always been her mother's favourite spot.

Caroline Beckford had created a little bower where she could sit, protected from rain and wind, and enjoy the scent of roses and the colours that ranged from palest pink to a deep red one with petals like velvet. It was here that Lucinda sat now, hoping that her mother's spirit would surround her and give a measure of calm. Nothing made sense any more. She could not believe that her life could have changed so much since the day of the Midsummer Fair. It was as if Giles had put her father under some sort of enchantment and Lucinda had no idea how to break the spell.

Chapter 17

Giles Milburn stood in the shrubbery observing Lucinda as she sat in the rose bower. The seat she was sitting on was surrounded by a climbing rose that was the same creamy-pink tone of her skin. He crept as close as he dared. Her eyes were closed and a pulse beat in her throat. A few tendrils of curly dark hair had escaped from her chignon and he longed to release it and see it tumble down her back. He imagined running its softness through his fingers. He wanted to make love to her here, in the privacy of the garden, their bodies crushing the grass and releasing its camomile scent.

In all his years of pursuing women, Giles had never before met a woman who had captured his mind and his heart. This time it wasn't just her fortune he craved - he would do anything in his power to get Lucinda Beckford into his bed.

As if sensing he was near, Lucinda's eyes opened, reminding Giles of sapphires glittering in a jeweller's window. The expression in them turned hostile when she caught sight of him.

"Mr Milburn," she said, getting to her feet and giving the briefest of curtsies.

"I'm sorry Miss Beckford – Lucinda – did I startle you?" Giles could barely contain himself at the thought of waking up to that face, those eyes, before many more weeks had passed.

She turned in the direction of the house, her dislike of him all too obvious. In spite of his optimism, Giles recalled Adam's words at the Midsummer Fair. *'If that's your intended, she doesn't seem any too fond of you.'*

No matter, thought Giles. He had no doubt that before long she would be eating out of his hand. There was something exciting about taming a woman – especially one as beautiful and passionate as Lucinda.

*

Lucinda went to her room, feeling exhausted. She was awoken from a fitful dream a few hours later where she was walking along an endless dusty road where the place she was trying to get to was tantalisingly out of reach.

The knock on her bedroom door came again. "Master says they're waiting dinner for you, Miss," said Tilly.

"If it's not too much trouble, could you bring me a tray up here please Tilly? Some bread and dripping will do." Lucinda couldn't bear the thought of having to face Giles across the dining table.

"I'll ask, Miss, but I think the Master will be none too happy."

Tilly's light footsteps tripped off down the stairs.

Josiah's heavy ones came up. He paused in Lucinda's bedroom doorway, his eyes lighting on the portrait of Caroline that Lucinda had rescued from downstairs.

"She was a truly beautiful woman," he said with a gleam of tears in his eyes. "And so are you, my dear."

"What is going on, father? Why are you allowing that – that woman to take over our house?"

"Sometimes in life our luck runs out," Josiah said wearily. "Sometimes things happen that are not of our choosing. We have to make the best of situations."

"What do you mean, father? What has happened? What are we going to do to help John and Charlie?"

"Lucinda – if you wish to help me and your brother, then please come downstairs and do your duty as my hostess at dinner."

Lucinda listened to his heavy footsteps going back down the stairs. Reluctantly she poured some cold water into the basin on her washstand and splashed some on her face. She brushed her hair and bundled it into a knot on the back of her head, not really caring what she looked like. She hoped that maybe later she would get the chance to talk to her father about getting John and Charlie released.

As Lucinda entered the dining room, the conflicting smells of potato and onion soup, roast beef, beeswax polish and Georgiana's sickly perfume assaulted her nostrils, making her feel queasy. Even though it was a long time since she'd eaten, her throat felt tight, as if she couldn't swallow a morsel.

The room appeared crowded. The candles had been lit, the flames reflecting in the dark wood of the polished oak table and in the glasses of claret that had been poured. It had been some time since Josiah had had company to dinner and this alone made Lucinda feel wary. She wished she'd taken the time to change her gown – but it was too late to do anything about that now.

Giles cleared his throat and Lucinda slid into the chair he was holding for her. She glanced at the faces round the table. Her father looked flushed and ill at ease despite his strong words to her.

Lucinda edged as close to the rector's wife as she could. They were tightly packed around the table and she did not want to touch Giles. As it was, she could feel the heat from his body, encased in dark green jacket and biscuit-coloured britches, radiating towards her. She was close enough to smell the stale wine on his breath and the cologne he wore.

A wave of nausea swept over Lucinda. The heat and the combined smells became unbearable and the room began to spin like a merry-go-round. However, she was determined not to let Giles see that she was upset. She ignored the bowl of cooling soup in front of her and sat with her hands in her lap, willing the feeling to subside. She was relieved when Tilly came to clear the plates.

"Our soldiers would be glad of bread like this," said the Rector. "I've heard tell they almost break their teeth on the hard-tack they're given. They're not doubt glad of the ale you supply, Josiah."

Josiah had the goodness to flush and look ill at ease. Lucinda was glad when the conversation moved on to other matters. To take her mind of the uneasy proximity of Giles Milburn, Lucinda tried to think what to do next. It was obvious her father wasn't going to be much help but she wondered about asking the Rector for aid. She resolved that in the morning she would go and ask him whether there was anybody she could write to in order to secure the release of the two men.

The meal dragged on for what seemed like hours. The sky outside the window turned to indigo. The dinner plates were cleared and the syllabub brought in. Lucinda looked forward to the time when Josiah would suggest that the gentlemen retire for port and cigars. However, Josiah was watching Giles as if he were now head of the house.

Giles waited until Tilly had cleared the syllabub dishes and her footsteps had faded away down the hall. He cleared his throat and stood up.

"There is a special reason for inviting you here this evening. Josiah and I have had much to discuss today – the most important thing being that he's given his blessing for me to marry his daughter Lucinda." The expression on Giles' face was like the cat that had just swallowed the canary.

He took Lucinda's unwilling hand in his. "Lucinda, I'm sure you have no doubt now of the depth of my feelings for you. I hope that in time you will come to feel the same for me." He pushed a gold ring with three rubies onto the third finger of her left hand.

Lucinda snatched her hand away, feeling scorched by his touch. The rubies reminded her of drops of blood and she wanted to pull the ring off her finger.

She got to her feet, feeling unsteady. "Doesn't my opinion count, father? I thought you understood that I have no wish to marry any man – ever."

She noticed the circle of shocked faces around the table but she didn't care. Lucinda pushed back her chair and headed towards the stairs. Black specks danced in front of her eyes and she felt as if she were about to faint.

"Disgraceful behaviour," she heard the Rector's wife murmur. "I've never seen the like of it before."

Lucinda held onto the newel post at the bottom of the stairs for a moment in order to steady herself.

"She has always been delicate," Josiah said. "She will get used to the idea."

Lucinda was about to go back and state that there was no way in the world that she would ever accept the idea of marrying Giles Milburn. She changed her mind when she saw Giles heading towards her but was too late to prevent him catching her in the circle of his arms as she swayed unsteadily.

She pushed him away. "I wouldn't marry you if you were the last man on earth," she spat.

"You are in no position to refuse," said Giles smugly, feeling a rush of excitement because she was so close to him. "I own this house now. If you consent to this marriage then you and your father may continue to live here. If you refuse, then you must go to the workhouse. The choice is yours."

"I would rather spend the rest of my days in the workhouse than consent to be your wife."

"You have no choice," Giles repeated. "Enjoy your solitary bed for now. It will not be for much longer."

Lucinda gathered up her skirts and hurried up to her bedroom. She shut the door and noticed that her bunch of household keys were missing from their place on her dressing table. She placed a wooden chair under the door handle – a trick she had learned from John – to prevent anyone from gaining entry.

She sat on her bed willing the dizzy feeling to settle down. For all her brave words, she was afraid of the workhouse. She'd often witnessed the lines of soberly clad men and women on their way to church. She knew her father wouldn't last long if he was sent there but she could not bear the thought of marrying Giles. She shuddered as she remembered the clammy feel of his hands and the urgent heat of his body as it pressed against hers.

It was getting dark and she had no means of lighting a candle. She caught sight of her mother's portrait, now propped against her washstand, and drew closer to it to gaze at the golden curls and the amused expression in the eyes that were so much like her own.

The expression reminded Lucinda of the way Caroline had looked that time she'd described Josiah's interview with Great Aunt Sophia prior to their wedding. Great Aunt Sophia was Caroline's guardian and had had great hopes for a spectacular marriage for her charge. She was therefore not at all impressed that Caroline was prepared to throw herself away on a lowly tradesman – even if he did own the brewery.

Caroline had hidden behind the long blue velvet curtains in the drawing room and had listened, stifling her giggles, to Josiah's stumbling declaration of love and devotion.

"My niece wouldn't look twice at a person like you," Great Aunt Sophia declared.

Both she and Josiah were shocked when Caroline emerged from behind the curtains.

"Mind you, I nearly changed my mind when he told me about how he nearly gambled away the brewery in order to get the ring he thought I deserved," her mother had said.

The only time that Lucinda had heard from Great Aunt Sophia since was the month after the devastating news about Reuben. She'd written to offer Lucinda the chance of a season in London.

"*It occurs to me that you must be close to the age at which your mother made her unfortunate misalliance with your father. I would hope to offer you the chance to improve yourself.*"

Lucinda had felt frustrated at the timing of the offer. Had it been when Reuben was in London, she'd have accepted the offer immediately. Receiving such an offer when he was no longer there was a bitter blow. She had written a curt letter back declining the offer and stating her intention of never wanting to marry.

As Lucinda sat in the darkness, watching the first stars appear like diamonds caught in the lattice of pear tree branches, it occurred to her that if she could send a message to Great Aunt Sophia – or better still, visit herself, then maybe she would help with the release of John and Charlie. The old lady was well-known for having a number of influential contacts – including, it was said, the Prince Regent himself – and would surely give them the help they needed.

Lucinda quaked inside at the enormity of what she was planning. She'd never travelled anywhere unchaperoned before but the alternative – staying where she was and marrying Giles – was equally unthinkable. She planned to escape and go as far as Hannah's cottage, intending to leave there at first light. She was sure that nobody would look for her until she failed to appear at breakfast time.

She dozed for a while, waking with a start at the sound of footsteps outside her door that had quickly moved away again. The sky was dark as Indian ink and the full moon appeared, spilling a fragmented pathway of light across her floor through the branches of the pear tree. The church clock struck eleven and she knew it was time to leave. She was certain that Hannah would be awake and worrying about Charlie and the fate of her unborn child.

The front door was certain to be locked but Lucinda was confident that the garden door would be left open. If it wasn't, then it was an easy matter to take the spare key from the hook in the scullery next to the mangle.

Lucinda quickly gathered some things into a bundle, laced her boots, put on her cloak and prepared to leave her childhood home. She took a last look at her mother's portrait, trying to draw courage from her smile.

She took the chair away from under the door handle and turned it carefully. It didn't move. She tried again. It occurred to her that what had woken her so suddenly was the sound of someone turning the key in the lock outside. Lucinda's first instinct was to pound on the door until someone came to unlock it. She forced herself to sit back on the bed and remain quiet until she decided what to do next.

She looked at her mother's portrait again. The eyes were looking past her and gave no clue as to what she should do.

A sudden breeze stirred the branches of the pear tree so that they tapped against her window, as if trying to attract her attention. Lucinda went to the window, pushed it open and looked out. The night air was soft and scented with the pink Persian roses that grew up the outside of the house. The tree had grown since her night-time adventures with John – but so had she. The distance to the ground seemed much greater than before and, looking down, Lucinda hoped she'd be able to reach the bottom safely. A glance back at the locked door stiffened her resolve.

She gathered her belongings, left Giles' ring on her pillow like a farewell note, and headed back to the window. She tossed her bundle down to the ground, hoping Giles hadn't decided to take a late night tour of the garden.

*

'*Don't think for too long or you won't move forward,*' she told herself.

Previously when she'd climbed down, she'd been wearing boy's clothes. She pushed up her dress and petticoats and sat astride the window-sill, one leg hanging in space, glad that nobody could see her making such a disgraceful exhibition of herself.

The most difficult part of the exercise was to move her other leg round so that she was facing forward and could then lean forward and take hold of the strong branch above her head and step onto the one below.

"Believe you can do it. Bring all your will to it." John had said the first time she'd attempted this.

The tree was bigger now, and its branches were closer than before, but this time it was in full leaf and bursting with half-formed fruit which was likely to fall to the ground and attract attention, should anyone be close enough to see or hear.

The first time she'd made the descent, she'd panicked, feeling she could go neither forwards nor back. Only John's threat that he'd go and fetch their father kept her moving.

Lucinda climbed down, testing each branch as she went, dreading the sudden crack that might alert the household. Her limbs felt weak and she prayed that she'd have the strength to reach the bottom. On reaching the lowest branches, she discovered another problem. When she'd gone on her escapades with John, he'd always climbed down first and was there on the ground ready to ease her down from the tree. Now there was a long drop that looked too far to jump without incurring injury.

Every muscle in her arms and shoulders screamed with pain as she lowered herself on her hands as far as she could and then shut her eyes and let go, hoping that she'd land on soft grass and not gravel. In the event, she landed awkwardly, jarring her ankle and grazing her left hand. She bit her lip in an effort not to cry out with pain. She sat for several moments feeling dazed with relief that she'd actually reached the ground without serious mishap.

The yowl of a cat reminded her of the necessity to be on her way. Lucinda gathered up her bundle from where she'd tossed it onto the grass and hurried down the driveway towards the main street that led through the middle of town. Moonlight silvered the trees and created its own magic. It was the first time she'd been out on her own at night and anxiety spiralled inside her like the white moths that flittered ghost-like amongst the shadows.

In a few moments, she told herself, she'd reach the shelter of Hannah's cottage. All she had to do was concentrate on getting there safely.

*

Giles wasn't at all dismayed at Lucinda's reluctance to marry him. It had been no more than he'd expected and would make things all the more exciting when the day arrived.

After her hurried departure from the dinner table, he'd tried to make light of any problems, making reference to the modesty and delicacy of his bride-to-be.

"We look forward to hearing the banns called – and to our wedding day three weeks hence, Rector."

The Rector looked as if he were about to say something, but changed his mind and made excuses for their early departure.

"You and Miss Beckford may have matters to discuss," was his only comment. His pale, sickly looking wife gave Giles a pinched, disapproving look down her long nose.

As soon as they had gone, Josiah pleaded tiredness and headed for his bed.

Georgiana could be heard berating Mrs Parsons and Tilly and there was more crashing of crockery and pans in the kitchen as they cleared away.

Giles sat alone in the dining room sipping port as the candle flames danced. He relived the sensation of holding Lucinda in his arms, however unwilling she'd been. The memory had an unsettling effect on the lower half of his body.

"*Be patient*," he told himself, "*she will be yours soon enough.*"

Then, the more port he drank, the more his body cried out for its usual release. He grew more belligerent. Why was he sat here waiting like some lackey? They were, after all, engaged with her father's blessing, however unwillingly given. He was entitled to enter her bedchamber if he chose.

He went quietly upstairs and tapped on her door. There was no response. He turned the handle. If she was asleep, he wouldn't wake her, but he felt the urge to look at her.

The door wouldn't open and he suspected she'd employed some trick like putting a chair under the door knob. He took the bunch of keys from his pocket that

Georgiana had taken possession of earlier and then had put down somewhere. Impatience surged within him as he selected a key and locked Lucinda's door. If she'd decided to withhold her presence, then he'd decide when she could come out. Three weeks from now, he would be master, and she would have to do his bidding. Giles felt a warm glow of anticipation as he went to his room.

Chapter 18

Lucinda huddled into her cloak as she hurried down the path and out of the gate, keeping to the shadows even though she was just as frightened of what might be lurking there.

The shadows at the edge of the path moved in the breeze and she thought she could hear footsteps behind her. She glanced back, certain that she was being followed, her spine prickling like a mouse about to be pounced on by a cat.

She felt even more nervous when she reached the main street and the market square. A group of drunkards wove their way past Lucinda arm in arm. They paid no heed to her as she stood motionless in a doorway.

She waited until they'd made their unsteady progress along the street before she hurried towards the cottage Hannah rented next to Widow Parker's millinery shop. The shop and Hannah's cottage were in darkness. The shop window was crammed with an array of bonnets and reticules all turned silver in the light of the full moon.

Lucinda knocked with all her might on the cottage door. She peered through windows but could see no sign of Hannah. She saw what looked like a half-prepared meal in the tiny front room and her mind spiralled into panic that Hannah may be lying somewhere ill or injured.

"Hannah, are you there? Let me in, it's Lucinda." She tried to keep her voice low, but to her dismay, noticed a candle flame flicker to life in the window above Widow Parker's shop. The window was flung open and a vinegary-looking face topped with a white nightcap glared down at Lucinda.

"What is the meaning of this outrage?" Widow Parker's nose quivered as she spoke. Her eyes gleamed like black coals in her pale face.

"I've come to see Hannah."

"At this hour?"

"I must speak with her urgently."

"Well she's not here! Please go away," said the Widow triumphantly and prepared to close the window.

"Wait – please," said Lucinda. "Why is she not here?"

"She's gone, and good riddance, I say. She failed to attend church this morning and then dared to ask me for a few day's grace before paying her rent."

"Where has she gone?"

"I neither know nor care."

"Her husband has just been conscripted into the Militia against his will and she is with child. Have you no pity?"

"I'm not running a charitable institution for tinkers' brats. Now be gone before I call the night watch."

This last was punctuated by a chamber pot being emptied from the window, the contents of which narrowly missed Lucinda. The window slammed shut.

"Wicked unchristian old woman," said Lucinda, but she was alone in a dark street.

Her indignation and sense of outrage was soon replaced by anxiety as to where Hannah had gone. There was no way of knowing how long ago she left the cottage – or which way she'd gone.

Lucinda was wary of attracting attention. The confrontation with Widow Parker had caused a few people in the surrounding houses and cottages to light candles and look out of windows. She shrank back into the shelter of the cottage doorway until the hubbub subsided.

If she was to carry out her plan to enlist the help of her Great Aunt then she would have to begin her journey now, even though her heart thudded with fear.

She gathered her cloak around her and headed out of town and along the lane that she and Hannah had walked earlier that day. The storm clouds had long since passed over but the lane still had milky-brown puddles in the cart tracks.

The moon cast a pathway of light along the road, casting the woodland on the one side into shadow. The undergrowth and hedgerows on each side rustled with secrets and night creatures. Lucinda heard the bark of a fox and the call of an owl. A branch cracked and she almost jumped out of her skin, fearing that the woods might be inhabited by gypsies or vagrants.

A hedgehog scuttled across her path and a barn owl swooped past her on silent wings.

Lucinda recalled the book of fairy tales her mother used to read from and every scary scene about travellers being bewitched in woodland flooded her mind. She tried to push these back, to forget the times she'd hidden under the covers so that these nameless fears could not reach her. She tried to think of all the happy endings – where the princess was rescued by a knight in shining armour – but the only face that came to mind was Reuben's and he was lost to her.

She was so lost in her thoughts that she didn't hear the hoof-beats at first – the sound of a horse approaching at steady pace from the direction she'd just come. Lucinda's heart clenched in panic. There was barely time to squeeze herself through a gap in the hedge and to fling herself down at the edge of a field of corn, keeping to the shadows so as not to be seen.

The corn was green and the hedge she'd just squeezed through prickly with brambles and wild roses. Lucinda's hair caught on the brambles and she had to wrench at it to free it. The scent of damp earth and the sharp stink of fox filled her nostrils. Her heart hammered frantically in her chest and she was sure it would be audible for miles around. She lay huddled under her cloak, peeping through the hedge as the rider paused his horse at the top of the slight rise.

Lucinda was certain that her pursuer was Giles and was therefore surprised to see Adam Lennox framed in the moonlight. Again, she wondered what he was doing here.

He paused and looked around him as if searching for something. Lucinda held her breath, fearing that her disappearance had already been discovered and that Adam's help had been enlisted to search for her. After what seemed like hours but was probably only a few minutes, he urged his horse forward and Lucinda let out a long, slow breath of relief.

*

Adam Lennox, on his return from visiting his patroness, had passed the turning for Marchington. It had taken all his self-control not to head for Orchard House and, despite the late hour, insist upon seeing Lucinda Beckford and demand that she come away with him now. He knew that to do so would ruin her reputation, but considered this preferable to the alternative.

The fear churned in his mind that Giles may have found the means to purchase a special licence and he would be too late.

'*You did your best,*' he told himself. '*If she would not accept your proposal yesterday, then why should she today?*'

There was nothing else he could have done to persuade her to marry him – and after all, what woman in her right mind would agree to a marriage with someone she didn't know and who blatantly admitted that he didn't love her?

Adam paused to rest his horse. His senses were well-developed from the time he'd spent on the Peninsula. He analysed each one – the path of moonlight that silvered everything it came into contact with, the scent of roses and elderflower, the texture of the night air against his skin, and the feeling he was being watched.

It was this last that persuaded him to move on. Woods like these could harbour gipsies and vagrants and he was tired and in no mood for a fight. It was no use turning back to Marchington. Lucinda Beckford was a lost cause and it was time he headed home.

*

Lucinda waited for some time after the sound of hoof-beats had died away before she rose from the damp earth. As soon as all was quiet, she proceeded on her way, alert now to every sound. She walked until her feet ached and her shoulders felt stiff from carrying her bundle. She was hungry and thirsty and wished she'd been able to take some provisions with her. She knew it wouldn't be long before Giles came looking for her, and that she would need to find somewhere to shelter during daylight hours.

Since her near encounter with Adam Lennox, Lucinda kept to the field edges and pathways, following familiar landmarks for as long as possible. She walked for hours, until she was exhausted and desperate to rest her aching feet for a while.

She approached a cross-roads and was uncertain which way to go. The road that crossed the one she was on was wider. She was wary of attracting attention to herself. In a field on the other side of the cross roads, she noticed a barn looking in a sorry state of neglect, surrounded by a rampant growth of docks and thistles.

Lucinda headed towards it intending to find shelter for a short while. It was only as she drew closer and saw the house that lay beyond that she remembered what this place was. The doors and windows had been boarded up and someone had painted a skull and cross-bones on one of the planks. There were massive holes in the roof and an air of sadness hung over the place.

Lucinda remembered a journey home from visiting her Great Aunt. She'd been a small child, anxious for the journey in the uncomfortable carriage to be over. Despite the fact that she was snuggled under a rug, her feet were cold and she felt queasy from the constant bouncing of the springs. The air was stale and she'd wished she could follow John's example and sleep.

It was winter and they'd been invited to attend Great Aunt Sophia's birthday party in the days when Laston House was the hub of fashion and interest. Great Uncle Harry was alive then and the day sparkled with happiness.

They'd departed from the festivities as late as they dared. The coachman and his assistant were anxious about highwaymen and footpads, not to mention the threat of bad weather closing in. Snow was threatened and would make the pot-holed roads treacherous.

They'd clambered back into the coach and were making good time, so the coachman said.

"With luck we'll outrun the weather," he said.

Lucinda remembered a squashed oval moon that kept appearing and then retreating behind storm clouds that were black as coal, as if it were playing a special game of hide and seek with her.

Then a problem had occurred in the form of the carriage wheel getting stuck in one of the deep ruts that patterned the roads. They jarred to a halt and John was thrown onto his mother's lap.

Josiah opened the window, letting in a blast of freezing air, and stuck his head out to address the coachman.

"What's the trouble, man?"

"Stuck in a rut, sir. Begging pardon sir, but I think you may all need to get out so's we can move her." The coachman's ruddy face was creased with concern.

"Stuff and nonsense, my wife and children could freeze. There's a farm over there – go and summon help."

The coachman shivered. "Not I, sir. Not for a king's ransom would I go and knock on that door – not as I'd find anyone there, sir."

The coachman told them the tale of No Gains Farm and how the farmer had been bewitched by one of the milkmaids one Hallowe'en. His wife – a shrewish woman - soon discovered what was going on and turned the young woman and her unborn child out into the cold night. When the farmer found out what had happened he went after the milkmaid but found her dead. He returned to his wife to find that she too had died – clearly frightened by something she'd seen. Shortly afterwards the farmer disappeared and was never seen again. When another farmer tried to buy the house and land, he was terrified by the appearance of a woman in white – said to be the milkmaid searching for her lost love.

"'Tis said, sir, that some nights when the moon is full, she can be seen waiting near the crossroads, trying to stop carriages heading this way to assist with her search.

A friend of mine who once tried to help such a woman reported that he helped her onto the seat beside him and she seemed real enough. However, when he turned to speak to her moments later, there was nobody there…,"

"Stuff and nonsense," said Josiah as he assisted his family from the carriage and helped the coachman and his assistant to move the wheel from the rut.

John had woken when the coachman was telling his tale and Lucinda remembered how a mischievous look had crept across his face. After they'd returned home, he would sometimes play tricks on her - hiding in the wardrobe and creaking it open slowly and emerging draped in a sheet and saying in a quavery voice: "*I'm the white lady – I'm looking for you.*" Such excitement before bedtime was enough to make both children unable to sleep until their nurse had given them hot milk with sugar and brandy.

Remembering the story and the place that had inspired it, Lucinda fought the urge to turn and run in the opposite direction. She was prevented from doing so by the sounds of a carriage heading along the road. For the second time that long night, she flung herself onto the ground, hoping that the tall weeds would hide her.

The carriage stopped and she heard the sounds of drunken laughter as a group of men got down to piss in the ditch. She was almost close enough to touch one of them and held her breath until he'd moved away. After much laughter and many ribald comments, she heard them get back into the carriage, the sound of the coachman urging the horses on when he realised where he was and the flare of a lantern making the shadows dance.

Lucinda headed across the rough ground to the barn door. The velvet darkness of the interior looked inviting and she felt she'd rather face a meeting with a ghost than with live revellers. All she craved was a few hours' rest before continuing her journey.

The inside of the barn smelled of old straw, sawdust, faded leather and dust. Small rustling sounds awakened

Lucinda's fear of rats and mice. The lower part of the building was divided into loose boxes for horses but clearly none had been in residence for some time. It looked as if the last occupants of the farm had indeed left without taking many possessions with them. Pitchforks and hay rakes were still attached to the walls. An iron ladder led to the upper floor and Lucinda headed towards it, trying to ignore the feeling she was being watched.

She detected a movement by one of the loose boxes and yelped in alarm as a grey-cloaked figure pushed her to the ground, knocking the breath from her body. The shadows tilted as she and her assailant rolled over and over on the dusty ground. A hand closed over Lucinda's throat and black specks danced in front of her eyes.

Lucinda made a final effort to fight off her attacker. As she pushed upwards with all her strength, the hood of the grey cloak fell back, exposing tangled fair hair and a familiar face.

"Hannah – what are you doing here?"

"Lucinda! Oh – I've been so frightened. I've sat here for hours feeling too scared to close my eyes. I don't like this place."

They embraced, their words tumbling over each other.

"Why did Widow Parker turn you out? Why didn't you come and tell me?"

"I did – and that Georgiana-woman said you were indisposed and not to be disturbed. She said there was no room for me at Orchard House."

"But you always worked so hard – how could she treat you so cruelly?"

"Widow Parker never liked Charlie and she's certainly never liked children. She'd already had her suspicions about the reason for me disappearing to the necessary house so often." Hannah drew herself up in perfect imitation of Widow Parker. '*So there you are, Mistress Marshall. I'd like to know the reason for your disgraceful conduct this morning – and why you've failed to attend church.*' I think she expected me to go straight to the workhouse."

"I told her she was a wicked unchristian old woman," said Lucinda with a grim smile. "She tipped the contents of her chamber pot out of the window."

"What happened to you, Lucinda?" Hannah indicated the scrapes and scratches on Lucinda's hands and arms.

Giles Milburn and half the county are probably going to be searching for me by morning," said Lucinda with a shudder. "I don't care what they do to me – I won't marry him."

"Marry Giles?"

"There was a 'betrothal party.' Giles put a ring on my finger. My father had given his permission." Lucinda's voice shook with emotion. "How could my father do that to me, Hannah? He knew how I felt when Reuben died."

"But they can't make you marry him against your will."

"I was locked in my room. I climbed out of the window."

"Oh Lucinda – they wouldn't be expecting that!" Hannah laughed softly before she grew serious again. "So what do we do now?"

Through the half open door they could see pink, gold and apricot light on the horizon that heralded the sunrise.

The two girls prepared to leave the barn with a feeling of relief, eager to reach the safety of Lucinda's Great Aunt's house.

"Wouldn't anyone else in Marchington help you?" asked Lucinda as they began their journey, keeping close to the shelter of woods and hedges.

"The innkeeper at *The King's Head* took pity on me. He said Charlie would be much missed and that he wished he could help me, but his wife wasn't happy to take me on with the baby coming. He gave me a sovereign and took me as far as the inn on the road to Tewkesbury. He said the carrier would take me on to Evesham the next day and I'd soon be with Charlie's family."

"So why didn't you stay there – at the inn?"

"My sovereign might have to last me a long time, especially if I can't find work. I thought I'd find a hedge to sleep under. I hadn't gone far when I saw a young girl heading this way and I followed her. I was a bit scared when I reached the barn and saw the state of things, but she didn't look as if she'd mean me any harm so I stayed. I didn't see which way she went."

Lucinda told Hannah the story of No Gains Farm.

"I'm glad I didn't know that before I went there." Hannah shuddered.

"I'm more scared of the living than the dead," said Lucinda casting a nervous glance behind her. "I have a feeling that Giles will stop at nothing until he finds me."

"They'll not be looking for two women," said Hannah. "Maybe your Great Aunt could find a position for me until Charlie comes back. If he survives…,"

"Hush, Hannah, of course he will come back to you." Lucinda wished she felt as confident as she sounded.

*

It was late into the morning when Giles overheard Tilly telling Mrs Parsons that she'd not seen Lucinda.

"Miss Lucinda's always one for being up and about early and I've not seen hide nor hair of her yet."

"She's allus one for her breakfast too," said Mrs Parsons, "and as far as I can see nothing's gone missing other than what Miss Georgiana's had." She sniffed as she said this, leaving the listener in no doubt as to what she thought of Georgiana.

Giles went upstairs and listened at Lucinda's door. He could hear nothing. He went back downstairs and ordered Tilly to prepare a breakfast tray for Lucinda. A vision stirred in his head of him unlocking the door and waking Lucinda with her breakfast. He imagined her waking, her dark hair spread on the pillow, and those incredible eyes looking at him.

He carried the tray containing thinly sliced bread and butter, honey and a cup of milk up the stairs. He put the tray down outside the door, got the key out of his pocket and unlocked the door. He turned the knob. The door remained closed.

As Giles had suspected last night, she'd wedged something against the door to stop it opening. He knocked on the door. He'd been patient long enough. There was no response. This produced a combination of lust and fury in Giles. He left the breakfast tray outside the door and headed downstairs, determined to get into the room even if he had to break the window to do so.

He went out into the garden and headed round to the side of the house below Lucinda's bedroom window. It was then that he experienced the first prickle of unease. The window was wide open and swinging on its hinges, in a way that could easily cause it to smash.

However, it wasn't just the open window that unsettled Giles. A tall pear tree grew outside Lucinda's window and this bore evidence of broken twigs and a large amount of unripe fruit scattered to the ground. It was true there had been a storm the day before, but this would not have caused a fragments of cloth to be caught on a branch – a fragments of yellow muslin that looked suspiciously like the gown Lucinda had worn yesterday. It fluttered there like a flag of defiance.

Giles roared like an injured bull for the gardener's boy to bring a ladder. The ladder was pushed up against the house and Giles, who had no head for heights, sent the gardener's boy up.

"The room be empty, sir," said the boy, looking down from the top of the ladder.

"Don't be a fool, boy, it can't be."

The boy came down and Giles, feeling distinctly queasy, climbed up. He looked in through the window. The room was indeed empty and neat as a nun's cell. A wooden chair was propped under the door knob. Something glittered on the white pillowcase – the ruby ring he'd pushed onto Lucinda's finger yesterday.

Boiling with temper, Giles climbed back down the ladder. He was too big to get through the window and open the door. He sent the gardener's boy back up the ladder to accomplish this. He fumed with anger as he planned what he'd do to Lucinda when he found her again. Their wedding would proceed three weeks from now. Giles was confident that Lucinda would be home again before many hours were passed. She would not escape again.

He called the gardener and gave orders for the pear tree to be chopped down.

*

Adam Lennox was on his way home from a visit to his patroness. She had summoned him for advice about a minor indisposition.

"You may need to accompany me to Bath," she said. "I thought my last hour had come yesterday, I felt all of a shiver and a quiver." She fanned herself energetically and helped herself to a sugared plum. Her plump cheeks wobbled like blancmange in a dish.

Adam felt his spirits plummet. He disliked Bath more and more every time he went there. The dandies taking every opportunity to show off the latest fashions irritated him and he was bored by the social calls he was expected to make. To add to his problem, he was viewed as a good catch by some predatory Mamas, despite the fact that he avoided ballrooms where possible.

Adam didn't want to go, but he didn't see how he could refuse because of all the help Lady Beeching had given him. He knew she enjoyed a certain notoriety because she had her own private physician; however he wasn't sure he wanted to become a rich woman's lapdog. He was thankful, therefore, that just before they were due to leave, two messengers arrived. One was from a friend of Lady Beeching asking if it was possible for her esteemed physician to call on him. The other was an invitation for Lady Beeching to a party that Beau Brummel himself was attending.

All torpor disappeared. Lady Beeching put aside the tincture of camomile and honey that Adam had given her and announced herself ready to travel to Bath with only her maid in attendance.

"It is gratifying, dear boy, to know that your talents are so much in demand," she said, tapping him playfully on the wrist with her fan. "I must tell the Prince Regent about you if I'm fortunate enough to speak with him again. Even half an hour in your company has made me feel so much better. I declare I'm quite well enough to travel immediately and will look forward to seeing you on my return."

Adam had bowed and exchanged the usual pleasantries and departed to see the gentleman who had sent such a timely message. He rode along the tree-lined drive, grateful not to be heading for Bath following Lady Beeching's black carriage with its silver monogram.

Since his first visit to Bath, he'd been plagued with a recurring nightmare. He was in a ballroom about to be dragged into a line of dancers. The orchestra were tuning up and it was a tune he was unfamiliar with. The room was stiflingly hot and smelled of lilies – a flower he always associated with funerals. The scent was overpowering as was the crush of bodies preventing him from making his exit. The music swelled louder and wilder. Couples circled the ballroom in a frenzied dance. Faces loomed close to him and receded, most wearing too much rouge. Hot hands clutched at him. He'd headed for the nearest door but his passage was blocked by a woman whose face he couldn't see… Adam had awoken on that occasion in a tangle of sheets, fearful that he may have a touch of the malaria fever he'd suffered from in Spain.

He'd had the dream on a number of occasions since, but lately there had been a new twist to the story. The woman blocking his way from the ballroom now had a face – and it had the sapphire blue eyes and dark hair of Lucinda Beckford.

*

He finished dealing with his new patient, refused the enthusiastic invitation to stay for dinner and took the road home.

He stopped at a roadside inn for some refreshment and to rest his horse and was directed towards the parlour which was divided into small sections not unlike the loose box his horse had been led into. The landlady brought Adam cold beef, pickles, bread and a glass of wine and he sat resting and enjoying his food.

Any hope of tranquillity was soon shattered by a traveller who arrived and was desperate to tell his tale to somebody. The man was a merchant clerk and was on his way to Bristol. He wore buff britches and a brown wool riding coat and had clearly been intrigued by what he heard. He sat down next to Adam and his voice grew louder as the story gained momentum.

"At the last toll house I came to I was talking to the keeper about a visitation he'd had the night before from a man on a black horse asking the whereabouts of a young woman. A young woman with dark hair and blue eyes. Well – the toll house keeper was afeared on account of his eldest daughter fitting that description – and he didn't like the way the man looked at him."

"What did he do?" Adam wished the clerk would take his hands from his sleeve. The man had edged closer to him and the sour smell of his clothes invaded Adam's nostrils.

"Do – what could he do sir? He had to let him search the place, but with fear and trembling in his heart that his daughter might be taken from him. He didn't like the way the man comported himself."

"What happened?" Adam knew the clerk would tell the end of the tale no matter what.

"The toll house keeper's daughter was not the one he sought. The keeper was so relieved he let the man go without charging the usual fee. He said the one he sought – his fiancée – had eyes like sapphires and he'd search until he found her. He'd marry her no matter what, whether she will or not. That's what he said sir."

A chill came over Adam. He was certain that the man the clerk described was his cousin Giles. If so, then he wondered how Lucinda had managed to escape and where she was now. He had no doubt that Giles would pursue her until he caught her and Adam didn't like to think of the consequences when that happened. A memory shone clear in his mind of a brindle puppy Giles had once been given that had run off. Giles had searched until he found it – and then he'd beaten it to death.

Chapter 19

Lucinda and Hannah were relieved to reach the imposing black wrought iron gates of Laston House. They'd taken two days to reach it, diving for cover whenever they heard hoof-beats approaching from either direction. Where possible they'd kept to fields and hedgerows, avoiding the bigger roads where they might attract notice.

At a remote farm they'd exchanged a few coins for a jug of milk and a loaf of bread. The woman had asked no questions and had not seemed curious as to who they were.

"You'll be catching up with the rest of your people," she'd said, putting the coins Hannah gave her into the bodice of her dress. "Mind – you'll have a job to catch them before nightfall. They went through here nearly two hours since a-clattering and a-clanking of their pots and pans."

"She thinks we're tinkers – and hardly surprising," said Hannah peering at her reflection in a cattle trough. "Heaven knows what your Great Aunt will think of us when she sees us."

Before they rounded the bend that led to the gates of Laston House, they tidied their hair as best they could and brushed the dust from their boots. It was late afternoon and the sky had turned a brooding, unwelcoming grey. Light drizzle beaded their cloaks. The huge black gates were locked against intruders.

The driveway beyond, overhung with chestnut trees, curved away from them, looking dark and forbidding in the fading light. They could not see the house, but the locked gates didn't look very welcoming.

Hannah shivered and looked at Lucinda. "What shall we do?"

Lucinda gestured towards the gatehouse that stood to one side of them. It looked like a miniature castle with mock battlements and was surrounded by a brick wall and a smaller version of the gate that barred the way to

Laston House. Through the gate they could see that the house was surrounded by a neatly-kept garden. A wisp of smoke rose from a bonfire presided over by a bent old man dressed in dark clothing.

"I can remember playing in that garden when I was very small," said Lucinda. "The custodian looked after John and I while everyone went to Great Uncle Harry's funeral. She let me pick flowers to take home and she gave us walnut cake and treacle toffee. Her name was Molly Preece."

They headed towards the gate and rang the rusty bell. A tantalising smell of rabbit stew drifted through the open door ahead of them.

A woman dressed in black with a white apron over it emerged from the house. She came over to the gate and surveyed them with folded arms. "Well? What is it you want? We don't allow no tramps or vagrants here."

"We're not tramps or vagrants," said Lucinda. "I am Lucinda Beckford. Lady Sophia is my Great Aunt."

"A likely tale," said the woman. "As if her ladyship'd be related to the likes of you."

"Where is Molly Preece? She'll vouch for me."

"She's been dead these five years. You'll not get past my door with tricks like that."

"I'm telling the truth," said Lucinda, her voice on the edge of tears. "I am Lucinda Beckford. I am in the gravest trouble and I must speak with my Great Aunt. May we please wait for her?"

"If you were a close relation you'd know her ladyship has been very ill and is now taking the waters at Bath on the advice of her physician. Now be off with you – and if I see you here again I'll send for the magistrate."

The woman stood glaring at them as they walked away in the direction they had just come, leaving no doubt that she would carry out her threat.

Lucinda's legs felt as if they were about to crumple from exhaustion and disappointment. She'd pinned all her hopes on reaching safety at Laston House. She hadn't expected her Great Aunt to welcome her with open arms – after all, Lucinda had refused her last offer of help. She'd expected the old lady to give her a scolding for her disgraceful appearance and for them both to be relegated to the servants' quarters until they'd had a bath.

They'd walked for miles on little more than bread and water and were now desperate for a proper meal and somewhere to sleep.

It was obvious that the custodian wasn't going to help them so all Lucinda and Hannah could do was to move on and try to find shelter.

The drizzle that had begun just before they reached Laston House had now turned into a downpour. They trudged on through the gathering dusk, taking a little lane that they hoped might lead to a farm that had an outbuilding where they could spend the night. It was a narrow lane with a ditch on one side half covered in brambles and overhung by trees that at least kept some of the rain off them. It was like walking along a dark tunnel with no end in sight.

"What was that noise?" asked Hannah.

"What noise?" Lucinda had been so deep in her anxious thoughts she hadn't heard anything.

"There it is again."

They stopped. It was a whimpering, snuffling sound like an animal caught in a trap.

"It's coming from the ditch over there," said Hannah, heading towards it.

"Wait – it could be something dangerous," said Lucinda.

"We can't leave the poor creature…,"

"Please help me. I be stuck," said a little voice.

Lucinda hung back, her mind focused on nursery tales of fairy curses and changelings and more recent stories about unwary travellers being tricked by tinkers' children into helping with a bogus rescue and then having their possessions stolen.

Hannah was less cautious. She went to look and turned back to Lucinda. "Lucinda – quick! There's a little girl in the ditch and she looks badly hurt. "Don't cry sweetheart," she said to the child. "We will help you out of there."

The crying and sniffing stopped.

Lucinda edged forward and looked into the ditch which was deep and not immediately visible on account of the brambles that edged it. The little girl looked just like the picture of Snow White in the book of fairy tales she'd had as a child. She had curly black hair and was wearing a white dress that was torn and covered with mud. Her left leg bore a jagged cut and the knee looked red and swollen.

Hannah crouched down to talk to the child. "What's your name and what were you doing out here on your own?" she asked.

Lucinda looked around warily, still alert to the possibility of meeting the family of tinkers who had been on the road earlier.

"My name's Ivy and I live over there," the child said, pointing towards the end of the lane where the dark tunnel opened into a field of green wheat. "I was running away with my dog Timmy but he saw a rabbit and runned after it and got isself stuck in a hole jus' by where you're standing. I got 'im out but then I fell over and he runned off. Then I tried to get out of 'ere and couldn't – and I've been here for hours." Ivy started crying again, wiping her freckled nose on the hem of her dress.

"Your mother would miss you if you ran away," said Hannah.

"I ain't got a mother," said Ivy, "and my step-mother's a mean ole toad. She never makes her Dora help with the washing – and she didn't tell her off when she dropped the line in the mud, just made me do it all again." She sniffed again. "I wish I'd brung some food with me. I'm ever so hungry. You got anything to eat?"

"We're hungry too," said Lucinda.

"Where you going' – can I come with you?"

"Let's see if we can get her out of there," said Hannah, anxious to escape any awkward questions.

"You'd best not in your condition," said Lucinda. "Let me try."

She found an ash branch and leaned forward so that Ivy could grasp the other end. Unfortunately, the rain had made the edges of the ditch slippery and Lucinda lost her footing and tumbled headlong into the ditch. She managed to avoid falling on top of Ivy, but in doing so, she cut her arm on a sharp piece of metal that looked like the remains of a trap. The cut bled and Hannah searched in her bundle for something to staunch the flow, eventually ripping a piece off the hem of her petticoat.

Dazed with pain and shock, Lucinda managed to gather Ivy into her arms and struggle to her feet. The bottom of the ditch was oozing black mud and she and the child were covered from head to foot. Lucinda thought grimly that even if Giles Milburn passed by at this very moment, she was so muddy he wouldn't recognise her.

She almost screamed from the pain in her arm as she pushed Ivy towards the safety of the pathway where Hannah was waiting to catch her. The effort of doing this had exhausted Lucinda and she struggled to drag herself up the steep sides of the ditch, her feet slipping back every time she thought she'd made progress. The smell of mud and old leaf mould was in her nostrils and the cut on her arm had bled through the makeshift bandage, making her feel dazed and sick. The light had faded now, bringing with it a drop in temperature and Lucinda shivered from cold and shock as she fell backwards into the ditch.

"What're you doing with that child?" bawled an angry voice. "If you've done her any harm then you'll pay for it, by Heaven you will."

Over the rim of the ditch, Lucinda noticed small lights moving towards them.

Ivy hobbled towards the lights. "These nice ladies have been helping me, Pa," she said. "They've not done me no 'arm. And now one of them's stuck in the ditch where I was and can't get out – and her arm's all bloody and horrible."

Lucinda and Hannah were relieved to notice that the big man in the billycock hat had a gentle expression despite the redness of his face. He wasted no time in instructing two of his men to lift Lucinda out of the ditch and carry her back to the farm.

"Be careful with the lady, mind," he said.

"Where are you bound for?" he asked Hannah.

Hannah hesitated. "We're heading for Evesham to look for work," she said.

"Are you now?" The farmer looked at her appraisingly and Hannah flushed under his scrutiny. "Well you'll be going nowhere tonight – not until I've repaid you for your kindness to my Ivy."

"A little food and a chance to wash ourselves would be most welcome, sir," said Hannah, bobbing a curtsey.

"From the look of my Ivy's leg and this young lady's arm I think we'll be sending for the doctor."

They went slowly back across the fields towards the farmhouse – a whitewashed house, the upstairs windows of which lay close under the thatched roof. It was surrounded by outbuildings – a barn, stables and sheds. There was a walled vegetable garden with a clothes line not far from the wash-house.

"I'm sure that's not necessary," protested Lucinda, who was being carried in a 'Queen's chair' – two men with crossed hands forming a makeshift carriage.

"You're bleeding like a stuck pig," said the farmer bluntly, "and such wounds can go to the bad."

On reaching the farmyard where a collection of tawny coloured hens scratched in the dust, he despatched a young boy to fetch the doctor.

They entered the farmhouse via the kitchen door and were enveloped in the smell of lamb stew.

"About time too," said a cross looking woman in a blue dress and white cap. "The stew is all but ruined." She caught sight of Ivy in her father's arms and her look turned even more hostile. "And look at the state of you, miss. Off to bed with you – now."

"Enough, Ella," said the farmer. "Leave the girl alone, she's suffered enough."

"Suffered enough!" echoed the woman. "She doesn't know the meaning of the word. Look at the state of her clothes. Who's going to remedy those, I'd like to know. My Dora'd never dream of getting herself in that state."

A prim looking girl with a pale face and white-blonde hair sat on a cushion working on a sampler. When she thought nobody was looking, she put out her tongue at Ivy.

The woman suddenly noticed Lucinda and Hannah. "And who are these people?" she asked.

"I am Mary Taylor and this is my cousin Jane Lucas," said Lucinda." Hannah shot her an amused glance.

"Set two extra places at the table, Ella. These ladies are in need of refreshment."

The woman clicked her tongue in irritation. "Let's hope there's enough stew to go round. It's all very well you inviting others to sit at our table but you don't have to do the work that goes with it."

"If it wasn't for your sharp tongue, Ella, the table would be full but I seem to remember you've scared off the scullery maid and the dairy maid in the last week – and we've still got two months yet before the hiring fair."

Ella crimped her lips shut but did as she was told.

"Where be ye from then?" Her tone was hostile and she looked Lucinda and Hannah up and down as if they'd just been dragged in by the cat.

"Somerset," said Lucinda, hoping the interrogation would soon be over – and that she would remember what she'd said.

"Not much alike are you?"

"L-Mary favours her father and I'm like my mother," said Hannah, thankful that was at least true.

"Enough questions Ella," said the farmer. "Find these ladies some clean clothes and give them some water to wash with."

A young girl with fair hair emerged from the scullery at the back of the kitchen with a jug of warm water and motioned them to follow her. They headed up the stairs to a room that smelled musty from being shut up, but otherwise looked clean.

"I'll take your clothes and launder them," she said, "and your boots look in need of a clean and some time by the fire to dry them. I've brought some fresh linen to bandage your arm but now the bleeding's stopped maybe 'tis best to leave it till after the doctor's seen it."

Hannah helped Lucinda to wash the mud off herself and change into the clothes they'd been given. The dresses had obviously belonged to a bigger woman and were plain and dark in colour but they were clean and neatly folded.

"I could just fall into that bed and sleep," said Lucinda looking at the bed she and Hannah were to share. The young girl had put a hot brick wrapped in a cloth into the bed to air it and all Lucinda craved was to lie down and close her eyes. She caught sight of herself in the cracked mirror on the wash-stand and was shocked at her appearance. Her face was pale and scratched with brambles from her recent escapade in the ditch. Her hair was snarled with knots and there were dark circles under her eyes.

"We should go downstairs and eat first," said Hannah. "The smell of that stew is fair making my mouth water. It will be hard for me to remember to call you Mary."

"I hope I remember too," said Lucinda. "I said the first names that came into my head."

They went downstairs to the big room where several farm hands were now gathered round the large table waiting for the arrival of their meal. Judging by the loud crashes and thumps from the kitchen beyond, it would not be long.

The farmer gestured for Hannah and Lucinda to take their places. Ivy had fallen asleep on his lap, the wound on her leg jagged and surrounded by plum-coloured bruising. The remains of a plate of bread and jam were on the small table next to her.

"The doctor's taking his time," grumbled the farmer, easing Ivy onto the couch at the far end of the room. He came across to the table, took his place and poured mugs of ale for Lucinda and Hannah.

The room was untidy – the wooden floor dusty and the windows in need of a clean. Hannah eyes lit up when she noticed an overflowing basket of what looked like mending.

"I have previously worked as a seamstress. I could help your wife with what needs to be done as a way of repaying your kindness," she said.

"That's more than kind of you," said the farmer. I'm sure my Ella will be delighted – her not being much of a needlewoman." Ella, coming in with a tray full of bowls of stew, looked fit to burst with anger as she slammed them down on the table.

Despite the appetising smell, the lamb stew was watery and bore a layer of grease on the surface. Hannah wolfed hers, but Lucinda, suffering from pain and shock, had little appetite. She'd knocked her arm on the newel post on the way down the stairs and the cut was oozing blood again.

Hannah tried to encourage Lucinda to eat a little of the hot meat and vegetables, feeding her with a spoon as she would a young infant. In the end, she finished Lucinda's bowl as well as her own.

They'd barely finished their meal when the sound of hooves on the cobbles outside heralded the arrival of the doctor. Lucinda didn't witness this as she'd ventured outside to the necessary house – the greasy lamb stew having had a disastrous effect on her stomach. She had no idea how long she was crouched in the filthy, spider-infested hut but she was alternating between boiling hot and shivering.

She headed back in through the kitchen, noting how the red floor tiles were caked in mud. The room smelled of rancid milk and rotten vegetables, which nearly made her heave again and head back towards the necessary house, her legs feeling as if they would no longer support her.

She hung onto the wall, breathing in fresh air from outside, willing her legs to carry her forward. The kitchen was lit by three candles, all of which highlighted festoons of cobwebs and walls in need of whitewash. Lucinda thought of the neat kitchen at Orchard House and how particular Mrs Parsons was and felt a twinge of longing to be back there as things used to be.

Looking into the living room from the kitchen, she could see a kindly looking elderly man bending over a drowsy looking Ivy.

"You're lucky young lady that this is no worse," he said in a voice as rich as plum cake. He rummaged in his bag for iodine. "Be a brave girl now."

Ivy yelped when he tipped it on.

"What do you say, Lennox?"

Lucinda nearly yelped louder than Ivy when she heard the name and then saw the back view of Adam Lennox standing by the table she'd been sitting at only a short time before. Her impulse was to turn and run, escape back into the tunnel of trees and hide until Adam Lennox had gone, but she couldn't possibly leave without Hannah, even if she did have the strength. Lucinda stood in the dark shadows near the kitchen door hoping they would forget about her.

"You have another patient for us your boy told us," barked Doctor Sanders. "Where is she?"

The farmer gestured towards the kitchen, causing Lucinda's heart to race with alarm. "Yes – Miss Mary Taylor. She went …,"

Adam Lennox headed towards the kitchen door. "How long ago?" His voice was soft with concern.

Lucinda was a bare few feet away from him in her hiding place crouched on the stone floor of the pantry.

Adam took another step towards the kitchen. He turned and spoke over his shoulder to Doctor Sanders. "The boy said she'd lost a lot of blood. I'd better check that she's not fainted away."

Lucinda's heart was beating into her throat as she edged towards the scullery that led off the kitchen. The slippers she'd been loaned made no sound but they were thin and the cold rose up into her body from the damp brick floor.

She heard Adam near the necessary house calling her name. She looked for a hiding place, tried to squeeze between the mangle and the wooden clothes horses. In doing so, she lost her balance and knocked her arm on the housing for the wash copper. Pain shot through her like an arrow, black dots danced in front of her eyes, and Lucinda fainted.

When she next opened her eyes, Adam was carrying her upstairs.

"Do not worry, you have nothing to fear," he said. "Your secrets are safe with me."

The voice was reassuring and she could feel its echo against her body. She could feel the heat of his body through the thin layers of clothing that separated them. Then she remembered his relationship to Giles and the fear spiralled again. He carried her to the room where she and Hannah had been directed earlier. The young girl had brought more water and cloth for bandages. She curtsied respectfully when Adam asked her to bring some boiled water and the black leather medical bag he'd left downstairs.

"Why are you here, Doctor Lennox?" Lucinda was aware she'd spoken abruptly but she didn't care.

"I might ask you the same question Miss – Taylor," said Adam. "But since you ask, I was attending an accouchement with my mentor Doctor Sanders when the boy brought the message about the accidents here. We both decided to attend as we had not seen each other for some time and the journey here and back would give an opportunity to discuss matters of interest to us both."

The girl brought the water and Adam sat beside Lucinda and gently peeled the soiled dressings away. The cut bled again. Adam pulled a wry face. "This will need stitching and I fear you will be lucky to escape without a scar."

Lucinda nodded, all her senses disturbed by his presence.

Adam opened his bag and prepared his equipment, laying it out methodically on the table next to them.

"I'll need more light," he said, heading downstairs for extra candles.

"We must leave here, Hannah," whispered Lucinda when he was out of earshot. "I am certain that as soon as Adam Lennox leaves here, he will go straight to his cousin Giles and inform him of our whereabouts."

"Lucinda, you are injured and ill. We cannot do anything other than trust him to look after you," whispered Hannah.

Adam returned to the room with a fresh supply of candles and there was no time to say more.

"This will hurt you," he said. "I could give you a tincture of laudanum."

Lucinda glared at him. "So that you can render me insensible and then send for your cousin Giles, I suppose?"

"Nothing was further from my intentions," said Adam, the colour rising in his cheeks. "Surely you are aware, that as a physician, it would be unprofessional of me to divulge information about my patients to a third party – whoever they are."

Adam cleaned the wound with iodine causing Lucinda to wince. He was about to say something else but the sound of footsteps bustling up the stairs prevented this. Ella came into the room without knocking.

"My husband wishes to know if you require any refreshment, sir," she asked Adam, a resentful expression on her face.

"For myself, no thank you," said Adam, "but Miss Taylor would benefit from a little brandy and sugar in hot water if you have any."

Ella gave off a sound like a kettle about to boil and stormed out of the room. The maidservant returned a short time later with the requested tonic.

"Drink a little of this," said Adam, propping her up so that she could do so. His arm was firm around her shoulders.

The strong liquor burned the back of Lucinda's throat and she almost choked. Soon after, a feeling of lassitude swept over her and the rest of what Adam was doing to her arm passed in a nightmare haze. His hands and voice were gentle. Hannah sat holding her other hand as he worked.

When he'd finished, Lucinda tried to stand, but exhaustion and pain got the better of her and for the second time that night she felt herself fainting away.

Adam was ready for her that time and caught her in his arms, laying her gently on the bed and checking for vital signs.

"She will recover," he said to Hannah. "It is better that she sleeps for now. Please send a message to Dr Sanders' house if you need me. I am staying with him for a short time. Send for me immediately if there is any sign of fever."

He gathered his equipment together, rinsing his things in the water and drying them on a clean cloth.

"I must ask you, Mistress Marshall," he said to Hannah, "what are you both doing here?"

"L – Mary had an unwelcome offer of marriage...," Hannah felt herself flushing red with embarrassment.

"You need say no more," said Adam, closing his medical bag. "What of your situation?" He checked to see that nobody was listening outside the door.

"I was turned out of my cottage when my husband was conscripted into the Militia against his will – along with L-Mary's brother John, sir."

"When did this occur?"

"The day of the Midsummer Fair, sir," said Hannah. "We went to the barracks to try and procure their release but we were told they'd already sworn the oath and were on their way to Bristol."

"Why did you say nothing of this when I met you on the road?"

Several answers bubbled into Hannah's mind – the main one being that Lucinda didn't trust him. She bit her lip and said nothing.

"You need say no more. I understand. I will endeavour to do what I can."

Adam Lennox rode away in the darkness with his friend Robert Sanders resolving not to return home until he knew that Lucinda Beckford had recovered. He hoped she'd have the sense to stay where she was until the wound had healed. He'd seen many such wounds on the Peninsula turn septic and in some cases, the unfortunate soldier had ended up losing the limb.

He had a good idea of the sequence of events that had led up to her flight from Orchard House. Giles had followed the same pattern as he had when he'd forced Amelia to marry him. A cloud went across the moon and reminded Adam of his journey to find Amelia – and the revelations she had made during her last few hours.

"*My father's business was failing*," she said. "*All his creditors were insisting on payment. I wrote to you every day but received no reply, asking for your help. Then Giles came and said he could save us from the workhouse – but only if I married him. I knew my mother would not have lasted a night in such a place – and my father's health was poor…,*"

Giles had ensured any letters Amelia had written to Adam were never posted – and that she never received any from him, either.

Chapter 20

The next day Hannah carried the basket of mending upstairs so that she could sit and watch Lucinda who was in bed recovering from the ordeal of the previous night.

"I don't think anyone's ever used this sewing box before," she said to Lucinda as she sorted through the various cottons and embroidery silks.

Half way through the morning, Ivy came up to join them, walking stiffly with her bandaged leg.

"Dora's playing with her doll," she said, "and she won't let my Nettie play. She says she's disgusting." She showed Lucinda and Hannah a much loved rag-doll with a face that had once been painted but was now faded to almost white.

Hannah drew out a pale yellow dress that Ivy had clearly damaged on another of her escapades. There was a tear near the neck where it had been caught on something.

"That was my favourite dress," said Ivy, "but my stepmother says it can't be repaired and must be used for rags. I didn't mean to damage it – the branch just got in the way."

She watched as Hannah found a small piece of yellow cloth to sew onto the back of the hole. "It shows," she said. "You can still see it's been torn."

"Just wait," said Hannah. She chose some embroidery silk in buttercup yellow, gold and green and proceeded to sew some flowers in a circle round the neckline, picking out the centres with a vibrant orange colour.

The little girl was so excited she almost forgot about her injured leg. "It's like magic," she said, a smile lighting up her face.

She insisted on wearing the dress when they sat down for their meal, arousing Dora's jealousy.

"I could embroider your dress if you'd like me to Dora," said Hannah, "or your doll's dress perhaps?

"No thank you," said Dora closing her mouth primly and sitting with her hands folded in her lap.

"You've been offered the same as your sister," said the farmer, "now don't you let me hear you complain, Dora."

Dora's eyes closed to slits like a cat about to strike. "She's not my sister," she hissed.

*

Adam Lennox returned to Manor Farm that evening, with news that his friend Dr Sanders had been out hunting that day and had sprained his wrist. Adam was therefore doing his best to attend to both sets of patients. Yesterday's rain had given way to searing heat that was now drying the grass and ripening the wheat. He reported that several patients that he'd seen were showing symptoms of a fever that was much like the malaria he had encountered on the Peninsula.

He was thankful that neither Lucinda nor Ivy showed any signs of fever, but there was something about Lucinda's appearance that aroused his concern. He repeated his instructions to send for him if there was a change in her condition.

Ella had viewed his ministrations with suspicion. "Who's going to pay for all these extra visits, I'd like to know," she said.

"Enough, Ella," said the farmer. "These two ladies saved my Ivy's life. She'd have died if she'd been left in that ditch all night."

Ella made a noise like a kettle building up steam. Nobody heard the remark she made under her breath, but the look she gave spoke volumes.

*

Adam left Manor Farm feeling frustrated that he hadn't managed to speak to Lucinda alone. There was always somebody nearby – Ella, the farmer's wife, the maidservant or the fair-haired child with the sneaky look who he didn't trust an inch.

He'd stayed awake long into the previous night trying to think of a way, other than marriage, that he could help Lucinda and her friend. He was in the process of setting up his new surgery at Court Green near the village of

Wick. The house was modest in size and he had already offered employment to his former nurse and her husband. He did not feel he could support two additional women on his current income, but determined to ask his patroness when she returned from Bath.

As he rode back to Doctor Sanders' house, he remembered the menagerie he'd set up in part of the stable block when he was a child. There were injured birds and hedgehogs, mice and voles. He'd wept bitterly when he discovered that one of the starlings had escaped and been eaten by a cat.

"*You can't help every creature you come into contact with,*" his uncle told him. "*Sometimes you have to let nature take its course.*"

Lucinda and Hannah were surprised to see Dora come into their room the next morning. They were both dressed and sitting either side of the mending basket. The mountain of work had decreased substantially and Lucinda was doing her best to help with the simpler tasks like sewing on buttons. The room was hot and stuffy and Hannah had opened the window, letting in the scent of hay and the sound of birdsong.

Dora walked in without asking permission, picking up things and putting them down – Lucinda's hairbrush, Hannah's reticule, a hat pin. She stood in front of them, hands folded demurely as if she was about to repeat her catechism.

"Good morning, Dora," said Lucinda, feeling uneasy at the way the child was staring at her.

"I heard you talking when you woke up this morning." Dora closed her lips primly and waited to see how they would react.

Lucinda's heart lurched as if she'd been bounced too fast on a see-saw. She tried not to look at Hannah, but could sense that she was holding her breath as she waited to hear what Dora said next.

"I heard you talking to each other," said the prim little voice. "You didn't call each other Mary and Jane – you said Lucinda and Hannah." Her eyes narrowed to slits as she stared at them. She stood still, hands folded in front of her, as if she was reciting a lesson.

Lucinda tried to think what to say. Her head felt as if it was stuffed with cotton wool. "We do call each other by different names sometimes. Doesn't your mother sometimes call you by a pet name or a middle name?"

Dora shook her head.

"We're cousins and we call each other all sorts of funny names. We always have done and sometimes we forget we're doing it. You must have been listening really hard to have heard us playing like that."

Dora's eyes narrowed suspiciously. "You're grown up. You're too big to play games," she said as she headed towards the door.

*

"We must leave here," said Lucinda when the sound of Dora's slow footsteps had faded down the stairs. She looked out of the window at the parched green and gold landscape. "We may be able to find work on another farm."

"You are not well enough yet, Lucinda. Your arm may yet become infected."

Hannah had changed the poultice on the wound as directed by Adam Lennox, but the area around the cut still looked a livid red. Lucinda was clearly unwell, no matter how much she protested she was feeling better.

That afternoon, an opportunity presented itself. Ella, Dora and Ivy had gone out in the pony and trap to visit the wife and daughters of a neighbouring farmer. The maidservant was working on the week's washing in the scullery. They could hear her voice raised in song as she pounded the sheets in the dolly tub.

"We may never have a better opportunity than this," said Lucinda. "I think we should leave before something terrible happens."

Hannah looked unhappy at the prospect of leaving. "To be truthful I've become fond of little Ivy and I've enjoyed the mending." She paused. "If we leave we may never know if Doctor Lennox found out anything about our menfolk."

Lucinda scoffed. "If he had any intention of doing so."

"I'm sure he did, Lucinda. He's very kind – and maybe you should have considered the proposal he made more seriously."

"I do not intend to marry anyone – ever."

In the finish, Lucinda got her way and they headed back along the track they'd followed when they'd first arrived. They hadn't gone far before Lucinda was lagging a long way behind Hannah.

"We should go back," said Hannah, taking in the sheen of perspiration on Lucinda's forehead and the feverish glitter of her eyes. "You are not well, Lucinda."

Lucinda shook her head. "I'll rest for a few minutes and then I'll be all right. I wish we had some water, Hannah. I'm so thirsty."

*

Adam Lennox had no idea what made him head towards Manor Farm that afternoon. He was on his way back from attending one of Doctor Sanders' patients and stopped to rest his horse in the shade of a willow tree. He paused, listening to the rustle of the wind in the leaves, certain that he could hear voices.

He hitched the horse to a low branch and edged slowly forward in order that he could see who they belonged to. He was amazed to see Lucinda Beckford and her friend sitting beside the path. Even from fifty paces away, he could see that the wound on her arm was infected and she was showing the first signs of fever. She looked up at him as he approached, her gaze hostile.

"Why have you left the farm?" he asked.

"We no longer felt safe there," she answered, her lips cracked and dry.

"Do they know you have left?"

She shook her head.

Adam felt a surge of impatience. "Your arm is showing signs of infection and you look feverish, Miss Beckford."

"I am well enough," she said, rising to her feet.

"I do not think you are," he said. "You need further treatment and if you do not have adequate care and shelter you could die."

He hadn't meant to speak so bluntly. He noticed how Hannah Marshall had whitened with shock at his words, but that Lucinda Beckford's mouth had tightened in determination. She picked up her bundle and stepped forward, her gait unsteady.

"Why will you not do the sensible thing and go back to Manor Farm?" he asked.

"Because I fear you will betray me to your cousin Giles."

"Don't be ridiculous. Why would I do such a thing?" Adam's voice cracked like a pistol shot. He felt as agitated as if a nest of soldier ants were marching all over his body.

He continued in a calmer tone. "Miss Beckford, I have no intention of betraying you to anybody – least of all my cousin Giles. I have my own personal reasons for not doing so." He turned away so she wouldn't see the tears in his eyes. Last night's dreams had awakened disturbing memories of Amelia.

"We should go back, Lucinda," said Hannah. "Doctor Lennox is right. You are not well."

"I am well enough," said Lucinda. "I wish to proceed on our journey."

Adam watched her as she tottered forward again, collapsed on all fours to the ground and vomited.

"Help me with her, please," he said to Hannah. "She is in no fit state to make any sort of journey." He lifted Lucinda into his arms. Her head lolled against his shoulder as he carried her to his pony and lifted her onto its back.

"With luck we'll get back to the farm before they are aware you have gone," he said.

When they reached the farmhouse, he tethered the pony in the shade and carried Lucinda up the stairs. Her skin burned with fever and yet she was shivering. He mixed her a draught of feverfew to bring the fever down and instructed Hannah to sponge her down with cool water if she got too hot. He opened the window to allow fresh air to circulate and told Hannah to leave it open day and night.

"Isn't the night air said to be harmful?" asked Hannah.

Adam shook his head. "I spoke to many foreign healers when I was with the Militia and they considered fresh air – whatever the time of day – was healing to the body."

He told Hannah about the Moorish healer he'd spent some time with who had such different ideas from the ones he had learned at the hospital in London. "Ashtar taught me a great deal about herbs and their uses," he said as he made a poultice of comfrey leaves for Lucinda's arm. "Do not allow the leaves to come into direct contact with the skin."

"What is the Peninsula like?" she asked.

Adam told her of the wide plains, the rivers and the birds and animals. "Storks nest on the roofs of houses," he said. "Many of the houses are white and the sky above is the bluest I've ever seen. He did not speak of the horror of battlefields and the men whose blood drained into the sun-baked ground.

He looked at Lucinda who was now tossing and turning. "It may take several hours for the fever to break," he said. Give her as much of the feverfew tea as she will drink."

Ella and the two girls returned in a flurry of raised voices. Ivy hurried upstairs to see Lucinda and Hannah. She paused, wide eyed in the doorway when she saw Lucinda.

"What's the matter with Mary? Is she going to die?"

Ella stormed up the stairs. "If she's infectious I want her out of my house."

Adam made her a curt bow. "I can assure you madam, that neither you nor your family are at any risk. However, Miss …Taylor will need careful nursing and you are to send for me day or night if her condition worsens."

Ella glared at him. "I suppose you expect me to wait on her? And who's goin' to pay for all this doctoring, that's what I want to know." She stood staring down at Lucinda as she writhed on the bed. "Them sheets'll need laundering an' all."

"I will do anything that is necessary to help my cousin," said Hannah.

Adam's instinct was to stay with Lucinda until her fever broke, but he didn't feel he could do so without incurring Ella's wrath and suspicion. As he rode back to Doctor Sanders' house he noticed the brilliant gold, pink and apricot sunset ahead of him. A chill settled over him as he remembered the colours of the sunrise on the morning Amelia died.

*

Hannah sat with Lucinda, not daring to leave her even to eat anything. She could smell the evening meal cooking and hear the tramp of boots as everyone gathered round the table.

The first stars were appearing when Ivy came upstairs bearing a plate of bread and jam and a mug of milk for Hannah.

"That mean ole toad said she weren't going to give you nothing," she said. "She wouldn't like it if anyone treated her like that."

"Thank you, Ivy," said Hannah. Now that her queasiness was past, she was hungry all the time. She devoured the bread and jam, keeping a watchful eye on Lucinda.

"I'm not supposed to be up here," said Ivy. "She thinks we're all going to catch whatever it is. Says the right place for you is the workhouse."

Ella's harsh voice summoned Ivy back downstairs.

Hannah's heart clenched as she looked at Lucinda who now seemed to be burning up with the fever that had come upon her so suddenly. Her face looked flushed and she lay tossing and turning as if in the grip of a nightmare.

Hannah sponged Lucinda with cool water and changed her nightgown. She held her and did her best to encourage her to drink more of the feverfew tea, but Lucinda's teeth chattered against the tin mug and the liquid spilled down her chin.

She was tossing and turning so much that it was difficult to change the comfrey poultice. Hannah followed the instructions Adam Lennox had given her, careful that the rough leaves did not touch Lucinda's inflamed skin.

As darkness fell, Hannah dozed fitfully, but woke when Lucinda startled her by rearing up out of the bed. Her shadow looked huge against the wall in the light of the stub of a candle. "Reuben," Lucinda yelled. Her eyes looked wild and unfocused and were following a presence that Hannah could not see.

Ella hammered on the door. "Keep the noise down. Some of us are trying to sleep."

Hannah opened the door. Ella stood there in voluminous nightgown and nightcap, her face sour.

"I think we should send for Doctor Lennox," said Hannah. "The fever isn't breaking."

"Oh you do, do you? Well let me tell you, our stable boy's got better things to do than worry about the likes of you when he should be asleep."

There was a flurry of activity and another door opened. Two faces looked out.

"See, you've woken Dora and Ivy with all your racketings. Back to bed you two or I'll take a stick to you," she said to the two children.

"She's very poorly," said Hannah. "I fear she might die."

"Then if you're so keen on the idea of fetching the doctor – go yourself. The only reason you want him here is because you're both sweet on him…."

"Enough, Ella." The sound filled the landing like the roar of a bull. "Don't worry about rousing young Benjamin. I'll go myself."

"Why should you go?" Ella looked truculent. "Don't tell me you're sweet on her yourself?"

She was silenced by a ringing slap as the farmer finally lost his temper with her, and she landed in a heap on the floor, nursing her reddened cheek.

"Keep your vicious tongue under control for once, woman, or I'll not answer for the consequences. You'd feel differently if it was your Dora whose life had been saved."

"My Dora's got more sense than to do stupid things."

The farmer had pulled a jacket and breeches over his nightshirt and was off down the stairs, his heavy boots clumping on each step. "I'll be as quick as I can," he said.

"You'll be sorry," hissed Ella when he was out of earshot. "I wish you two had never come here." She went to her room and slammed the door.

The sound of hoof-beats on cobbles echoed into the night. Hannah went back to sit with Lucinda feeling relieved that she wouldn't have to face this battle alone.

*

Adam arrived just as the stub of candle that was all that lit Lucinda and Hannah's room guttered and died.

"Bring more candles please – and fresh water." He spoke with quiet authority.

Hannah hurried down to the kitchen to attend to both requests. As she came upstairs she heard Ella's low tones bickering with her husband. "You must think we're made of money, husband. More candles… I ask you – and her being left unchaperoned."

"Well, get up yourself and help then," said the farmer.

"Don't blame me when there's no money for food." There was a loud bang as Ella got out of bed and slammed their bedroom door, and then silence.

*

Adam Lennox's heart clenched with anxiety as he watched Lucinda Beckford. He'd checked her arm for signs of further infection, relieved to see that the comfrey poultice had done its job and the wound looked less livid. He replaced this with some calendula salve that he carried in his bag, wrapping the arm in clean bandages. He was well aware that he was just keeping himself occupied. He'd seen men on the battlefields with fevers like this – and mostly they were dead by morning.

The fresh candles that Hannah brought merely highlighted the problems they were facing. Lucinda's shadow loomed large against the whitewashed walls as she raved and babbled. "Reuben, don't leave me," she'd implored, reaching out to someone that neither Adam nor Hannah could see. She'd tried to throw herself from the bed in order to follow this presence. It took all Adam's strength to hold her until she quietened and sagged into his arms.

"Who is Reuben?" asked Adam.

"Lucinda was in love with him. He died."

Adam said nothing but he sensed that Lucinda's pain must be as great as his own. He envied her that she would at least be reunited with the one she loved.

Hannah watched as Adam gave Lucinda a dose of laudanum and settled her down. He knew he couldn't face waiting for another dawn that heralded the death of another young woman. He rode away from Manor Farm with a heavy heart and sat for the rest of the night in the blue velvet armchair in his bedroom at Doctor Sanders' house, watching the movement of grey clouds against indigo sky.

*

In Lucinda's fevered mind, past and present became confused. She was back in Marchington with Reuben and the stolen moments they'd shared at the ball. Her senses remembered the touch of his hand on hers, his kisses – and the aching sense of loss when he was sent away. The fever carried her to a dream space between the worlds. She watched Reuben's carriage drive away, ran after it, her gown tangling round her legs, determined this time not to be parted from him.

The road narrowed to a green pathway edged by brambles that tangled in her hair and around her limbs and wouldn't let her go. She shouted to Reuben to wait for her but the black coach drew further away from her.

Then she noticed that there were trees behind the brambles, pressing in on the pathway, their canopies dense with leaves. Some of the trunks had faces on them – the same face. Giles. Then she remembered that Reuben was dead and she'd never see him again. Grief swamped her like a river in flood.

She'd slumped back, tried to turn back from the pathway, but the trees had closed behind her. There was no way back. Then, to her joy, she noticed that the coach had stopped. Reuben got out and was walking towards her, his face alight with love. They got so close that they could almost touch – but there was a sheet of glass separating them. They were unable to touch each other.

Lucinda noticed that the path on Reuben's side of the glass led to a gateway surrounded by golden light. Reuben reached for her but he was unable to grasp her outstretched hands. The golden light was drawing him towards the gateway. Before he left her, he pointed to another pathway that she'd not noticed before that meandered along the bank of a peaceful river edged with trees. The upper windows and roof of a square white house showed beyond the tree-tops in the distance.

"There is your pathway, Lucinda," he said. "Be happy and know I loved you truly, but now you are free to live and love again."

Then he passed through the gate, closing it behind him.

Lucinda pounded on the sheet of glass with her fists but it would not break.

"Reuben, take me with you," she cried, "Let me stay with you."

Strong arms held her, she heard a soothing voice that was like the murmur of the river in her ears. She felt the cool taste of something against her lips and then the darkness claimed her, dragging her down into its velvet softness. She tried to open her eyes but her eyelids felt heavy as lead. Lucinda gave up and surrendered to a greater will than her own.

Reuben was back with her again, the dream sequence replaying endlessly in her fevered mind.

Somewhere beyond the dark space inside her head, a voice she recognised said: "You'll know by morning."

*

The next time Lucinda opened her eyes, she was in the bedroom she shared with Hannah at the farm. From the direction of the sun, it was nearly noon. Hannah was sitting by the bed weeping silent tears.

Lucinda had only a vague memory of the terror she had struck into Hannah's loving heart.

The last thing she remembered was her desperate need to escape from Manor Farm and she was puzzled to discover that they were still there. With a little prompting from Hannah she was able to piece together what had happened – how she'd walked away from the farm on legs that felt too weak to support her weight. She'd sat at the edge of the field feeling as if her head was stuffed with the seed-heads of old man's beard and then she'd come face to face with Adam Lennox, feeling as if she was in the middle of a dream.

Gradually, she pieced events back together like a series of pictures in her mind. Her legs had collapsed under her and she felt mortified as she remembered vomiting a stream of yellow bile.

He'd picked her up as if she weighed no more than a sack of feathers. His sweat smelled salty and the texture of his shirt was soft against her hot skin. She remembered the way his heart beat against hers and his warm breath on her cheek.

*

Adam Lennox felt certain that the next news he received would be that Lucinda Beckford had died.

However, there were several reasons why he did not return the next morning to find out how she fared. He'd gone back to Doctor Sanders' house the previous night, following the pathway carefully because there was no moon. When he arrived back, he'd sat in the chair brooding. When he did sleep, an unpleasant voice wove through his dreams. "*You're sweet on her*," it said.

Doctor Sanders had asked over bacon and kidneys at breakfast how his favourite patient was. Adam had felt his face flush as he denied the accusation.

"It does not do to become too attached, Adam. It is unfortunate that people gossip and it may do your reputation no good. No good at all."

Adam's appetite disappeared. He pushed the food to one side of his plate. He sat toying with a slice of bread and sipping his coffee. He knew that his friend was right. He knew now that he'd been making excuses and inventing delays to prevent him from properly moving into his new house and surgery. He admitted to himself that the reason for this was his growing feelings for Lucinda Beckford.

Chapter 21

Doctor Sanders called at Manor Farm that afternoon to see how Lucinda was faring.

"Where is Doctor Lennox?" asked Hannah.

"He ... ahem ... decided to return home."

Doctor Sanders didn't look at Hannah as he said this. He took his time checking Lucinda's wound, feeling her pulse, asking a few perfunctory questions and prescribing a special salve. Then he bowed politely, wished both of them good day and left. They heard his heavy footsteps moving slowly down the wooden stairs.

"Well!" said Hannah. "Doctor Lennox said nothing yesterday about having to leave us – and he's gone with no word of anything he may have discovered about Charlie and John."

"What people promise to do and what they actually do are not always the same," said Lucinda. She was surprised at how disappointed she'd been to see Doctor Sanders instead of Adam Lennox.

"Your handsome doctor wasn't that much in love then," taunted Ella. "They say he's moved on to his fancy new house – and no doubt he'll be finding himself a pretty young wife."

Lucinda flushed as if she'd been slapped. "My cousin and I had no expectations of any sort from Doctor Lennox." She was surprised at the shaft of jealousy she felt at the thought of Adam Lennox being married to someone else.

"Then no doubt you'll be moving on soon," said Ella, dusting her hands on her grubby apron. "Don't expect us to feed another mouth." She nodded towards Hannah's growing waistline.

Hannah opened her mouth to protest. At that moment, the farmer came clumping up the stairs.

"Guard that vicious tongue of yours, Ella. 'Tis little wonder any help we hire doesn't stay long. These ladies are welcome to stay until Miss Taylor is fully recovered.

Miss Jane has done more mending in the short time she's been here than you've done since our wedding."

Ella flounced down the stairs and Lucinda and Hannah heard her banging around in the kitchen.

"I wish the farmer hadn't spoken up for us like that," said Hannah. "I fear it will only make things more difficult between us and Ella.

*

The days continued long and hot, with the crops ripening and the promise of an early harvest.

Lucinda and Hannah tried not to incur the wrath of Ella any further. Hannah had completed the enormous pile of mending and now spent the time in between helping with the household chores making little pincushions, baby's bonnets and the like from fabric she'd purchased from the market.

To Hannah's surprise, it was Ella who praised the work and suggested that she take some of it to the weekly market in the local town to try and sell it.

"Perhaps she's turning over a new leaf," she said to Lucinda.

"I don't trust her," replied Lucinda. "Make sure you get the money that is due to you."

On market day, Ivy complained of stomach pains, so it was decided that she should stay at home with Lucinda while Hannah accompanied Ella and Dora to the market.

*

Hannah didn't particularly enjoy the company of either of them – she always felt they were testing her out, trying to make her say something out of place. There was no doubt that Ella's nose was also put out of joint when the beautifully stitched baby clothes and aprons sold rapidly and the coins in Hannah's pocket accumulated. She gave some of the money to Ella, who shoved the money into her own purse without a word of thanks.

The crowds of people buying from the market increased as the day went on. Hannah was kept busy selling their wares. Ella, almost as soon as they had arrived, had snatched up the butter and cheese that had been ordered by the landlady at *The Saracen's Head* and had departed to spend time chattering with her old friend. Dora had remained behind on the stall, sitting silently beside Hannah.

Just after Ella had gone, Hannah felt uneasy because she spotted a man on a black horse. She only saw him silhouetted against the sun but what she did see reminded her of Giles. She hoped that Lucinda, preparing the evening meal at the farm, would be safe. Hannah knew it was probably her imagination getting the better of her, but even so, she made sure the brim of her bonnet shaded her face.

She was surprised when Ella returned sooner than she expected.

Hannah had requested time to look round some of the other stalls and exchange some of her own money for fabric and embroidery silk so that she could make more items for sale.

"You'll have to be quick. I'm ready to go home," said Ella.

"But we haven't sold all our goods yet."

"It's time we went home." Ella had previously always made a point of being the first to arrive at the market and grabbing the best pitch, and the last to leave. She was up to something, Hannah was sure. Ella had a gleam in her eye and looked more cheerful than usual.

Hannah hurried round the stalls, collecting the things she needed. When she returned, Ella and Dora had packed up their stall and were whispering to each other. They stopped abruptly when Hannah returned and the journey home passed in an uneasy silence.

*

Giles felt it was a stroke of luck that he'd stopped to rest his horse in the small market town. He was on his way back from settling more tedious matters to do with his father's estate and had been drawn by the prospect of refreshment at the local inn. The groom had taken charge of his horse and Giles had been ushered into the dining room – a long, low building with oak beams divided into separate booths for privacy.

He hadn't been there long, tucking into a glass of ale and a large plate of thickly sliced ham, cheese and bread, when he overheard a conversation behind him that held his attention.

Two well-dressed men were just leaving the inn. It was the words of the older man with the rich, plummy voice that caught Giles's attention.

"Yes, I've lost the services of my assistant physician now that my injury has healed. I miss him, in truth. I expect one of his patients does, too. He was forming quite an attachment by all accounts. Mind you, if I was younger I'd have had a crack at her myself. Handsome young filly – dark hair and eyes like sapphires…,"

"Women are still more trouble than they're worth," said the other voice, the sound fading as they moved further away.

Giles sat bolt upright. He'd been searching fruitlessly for Lucinda for weeks and had been growing increasingly frustrated. He'd searched the countryside asking for information at farms and tollhouses, unable to understand how she could've disappeared so completely. He pushed his plate aside and headed after the two men, his attempts to reach them blocked by the crowd of farmers quenching their thirst in the low-ceilinged taproom. He reached the inn yard in time to see their carriage depart.

He returned to his seat. When the landlady came to clear his plate, he asked her who the two men were and if she knew the whereabouts of a young lady answering that description.

"A matter of the heart would it be, sir?" she asked.

"Quite so." He tried to look suitably lovelorn.

"I'm sorry, sir, I don't know who the gentlemen were and I've not met a young lady meeting that description." She bustled off, promising to find out what she could. "Maybe by the time you've spent a few days here, you'll have found her, sir." She hurried off to share this latest titbit of gossip with her friend Ella.

*

Lucinda had spent a peaceful day at the farm looking after Ivy who had miraculously recovered the minute the others had departed.

"I like the market itself," she'd confided to Lucinda, "but it's going with them I don't like. I'd much rather stay with you. I like you better than Ella or Dora. I wish you were my stepmother."

"Hush, you shouldn't say such things," said Lucinda.

"Why not? It's true. She's a mean ole toad and she's never liked me."

Lucinda prepared a stew for the evening meal, chopping meat and vegetables and adding fresh herbs from the kitchen garden. Then they made raspberry tarts – Lucinda allowing Ivy her own piece of pastry to make something special for her father.

By the time Hannah, Ella and Dora came home, eager for a cool drink and a rest from the heat, Ivy was looking happier than she had for some time. Her special pie was cooling on a rack near the open kitchen window. Dora spotted it and snatched it up greedily, biting into it.

Ivy yelled in protest, earning a slap from Ella.

"That's not fair," said Lucinda. "Ivy made that for her father."

"Whose ingredients are they, might I ask?" Ella glared at Lucinda. "There's been nothing but trouble in this house since you two arrived. Well – let me tell you, I won't stand no more of it." She folded her lips as if she was about to say something else but changed her mind.

*

Lucinda and Hannah were in their own room when they heard Ella come up the stairs with Dora.

"Did you see the man at the inn, Ma?" Dora whispered.

"Hush, they'll hear you," said Ella.

Lucinda and Hannah stood still, almost not daring to breathe.

"No, but I've sent young Dick to find him and bring him back here – especially now I've heard there's a reward."

There was the sound of Ella and Dora going into Ella's room and shutting the door. Hannah looked out of the window.

"The yard is clear," she said. "If we can get through the kitchen, then we may be able to escape before the men come back."

They gathered their belongings and crept quietly down the stairs. They'd almost made their escape when their way was blocked by Daniel, one of the farm hands.

"Going somewhere, ladies?" he asked.

Ella came up behind them, grabbing Lucinda by her injured arm.

"They most certainly are not. There's someone who very much wants to see you – Lucinda isn't it? Give me a hand to shut them in the store shed, Daniel."

Ella and Daniel bundled them and their belongings into the small brick-built shed at the far end of the farmyard that was used to store tools for the kitchen garden, ropes of onions and sacks of potatoes.

"Shout as much as you like," she said. "Nobody from the house will hear you."

"This is disgraceful," said Lucinda. "Please let us go." Her arm was throbbing from the rough treatment she'd received.

They heard the sound of the key turning in the lock. A small amount of light filtered in through a gap at the top of the door.

Lucinda beat on the door with her fists. "Let us out, Ella. You have no right to lock us in here."

There was no answer from Ella or Daniel. They heard the sound of their footsteps going away from them in the direction of the barn.

Lucinda hoped the farmer might comment on their absence at dinner and ask where they were. "If Giles doesn't arrive before then," she said, her whole body recoiling at the thought of his clammy hands on her skin.

"I can smell smoke," said Hannah. "Maybe Ella's burned the dinner again."

"That's not coming from the farmhouse kitchen," said Lucinda. "The barn's on fire. Listen."

The smoke was now accompanied by a crackling sound that was getting louder. They could hear the whinnying of horses and the running of feet, followed by the yell of "Fire!" The hayrick's on fire."

The yell was taken up by other farmhands coming in from their day in the fields. The smell of smoke drifted through the gap in the door. Lucinda and Hannah had sunk down on a pile of dusty hessian sacks. They'd clearly been forgotten in this latest emergency.

Lucinda piled up anything she could find in the shed that she could scramble onto in order to see what was happening. Clutching her shawl over her mouth, choking on the acrid smoke, eyes smarting, she peered through the tiny gap at the top of the door trying to see what was going on.

"They can't stop it," she said. "It's spreading to the barn."

She saw one of the horses being led out of the stables, its head covered in a cloth so it wouldn't see the flames and be spooked.

They heard a loud crash as part of the barn collapsed followed by a rising tide of voices, a woman's voice screaming and the desperate sound of frightened horses.

"We'll die if we don't get out of here," said Lucinda sinking down next to Hannah on the hessian sacks and covering her face to stop inhaling too much smoke.

At that moment, there was the sound of a key in the lock. The two women clutched at each other. Lucinda fully expected to come face to face with Giles Milburn with the prospect of no escape this time. The time it took for the key to turn seemed to go on for ever. The door swung open letting in smoke and heat. Ivy stood there clutching a package in her arms.

"I stole the keys," she said. Her blue eyes filled with tears as she flung her arms round Lucinda. "I knows I can't come with you 'cos you'd get into even more trouble but I wish I could." She pushed the package into Lucinda's arms. "I got you some food."

"Won't Ella miss it? We wouldn't want you to get into trouble," said Lucinda.

A mischievous smile crossed the little girl's face before being replaced with a more serious expression. "She's lying upstairs injured – some burning straw fell on her and Daniel when they was doing something they shouldn't. They've sent for Doctor Sanders. That's how I managed to get the key. It fell out of her pocket when they carried her into the house."

Lucinda and Hannah hugged her and hurried along the pathway, keeping themselves hidden amongst the trees. The sky was darkening again and they needed to find a place to hide. They'd agreed it was safer to keep to the fields where possible and make their way to the village where Charlie's mother lived.

*

They heard the sound of hooves moving quickly across hard ground and shrank into the bushes. Giles and the stable boy galloped past them. Giles looked like the cat that was about to eat the canary.

"It'll be sometime before he finds out we've gone," said Lucinda. "If what Ivy says is true and Ella and Daniel are injured then it may take time for him to find out what she'd done with us."

*

Giles could barely contain his excitement when the boy from the farm called at *The Saracen's Head* with a message for him. He tried not to build his hopes up as he questioned the boy who hung his head nervously as if Giles was about to strike him.

Nothing had been written down – Ella wasn't gifted in that way – but she'd given a clear message to be passed on. '*The lady you are looking for is at Manor Farm.*'

"What does this lady look like?" asked Giles.

The boy scraped his toe on the carpet as if trying to rub a hole in it. His boots were dusty and cracked.

"What lady?"

"The one you're telling me is at Manor Farm."

"There's two."

Giles took a deep breath and tried again.

"What does the prettiest one look like?"

The boy shot him a helpless look. "I dunno, sir. Golden hair, what you can see of it under her cap, and she be having a child."

Giles turned away. The boy, obviously hopeful of at least a penny for having ridden hard to reach the inn as soon as possible, sensed that he'd failed.

"The other has dark hair and her name's Mary."

Disappointment flooded Giles combined with a searing tremor of frustration in the area of his britches.

"Thank you for your trouble but she cannot be the lady I am seeking."

"She got blue eyes," said the boy, digging deep in his ideas of what grown-ups got excited about. "They glitter just like Crow Pool on a hot day."

Giles' excitement returned. This sounded more promising.

"Show me where Manor Farm is. If she turns out to be the lady I'm looking for, then I'll give you a florin."

"The mistress said I'd get a guinea," said the boy.

"Go and get my horse saddled," said Giles. "If your story is true then we'll see."

Chapter 22

When Giles reached Manor Farm, everything was in chaos. Nobody was prepared to stop their efforts to get the blaze under control, even for a fine looking gentleman like him. The air was full of smoke and ash and everyone he encountered looked dirty and exhausted.

Thankfully, because there was no wind to stir the blaze, the farmhouse was untouched – the main damage had been to the hayrick, the roof of the barn and part of the stable building.

Giles dismounted and handed Black Boy's reins to the stable boy so he could take care of him while he went in search of Lucinda. Black Boy, upset by the smoke and the sound of other horses in distress, sidestepped and bucked causing the stable boy to shout in alarm so that Giles had to take the reins from him and lead the horse to a quiet place behind the farmhouse where he could tether him.

The farmhouse door was open and Giles made his way through the cluttered kitchen where it looked like a meal had been in the process of preparation and then abandoned. A cat was lapping from a bowl of cream and a cooking pot containing potatoes had been overturned in someone's haste to leave the kitchen.

Giles paused in the doorway leading to a long, low room with a big table running down the centre of it. A man – he assumed the farmer - was sitting at the table taking a long draught of ale and talking to a man who looked like a physician. His face was streaked with dirt and ashes.

"It's God's punishment that their sin should be discovered in this way," the farmer was saying. "When they're well enough – if they survive – then they must both leave here. You need not bother to call again, Doctor Sanders. They can take their chances with life or death." He handed the doctor some coins and took another draught of ale, wiping his mouth with the back of his hand.

"There is someone else to see you," said the doctor as he took his leave.

The farmer turned and noticed Giles. He got to his feet. "What can I do for you, sir? Are you another man seeking my wife's favours?"

"I am seeking a young woman named Lucinda Beckford," said Giles. "I am reliably informed that she has been living under your roof."

"There's nobody of that name here," said the farmer.

"She may be here under an assumed name."

"What is she to you?" asked the farmer, his eyes narrowed with suspicion.

"We are engaged to be married," said Giles.

"So why have you come looking for her – and what makes you so sure she is here?"

"I am reliably informed so by your wife. I paid her good money for the information."

"I know nothing of this." The farmer's face flushed with anger.

"Look man, are you going to show me where she is or do I have to get a magistrate with a search warrant?"

"This is my property," said the farmer, "and if I say there's nobody of that name here, then there isn't."

Two burly farmhands blocked the doorway and Giles looked less sure of himself. He'd heard of situations like this where wealthy young men had been lured to a remote place and then 'disappeared' – to be found later stripped of their belongings and dead in a ditch. He swallowed. His neck-cloth suddenly felt too tight. He and the two farmhands eyed each other.

Dora came into the room. From the look on her face, she'd obviously been eavesdropping outside the door.

She looked at Giles and gave him a sickly smile. "What'll you give me, sir, if I tells you where the lady is?"

"Dora, go to your room and stay there," growled the farmer, "this is no concern of yours."

"They're probably dead by now anyway," said Dora – a look of morbid satisfaction on her pale face.

"What are you talking about, Dora?" bawled the farmer.

"Mother put them in the outhouse," said Dora. She picked up her doll and rocked it in her arms, singing softly to it, clearly enjoying the sensation she was causing. "Shall I go to my room now?"

"You'll go upstairs and you'll find the key to the outhouse and bring it down here – and be quick about it."

"If she's dead then you'll all hang for this," blustered Giles.

The farmhands stepped back looking less sure of themselves.

Dora hurried upstairs and they could hear her rummaging about in the room above. She came back downstairs with the key and handed it to the farmer.

The farmer led the way to the outhouse. The air outside was still thick with smoke and ash. It had begun to rain which had helped to damp down the last vestiges of fire. The heavy wooden door of the store shed was hot to the touch and the area around the outside of it littered with debris.

He put the key into the lock and turned it. The door swung open showing a dark, smoky, empty space beyond.

Giles looked around it, an expression of disbelief on his flushed face. "I've been hoodwinked by your wife and child," he said. "They are both liars and should both be severely beaten. I very much doubt that my fiancée was ever here at all. I should never have wasted my time by coming here. Please fetch my horse."

Dora had followed them to the outhouse, her small face pinched and white. She stepped in front of Giles. "Me and my Ma are not liars, sir. Them two ladies was here. Look." She gave a white lace handkerchief to Giles embroidered with the letter 'L.' "They left this in their room."

Giles eyed her warily. "How do I know you didn't steal this from some unsuspecting lady?"

"'Ere – don't you go accusing my girl of stealing when she's doing her best to help you," said the farmer.

Dora stood still, as if she were repeating a Sunday School catechism. "They said their names were Mary and Jane but when they thought nobody could hear they called each other Lucinda and Hannah." She curtsied and then skittered away like a kitten, avoiding the farmer's fist as she passed.

Giles grabbed Black Boy's reins from the farm hand who had fetched him and threw himself up into the saddle. "I pray for all your sakes that I find her quickly," he said with a menacing look. He left the farm at the gallop, raising a cloud of dust and ash.

Chapter 23

Adam was tired. He'd slept badly since he arrived back at his own house, plagued by guilt that he hadn't done more to help and protect Lucinda Beckford. He'd valued his own reputation and had been scared away by gossip-mongers when he should have stayed and made sure she was safe.

He wasn't expecting visitors, so was surprised to hear a heavy knocking on the front door.

The house was square, brick-built and had several outbuildings. One of these had been white-washed and turned into a makeshift surgery where poorer patients could be examined. His wealthier patients were, of course, visited in their own homes.

Adam could hear his housekeeper Rose Dennett's footsteps along the stone flagged hallway and her muffled exclamation as she opened the door. He got to his feet, wondering what had happened that had caused her such distress.

The last person he expected to see was his cousin Giles.

"Where is she?" Giles looked belligerent. He was leaning on the door-frame, his eyes were blood-shot and his breath stank of wine and brandy. He usually held his drink well, but this time he'd obviously had more than usual.

"What are you talking about?" Adam's voice cracked like a pistol shot.

The housekeeper scuttled back towards the safety of the kitchen.

"Don't play the innocent." Giles staggered slightly. "You know quite well who I mean. Lu-cin-da – my betrothed."

"I don't know what you're talking about," said Adam, desperately wanting to know where Lucinda was now.

Rose reappeared, her arms full of freshly laundered white sheets. "Is everything all right sir?"

Giles recognised their old nurse.

He turned to Adam. "Well, well. Saint Adam. Never could resist taking in lame ducks could you?" he sneered.

"I'll not stand by and see a good servant on the streets," said Adam, glad that the subject had been changed slightly.

"I'll wager she's not all you're harbouring in this fancy new house of yours. Was it you that rescued Lucinda from the fire?" Giles leaned against the door frame. "Because she and her friend had disappeared by the time the farmer opened the door."

"What fire?" Adam's heart clenched with anxiety but he tried not to show it. "I have no idea what you're talking about."

"You're a good actor, man, I'll give you that!" Giles paused. "The fire at Manor Farm. The farmer's wife was keeping her locked up for me – but somebody let her out before I got there. Wasn't you by any chance was it?" Giles lurched forward, pushing Adam out of the way as he tried to force his way into the house.

The commotion brought Rose's husband Matthew hurrying in. He'd been a prize fighter in his youth and had no trouble in bundling Giles out of the door and deposited him on his backside on the cobbles.

"You'll be sorry," Giles spluttered as he staggered to his feet, realising as he did so that he'd jarred his ankle. He hobbled towards where he'd tethered Black Boy but to his horror, an old crone in tattered clothes had hold of his bridle.

"I saw you here afore," she said, looking up at him through her thatch of white hair. "I knowed you'd not drowned like they said. I knowed you'd come back like Moses in the bulrushes…,"

The horror of madness Giles had witnessed in the asylum to which he'd committed Amelia surfaced and he wrenched the old crone's bony hands off Black Boy's bridle, raising his whip in a threatening gesture.

The old crone's yells brought a pale young woman running from the direction of the dilapidated cottage near the brook.

"Come along with me, grandmother, and stop a-bothering this gentleman."

She tugged gently at the old woman's arm and led her back towards the cottage.

With a sigh of relief, Giles mounted Black Boy. As he rode away he was aware that Rose's husband Matthew was still watching him from the doorway of his cousin's house, a disrespectful grin on his weather-beaten face.

"Looks as if old Agatha Dixon has given him more of a fright than we could have done," he said.

"Poor old lady," said Rose. "She never got over losing her little boy all those years ago when he got swept away in the floods. Every stranger that arrives here she thinks is her missing Daniel."

Matthew shut the front door and barred it.

"I fear we've not seen the last of Mr Giles though," said Rose. "He's always had a nasty temper and if there's something he wants he'll stop at nothing until he gets his way."

Adam, overhearing this, knew it to be true and hoped with all his heart that Lucinda Beckford managed to stay out of his cousin's clutches. He would not want to be in her shoes if Giles caught up with her.

Chapter 24

Lucinda and Hannah were no more than five miles away from Lower Warren when they heard hurdy-gurdy music and noticed a commotion of carts and people heading along a narrow lane. The sense of excitement in the air reminded Lucinda of the Midsummer Fair and the events following it that led to their lives being turned upside down. She felt cold, as if a cloud had blotted out the sunshine.

The dusty green and gold summer had changed to a vibrant autumn with the hedgerows glowing russet and orange and heavy with elderberries, sloes and rosehips. There were pale mushrooms and red and white toadstools and the scent of apples and bonfire smoke on the early morning air.

"What's going on in that field?" Lucinda asked three young girls who were hurrying down the lane, arm in arm and giggling.

"Why, 'tis the Hiring Fair," said one of them, "where have you been that you don't know about it? 'Tis the best place in the county to find whatever you lack – a situation, a new bonnet or a handsome young man."

"We all know which of those you want," teased her friends, nudging her and laughing.

"What do we have to do to find a new situation?" asked Lucinda.

"Give your names to Squire Lawrence's Steward and do as he bids you," said the girl with a friendly smile.

Lucinda thanked them and the three girls ran off down the lane. She and Hannah proceeded more slowly, taking time to look around the various stalls.

The smells of roasting meat, fresh bread and cakes hung in the air and Lucinda and Hannah refreshed themselves with lemonade and plum cake. Then they headed towards the far side of the field where a man was ordering people to stand in a circle.

On the way there, they noticed the fake doctor with his little pink pills. He was having a better day today. The audience were more receptive and there was no hint that he would have to beat a hasty retreat. They crowded round, queuing for bottles of pills. The girls were obviously still sharing the blue-trimmed white dress and bonnet – although close inspection showed it to be in need of a wash.

The wagon flaps remained carefully closed at the back and a young man was doing guard duty. Even so, Lucinda noticed that once the bottles were all sold, they wasted no time in moving on.

Lucinda and Hannah walked past the section where horses were being bought and sold – prospective buyers looking carefully over a horse's points and watching as they were put through their paces. The ground was tinder dry under their feet and the air smelled of human sweat, horse-shit and leather. The sound of raised voices conflicted with the hurdy-gurdy music as they headed towards where an official-looking man with a malacca cane was directing people to their places.

Lucinda and Hannah stood side by side in the circle of shepherds with their crooks, housemaids with feather dusters and dairymaids with three-legged stools. They stood as the farmers and their ladies circulated, picking people out – in some cases poking and prodding them as if they were cattle.

"I could never employ a dairymaid with red hair," said a stout farmer's wife. "It would dry the cows' milk."

"Just as well I didn't want to go there then," said the red-haired dairymaid to Hannah. "One thing I hate about hiring fairs is the way they talk about you like you're deaf or silly in the head. I wouldn't have left my last situation at all if my mistress hadn't died."

A man dressed in a brown woollen topcoat and buff coloured breeches looked Lucinda up and down. "I have a vacancy for a cook-housekeeper," he said. "Would you be interested?" He was an older man with iron grey hair.

"Only if you'll take my friend as well," said Lucinda. "She's a good seamstress."

The man looked Hannah up and down with grey eyes hard as stones. "In the family way is she?"

"She is legally married," said Lucinda primly. "Her husband is currently serving with Wellington's forces."

"That may be so, but I cannot afford to carry anybody – not with my wife being so ill." The man turned away.

"You had a lucky escape there," said a shepherd standing on the other side of Hannah. "Farmer Braithwaite is well-known for wanting a week's work for a day's pay."

"I'd have accepted his offer if he'd have taken both of us," said Lucinda.

"Don't worry about me. I'm sure Charlie's mother will take me in," said Hannah.

"We don't know that for certain," said Lucinda. She'd been sure that her Great Aunt would help them but those hopes had been dashed.

The shepherd winked at Hannah and told her he'd just been offered a situation on a nearby farm. "The dairymaid they've hired looks a bit of all right too – and if it's not to my liking there's the runaway mop at Casterton next week."

"What's the runaway mop?" asked Lucinda.

"It's when all those who've made a wrong choice can change their minds and try a new employer," said the shepherd cheerfully. "Although looking at that dairymaid, I think I'm right suited this time." He looked at the red-haired dairymaid and she looked back at him and then quickly turned away, a flush staining her cheeks pink.

It was late afternoon when the stall-holders began packing up their wares and making their way along the narrow lane. The large field was nearly empty and Lucinda and Hannah were among a few who had not accepted offers of work.

"What do we do now?" asked Lucinda.

"See if Charlie's mother will help us, I suppose," said Hannah. "Although from the little he has said about her I don't expect a very warm welcome."

Chapter 25

It was early evening when they reached Lower Warren. The village was no more than two streets and a village green with a stagnant-looking pond where the horses drank and a well where the village women collected their water. There were a collection of them now gossiping and looking at Lucinda and Hannah as if they'd just arrived from the moon.

They asked a young woman for directions to Mrs Marshall's house and she pointed down the narrow street edged with small cottages. "Last one on the right."

The young woman had a sharp face and she eyed Lucinda and Hannah curiously. "Things must be looking up for Old Matilda if she's taking on more girls," she said to one of her friends, obviously not caring if Lucinda and Hannah heard her.

"What on earth did she mean?" asked Hannah. "She acted as if we'd got the plague."

"I have no idea," said Lucinda, "but she didn't make me feel very welcome here."

They picked their way down the muddy lane, careful not to turn their ankles in the many potholes. The last cottage looked so dilapidated they doubted if it was occupied. It was in desperate need of a coat of whitewash and the garden was neglected and full of weeds. They were about to turn away until they noticed a little girl crouching just inside the rough wooden gate.

She was wearing a blue cotton gown several sizes too big for her. The fabric was so faded in places it was almost white. Her feet were bare, her fair hair a mass of tangles, and her face was dirty and smudged with tears.

"What's the matter?" asked Lucinda.

"My Ma's sent me to buy ale," the little girl showed the chipped earthenware jug that she'd set down by the gate, "but I dropped the penny she give me. She'll give me a whipping if I go back and tell her."

"Jessie," yelled a harsh female voice from somewhere inside the cottage, "where's my ale? Don't take all day about it."

Jessie's blue eyes were huge in her small face. "What shall I do? She's mad enough to bust something."

Lucinda noticed Hannah searching her reticule and she frowned at her. If she supplied a penny this time, the other occupants of the cottage might think things could go on that way. Just then a shaft of late afternoon sun split the grey clouds that had gathered and Hannah noticed the penny caught in a crevice on her side of the gate. She bent down and picked it up and handed it to Jessie. A big smile lit up the little girl's face.

"She looks just like Charlie," said Hannah, her eyes filling with tears.

They watched Jessie run up the street in the direction they'd just come, skinny legs flashing under the ragged hem of the gown. Within minutes they saw her return, walking carefully this time so as not to spill the contents of the jug.

Lucinda and Hannah followed her up the mossy pathway to the cottage door. They found themselves in a small room where watery-looking gruel in a black cooking pot bubbled over a smoky fire. The flagstone floor was caked in mud and the room smelled of mice and unwashed bodies.

A big woman in a rusty black gown and a greasy looking mobcap sat in a wooden chair beside a fire that was more smoke than flames. She snatched the jug of ale from Jessie and drank from it greedily, her eyes closed. It was some minutes before she opened them and noticed Lucinda and Hannah standing by the open door.

"'Oo might you be?" Her grey eyes were cold as a fish on a marble slab as she looked them up and down.

"I'm Hannah, your son Charlie's wife."

The woman spat into the fire, narrowly missing the cooking pot. "Charlie – that good-for-nothink. He's never sent me any money since he left here." The woman's lower lip stuck out like a shelf.

"He is unable to send you or me anything," said Hannah. "The Militia have taken him."

"I s'pose you put him up to it?"

"No! He was taken against his will."

"I wondered why he'd not sent me nuffink. I might've known he'd got mixed up with some doxy." She swept Hannah an appraising glance from her head to her feet, her eyes drawn to her belly. "There's two or three girls in the village claim to have had a brat by Charlie. You won't be the last."

Hannah's cheeks flushed. "Charlie and I were married in church."

"If it's money you're after, we ain't got none. There's no room here neither, so you'd better be on your way." The woman turned her attention back to the jug of ale.

"Come along, Hannah, we'll go to the vicarage," said Lucinda. "I'm sure they'll know someone who'll let us pay for a bed until we can find work." She said this with more confidence than she felt. She couldn't face the thought of walking another step. Dusk was gathering along with rain clouds on the horizon.

They picked up their bundles and prepared to leave.

Jessie emerged from behind the door where she'd been listening to their conversation. "I know someone who'd give you board and lodging," she said. "Will you give me a ha'penny if I takes you there?"

"'Ere," said Charlie's mother, getting to her feet and aiming a swipe at Jessie," if anyone's getting any coppers for putting these two up, it'll be me." A crafty expression crossed her face. "Now don't be hasty ladies. Sit down and take a glass of ale with me. You can share the girls' room upstairs."

Lucinda and Hannah sat down, careful not to make the mistake of looking too grateful.

Chapter 26

Lucinda and Hannah shared a room with Charlie's three younger sisters. Matilda Marshall grudgingly provided them with a straw-filled mattress and a thin blanket. The room was full of draughts. Lucinda and Hannah huddled together for warmth and slept badly because of the cold. Hannah developed a troublesome cough and Lucinda was concerned by the high spots of colour on her otherwise pale cheeks.

"Is there an apothecary in the village?" she'd asked Matilda.

"You've got ideas above your station and no mistake!" Matilda looked scornful. "We don't have any of that nonsense here – couldn't afford it if we did. Give her raw onion in honey – mind it'll cost you extra!"

*

Lucinda walked the five miles into Bridgeton, entering the town by crossing the narrow bridge over the Avon. She had to squeeze into one of the triangular shaped spaces to allow horses and carts to pass by. The river meadows were grazed by sheep and the river meandered peacefully between its banks, edged by willows that glowed orange in the morning sunlight. She'd heard from Matilda Marshall that there were times when the river became a raging torrent and the water levels rose to flood the low-lying meadows and houses nearby.

"When I was a child," Matilda said, "the flood water covered the bridge so you couldn't see it and everyone thought it had been washed away. It was a week 'fore we could get anywhere near the town."

Lucinda covered her head and kept her eyes cast down as she passed the tollhouse keeper. Thankfully, he was busy talking to a man with a flock of geese that had clearly walked some miles on their flat yellow feet.

"I'd have flat feet if I'd walked as far as them," the tollhouse keeper said.

"That's why I keep me boots on," said the goose-man with a chuckle.

Judging by the volume of livestock heading into the town, it was clearly market day. Lucinda thought this was a good thing as it would make her less conspicuous.

She found herself in a street edged by elegant buildings. The town also had two coaching inns *The Three Tuns* and *The Angel*. Lucinda gazed around at the bustle of life - fashionable women stepping carefully along the pavement and elegantly dressed men picking their way across the manure-filled street. She realised how much she'd missed the day to day life in Marchington.

It was tempting to stop and look at the shops, but Lucinda went into the coffee room at *The Three Tuns* to ask if it was possible to purchase writing materials. Travellers were awaiting the arrival of the Mail Coach and she hoped it would be possible to send a letter to Great Aunt Sophia. The landlord looked surprised at her request, as did an elderly man who was dressed like a lawyer's clerk.

"May I be of assistance?" he asked. "I could write a letter to your dictation. Perhaps we could discuss your requirements in a private room?" His pale eyes slithered over her body in a way that made Lucinda feel uncomfortable.

"Thank you, sir, but I can manage by myself somewhere a little more public," she said. She turned to the landlord who was hovering near the door, an amused grin on his face. "That is, if the landlord can supply me with the necessary items."

Something in her tone of voice galvanised him into action although the piece of paper he gave her was torn and ragged on the edges, and the quill looked as if it had been in constant service for more than a fortnight.

Lucinda did her best with it, wishing she could have made fewer blots.

"*I pray that you will overlook my previous refusal of the help you offered and come to our assistance now. Your loving niece Lucinda.*" She dusted the letter with sand, folded and sealed it and handed it over to the landlord. She had a feeling that if her Great Aunt saw the state of the letter, she would refuse to pay the delivery charge, assuming it was from a vagabond or ne'er-do-well.

She asked the landlord for directions to the nearest apothecary's shop. The instructions took her into a series of winding lanes that made her feel nervous because it seemed that the alleyways that ran between the old black and white houses could harbour cutpurses and thieves. She began to wonder if she'd interpreted the instructions correctly and then, just as she was about to turn back and try another street, she saw the familiar sign swinging above a low doorway and headed towards it. She opened the door and stepped down into a room with oak beams that smelled of a mixture of garlic, aniseed, mint and rosemary. A fire burned at one end, adding the smell of apple-wood smoke to the concoction.

The apothecary, who wore black breeches and jacket, listened to her account of Hannah's condition.

"You say your friend is with child?"

Lucinda nodded, feeling a flush of embarrassment at discussing something so personal with a man, even if he was an apothecary.

"When is the child due to be born?"

"At Christmas."

"Has she been well up until now?"

"The place we are living is very cold and damp, sir."

"Such places are best avoided for the good of the child."

He mixed a special tincture the colour of pale Madeira wine and gave it to Lucinda with instructions for its use.

"If this does not work, then please come back. Bring the lady with you if she is able to walk that far." His dark eyes were kind behind round spectacles.

*

Everyone except Matilda and Hannah went to work in the fields, helping to gather the potato crop into large baskets. It was dirty, back-breaking work, but Lucinda was eager to earn some money. She'd hoped that she and

Hannah could move into a cottage of their own, but enquiries revealed nothing available at the moment – and not enough work to be able to support themselves.

The day was damp and chilly with clouds gathering over the distant hills like grey blankets.

They'd not been working for more than an hour when a whisper came along the rows that Farmer Braithwaite was on his way. He looked an imposing figure on the back of his grey mare.

He stopped when he reached Lucinda.

"I'll wager you wish you'd taken my offer at the hiring fair," he said staring down at her. His cold grey eyes scanned her body, taking in her muddy hands and clothes.

Lucinda shook her head. "I do not regret my decision, sir. I would not be parted from my friend."

"You may change your mind when the snow comes and food becomes scarce." He gave a curt nod and passed on along the row.

As soon as everyone had left the house, Hannah headed towards the vicarage to ask if the vicar's wife had need of any sewing work. She took with her some examples of her handiwork left over from the market she'd gone to with Ella.

"Mrs Temple would want nothing to do with a person like you," the housekeeper said as she prepared to shut the door on Hannah. She was dressed in black and the expression on her face looked as if she'd been drinking vinegar.

"Please may I speak to her?"

"She is far too busy to be bothered with you." The housekeeper's tone was harsh and Hannah had a feeling that if she'd been holding a broom she'd have swept her out of the door.

"What's going on, Mrs Hoskins?" asked a nervous voice.

"Some vagabond making a nuisance of herself, Madam"

"If you please, Madam, I only wanted to speak to you," said Hannah.

The owner of the voice came forward and Hannah saw a woman of about her own age, also about to bear a child in the near future.

"What is it you wish to speak to me about?" she asked.

Mrs Hoskins the housekeeper stood guarding the doorway, her arms folded and the expression on her face mutinous.

"I wanted to show you some of my needlework," said Hannah, "and to ask if there is any work I could do for you."

She passed the lady an embroidered nightgown she'd been making for her baby from the remnants of one of her petticoats.

"She has no doubt stolen it from some unfortunate person," grumbled Mrs Hoskins.

"Mrs – what is your name my dear? – wouldn't be offering to do more work for me if that were so," said Mrs Temple.

"It's a trick," said the housekeeper. "You wait, she'll worm her way inside the house and then we'll all be murdered in our beds."

"Stuff and nonsense, Mrs Hoskins. Bring us some tea in the morning room please and shut the front door. The draught's enough to cut us all in half."

"I don't know what the vicar will make of this," grumbled the housekeeper as she headed along a passageway.

Mrs Temple led Hannah into a room with two bay windows that was decorated in the shade of dark green that had been fashionable five years ago. The lace curtains, she could see, had been mended by someone with darning skills that left a lot to be desired. Hannah's fingers itched to be able to unpick the ungainly white stitching and replace it with something that would be less noticeable.

Hannah sat opposite the vicar's wife while she poured tea and offered small cakes.

"My Christian name is Florence," she said. "I am named for the place where I was born. I am thankful that my parents had moved on from Assisi or that would have been my given name." She rattled on, not giving Hannah much chance to get a word in edgeways.

"This is beautiful work," she said as she examined Hannah's stitching. "I confess to being very stupid with my needle."

"I learned the skill from my mother," said Hannah. "One of my earliest memories is of sorting the buttons in her special box into different colours and patterns."

"What happened to her?"

"She died in the typhus epidemic that ravished our town."

"I fear death more than anything," said Florence, drawing closer to Hannah. "Especially death in childbirth." She looked out of the window at the gravestones that were visible on that side of the house. "I detest the view from that window more than any other from this house."

"I envy you this house, whatever the view," said Hannah. "My husband was taken by the Militia and is somewhere on the Peninsula. Until he returns or I can find something better I must remain with my mother-in-law and her cottage is very cramped."

Florence looked at her. "You are right. In my situation, I should be thinking more of others – but it is difficult to behave as a true Christian, especially when my dear sister…," She broke off suddenly at the sound of a key turning and the front door opening.

Heavy footsteps sounded in the hallway.

"My husband does not like me to speak of such matters," said Florence, looking nervously towards the door.

Hannah gathered her needlework together not knowing what to do next.

The footsteps headed past the morning room door and there was the sound of another door opening and closing.

Hannah stood up, preparing to thank Florence Temple for her hospitality.

"Hannah – Mrs Marshall – will you please come again and help me stitch some garments for my baby? I will of course pay you for your efforts. I have a little money of my own." She flushed and looked down at her lap.

*

It was arranged that Hannah would work at the vicarage for two days a week. As expected, Matilda Marshall immediately demanded more rent "to provide better victuals," she said. However it was noticeable that the only thing that increased was her consumption of ale.

*

The younger children were eager for details of life in the vicarage – surprised to hear that the new baby was having a whole room to itself.

"The housekeeper, Mrs Hoskins, certainly keeps an eye on me," Hannah reported after her first day there. "I am not able to visit the necessary house without her wanting to know where I am. I'm surprised she doesn't check my petticoats to make sure I'm not trying to escape with the silver."

If the housekeeper was a little frosty, the vicar seemed pleased that his wife had found a diversion.

"She was spending too long on her own," he confided to Hannah one day as she was leaving. "I thank you for helping her forget her fears for a while."

Hannah curtsied, wishing there was more work for both her and Lucinda and that they could stay permanently at the vicarage. The smell of stewed lamb and baked apples drifted along the passageway from the kitchen and her stomach growled with hunger. She turned towards the door, bracing herself to step into the cold wind and drizzle.

That afternoon, Florence Temple had given her the disappointing news that her husband's cousin was coming after the birth to act as nursemaid-companion.

"I must confess I do not warm to Cousin Drusilla," she said. "I would rather have you to help me, Hannah. We could watch our babies grow together."

*

It was a few weeks later while Hannah put the finishing touches to a tiny white cotton nightgown that Florence imparted some startling news.

"I am, as you know, still facing the birth of my baby with a great deal of fear, despite my dear husband's efforts to calm me. He is at such pains to help me that he has consulted a local doctor on my behalf and I am expecting a visit from him." She paused, her face flushed with agitation, to fan herself. "His name is Adam Lennox and he has some experience as an accoucheur, having trained with an eminent physician in London. I gather he has also seen some service on the Peninsula with our gallant soldiers."

Hannah pricked her finger when she heard the name, narrowly avoiding getting a spot of blood on the delicate lace of the nightgown. She gave a yelp of surprise.

"My dear, I had no wish to distress you," said Florence. "It is my own fear I am trying to overcome. My beloved sister and her babe died last year and I greatly fear suffering the same fate." She wiped tears from her eyes with a lace edged handkerchief. "I know I shouldn't make a fuss and my husband bids me submit to the will of God, but sometimes it is good to have some extra help."

Florence chattered on, obviously taking Hannah's silence for shock at what she had just said.

"I realise my dear that you may be shocked at the prospect of a man attending a lying in, but I am assured that this is becoming quite fashionable amongst the nobility and we are lucky to have such an eminent physician so close to us. You may possibly meet him when he calls to visit me today – although of course his services would be beyond anything you could possibly afford."

Hannah busied herself tidying away her sewing things, aware that her hands were shaking.

The afternoon was fading when they heard the clatter of hooves outside. Shortly afterwards the doorbell rang, the sound echoing through the house. The housekeeper ushered the visitor in with much pomp and circumstance. Hannah was about to hide herself away in the window seat overlooking the garden, but Florence had other ideas.

"This is my companion, Mrs Marshall," she said.

Hannah bobbed a curtsey and could feel her face flushing.

Adam Lennox bowed to both ladies and sat on the chair indicated. Florence rang for tea to be brought in. They sat making polite conversation while they were waiting. Hannah tried to stop herself from coughing. The atmosphere in the drawing room was hot and stuffy and her added nervousness made things worse.

"I see you are also to be congratulated on your future expectations, Mrs Marshall," said Adam Lennox.

"I am sure Mrs Marshall is awaiting events with far less trepidation than I am," said Florence.

"As your husband says, you should not dwell on your sister's unhappy experience," said Adam Lennox. His voice was gentle, reassuring. "Think of happy times to come with your new baby."

*

It was growing dark when Hannah left the vicarage, feeling reluctant to leave the appetising smells and rich fabrics that surrounded her together with the gleam of polished wood. Hannah had been a tiny child when she'd last lived in such opulence. It hadn't lasted long. The money her father had inherited had gradually been frittered away on various money-making schemes that did not work. When he died, the creditors came calling and her mother was forced to sell most of their treasured possessions and to take work as a seamstress.

She knew what Florence said was true – death could strike quickly and change lives for people in the blink of an eye. After all, it was the death of her father that had led to the reduction in circumstances for herself and her mother –and to that beloved person dying of a broken heart.

*

Adam Lennox was waiting for her further down the lane in the shadow of an oak tree. His horse was tethered to a fence and cropping grass.

"I do not wish to upset or frighten you, Mrs Marshall, but I am concerned to know how you and Miss Beck…Taylor are."

"We are well, sir."

"Miss Taylor's arm – how is it?"

"It sometimes troubles her a little. She hopes in time that the scar will fade."

"My house is at Court Green if you should need my help." He paused. "I did write to one of my acquaintances requesting news of your menfolk. It appears that Miss Taylor's brother is using his artistic talents in Wellington's service. He has been creating drawings of the soldiers and the battlefields that have been very well received. Your husband was also in good health at the time of enquiry."

"When might we expect their return?"

"That I cannot say."

Hannah saw young Jessie running along the lane, skirt flying around skinny legs – no doubt on an errand to fetch ale for her mother. She turned and ran back the way she'd come and Hannah knew that being seen conversing with Adam Lennox would excite comment.

*

By the time Hannah reached the cottage, Matilda and the other children had all heard about the fine gentleman she'd been talking to.

"What was he doing, talking to the likes of you?" asked Matilda as she took a swig of ale and wiped her mouth with the back of her hand.

"He'd lost his way and was asking directions to the nearest coaching inn," said Hannah, wondering why she hadn't just been honest and said he was the vicar's wife's physician. It was bound to become common knowledge soon enough.

"He must be lost indeed if he's come to Lower Warren," said Matilda who was in a good mood now she'd drunk a tankard of ale. "Did he give you a coin for your trouble?"

Lucinda was staring in a way that reminded Hannah of a rabbit she'd once seen caught in the gaze of a weasel. It wasn't until the children were asleep on the straw mattress next to theirs that they were able to talk about what had happened.

"When will we ever be free of that family," hissed Lucinda.

"I do not believe Adam Lennox is a threat to us," said Hannah. "He asked about the injury to your arm and whether you were fully recovered. And – oh Lucinda – he's had news of our menfolk. He said that John's skill as an artist was being of use to Wellington and that Charlie was well."

"So when are they coming home to us?"

"That he couldn't say."

"Exactly," said Lucinda. "He tells a good story just to keep us waiting until his cousin Giles arrives. We must get away from here."

"Where to?" asked Hannah – and with what? We have little money between us, and if we leave here, Charlie will not know where to find us."

"I have a plan," said Lucinda. "Tomorrow, while you are at the vicarage, I will walk into town and sell my mother's ring. It will give us enough money to live on until John and Charlie return."

"Lucinda, you must not do such a thing."

Hannah spoke louder than she intended and one of the children woke up crying. This resulted in Matilda Marshall banging on the wall with her stick and warning the culprit to shut up. By this time Lucinda and Hannah had subsided and were feigning sleep. Hannah could feel Lucinda's tears dampen the pillow and she ached for her.

Chapter 27

Adam Lennox received another unwanted visit from his cousin Giles. He'd returned from making house calls in the locality to find the house ransacked and Rose Dennett sitting hunched on a kitchen chair in a state of extreme distress.

The beef she'd been cooking for Adam's evening meal had been sliced into and discarded. There was a trail of grease across the stone flagged floor.

There were muddy footprints along the hall and up the stairs. Adam followed the trail of destruction. Cupboards and wardrobes had been opened and their contents thrown out.

"What happened?" Adam plied Rose with hot tea laced with brandy and wrapped a woollen shawl round her shoulders. He was glad when the colour returned to her cheeks and she was able to tell him what had happened.

"Mr Giles came with a friend of his. I can't say as I took to him. Ugly looking fellow. They must've been watching to see when I was on my own – my Matthew having gone to run some errands for you. They burst their way in here without so much as a 'by your leave' and they rampaged through the place worse than Napoleon's army. They wouldn't believe me when I said you'd not hidden Mr Giles' fiancée here." She stopped to gulp at her tea and draw breath before she continued. "It only came to a stop when my Matthew came back with our son Tom. They threw them out and threatened to fetch the magistrate. I'm sorry sir, I've felt that bad I've not managed to put anything to rights yet."

"All in good time," said Adam trying to keep his voice calm. "It is not your fault."

"Be careful, Mr Adam. You knows what Mr Giles is like - always had a temper right from when he was a babe. Always had to have his own way. He and Miss Georgiana used to near drive me to distraction."

Adam poured himself some tea and laced it with brandy. He sat down on another of the kitchen chairs.

His head ached and he felt weary. He'd heard rumours that Giles had joined forces with a strange character who had recently returned from the colonies. This man had won himself the dubious reputation of being known as 'Twister' and he was said to have hunted down and killed at least twenty wanted men on both sides of the ocean. Adam didn't like to think of what might have happened to Lucinda Beckford if Giles had found her in his house.

*

Adam thought he'd seen an end to the disturbing dreams he'd had since Amelia died, but they'd begun again the night after he'd seen Hannah at the vicarage.

He was wandering a dark moonless landscape on a wild stormy night searching for Amelia, knowing he'd never find her, but unable to move away from the place he was in.

He called her name but there was no answer. His boots were sinking into mud the consistency of treacle and he could feel it dragging him downwards. His nostrils were full of the stink of rotting vegetation and he could hear the sound of water as if it were pouring over a weir or mill-race.

A few steps more and he'd almost toppled into it. Then he heard a woman's cry for help. She was close to him, being tossed by the violent torrent of water, her violet eyes fixed on his. He lay down on the bank, feeling the chilling mud soaking into his clothes and reached out his hands, caught her icy ones in a firm grip, pulling her towards him.

Her face changed as he did so and he found himself looking into the eyes of Lucinda Beckford.

Adam was roused from the dream by an urgent knocking on his front door. He got out of bed and went to the window, throwing open the sash and leaning out to see who was below.

The vicar's servant stood there, twisting his cap in agitation. It was barely dawn and the shadow of the moon hung in the pearl grey sky.

"Can you please come, sir? Mrs Temple's baby is coming full early – and her screams are like nothing I've heard before on this earth. The vicar's in church praying and they've sent for young Mrs Marshall from along the lane."

Chapter 28

Giles had despaired of getting his hands on Lucinda Beckford until he'd heard rumours about the man called Twister during a poker game. He'd sat bland-faced listening to the conversation on the table behind his. During a suitable interval, he had made his enquiries and set up a meeting.

"He's a bad person to cross," his informant had told him. "Made his fortune in the colonies hunting down runaways. He lived with the Indians for a while and learned their tracking skills – so don't expect much conversation. Be sure to pay him or he'll kill you."

Giles did indeed find Twister a scary person to deal with. He had a sharp face, with flinty blue eyes that missed nothing. They met in an ale house that smelled of rancid fat and unwashed bodies and had sat on stools in a corner of the bar. The light was poor and the air stuffy from the smoking fire. Twister had listened silently while Giles outlined his problem.

"One hundred guineas. Half now. Half when I've found her." He took a long drink at his ale.

Giles almost choked. "That's preposterous! How do I know you won't disappear with my money and never come back?"

"Those is my terms. Take them or leave them. As I see it, you ain't got much choice."

"But fifty guineas!"

"I don't exactly trust you to deliver the rest of the money once you've got your hands on the lady. She must have something real sweet between her legs for you to go to this much trouble. I can see you're real eaten up with her." Twister finished the last of his ale, wiping his dirty hand across his mouth. "You know where to find me when you've made up your mind."

Giles hesitated.

Twister stood up, his eyes bright as a cat's in the gloomy interior of the ale house. "Look, I've got other people to see who'll pay up without quibbling. I don't like or trust you any more than you trust me, but if you want me to find her for you then bring the fifty guineas to me here by midday tomorrow. If you're not here by then I'm leaving this town."

"Very well." Giles knew when he was beaten. "Fifty guineas by midday tomorrow." He held out his hand. Twister hesitated before shaking it.

Giles waited a full five minutes before leaving the ale house, his thoughts a mixture of anticipation that he would soon get his hands on Lucinda Beckford – less than a week was Twister's estimate – and frustration that he hadn't been able to find her himself.

Chapter 29

When Adam reached the vicarage a fire had been lit in Florence Temple's bedroom. That lady was in bed, clearly in a state of distress. The housekeeper showed him in, obviously relishing her position of authority.

"Please to come upstairs, sir," she said, taking his hat and topcoat. "The vicar's gone to church to pray – and well he might. The mistress asked for young Mrs Marshall to be fetched. Struck up quite an affection for each other they have, although personally I'd have nothing to do with anyone from that cottage. In my opinion, me havin' had ten young uns, we'll still be waiting this time tomorrow and you shouldn't of been troubled."

A look from Adam silenced her.

"I'd like hot water if you please," he said. "Lots of it. And clean sheets if you have them."

"The sheets in this house are always clean," said the housekeeper huffily, still hovering on the landing. "Let me show you to the mistress's room."

"I believe I can find that well enough," said Adam. "The hot water and sheets if you please, Mrs Hoskins."

The housekeeper headed downstairs clearly upset at being left out of the action.

Adam followed the sound of voices into Florence Temple's room. Florence herself was crouched on the bed, clearly in the throes of strong labour. Hannah, looking ragged from being summoned from sleep, was rubbing her back and talking in low tones.

As he entered the room, Florence was seized by another contraction and some ungodly language filled the room, betraying her thinly disguised northern roots. The room was stiflingly hot. A fire had been lit in the grate, filling the room with the scent of apple-wood and smoke. The curtains were half-drawn and candles lit.

Adam opened the curtains and blew out the candles. He noticed the mirrors had also been covered.

"Mrs Hoskins says if the mirrors are uncovered then the fairy-folk could come and take the baby and leave a changeling in its place," said Hannah. "That's why she's lit a fire – so as they can't come down the chimney."

She and Adam exchanged conspiratorial looks over Florence's hunched body.

"I think those are the last things we need worry about for now," said Adam.

He took Florence's pulse and noted the time between the contractions which seemed remarkably short given that she'd said the pains had only begun a couple of hours before.

"Mrs Hoskins said not to bother you because first babies always took more than twelve hours. I cannot stand this pain for nine more hours…" Her words ended in a banshee-like wail.

"With your permission, I must examine you," said Adam. He and Hannah eased Florence onto her back, causing her to draw her knees up in pain. Hannah sat holding onto her hand and soothing her as if she were talking to a child. Florence's face was flushed scarlet and slick with sweat. Hannah wiped her face with a damp cloth and gave her sips of water.

"You're a good nurse," said Adam.

"My mother suffered so when she had her babies," said Hannah, "but Mrs Temple is doing so much better than she ever did."

"She is indeed," said Adam as Florence gathered herself on all fours again on the middle of the bed and howled as another contraction took over her body. "This baby will be here before we know it. I feel my services are surplus to requirements."

"Don't leave me," said Florence, shooting him an agonised glance.

Mrs Hoskins came puffing up the stairs with a large can full of hot water. "Beats me as to why you wants all this water," she grumbled. "As if a body hasn't enough to do." She looked at Florence's undignified position. "If

I may say doctor, I don't think you're going about things the right way."

Adam ignored her. He was sorting through his medical bag and had tipped some of the hot water into the basin on the washstand and was rinsing some of his instruments in it and drying them on a soft cloth.

"I'd have not rushed with the water if that's all you were going to do with it. Waste of good water and me having to make a special trip to the well…,"

Adam took no notice of her grumbling and Mrs Hoskins stomped off downstairs.

"It probably doesn't make much difference," he said, "but a Moorish doctor I met in Spain had an interesting theory about washing instruments. I tried it and was successful with the patients I treated."

Florence was screaming by now with Hannah trying to calm her.

"The child is almost here," said Adam.

Hannah's hand was squeezed so hard she felt it would break. There was a yell from Florence that the vicar must surely have heard inside the church – and then silence that was broken by the thin high-pitched wail of a newborn baby.

"A fine boy," said Adam, a feeling of relief surging inside him.

Mrs Hoskins, despite her words about having lots to do, puffed back up the stairs eager to know what was happening. She and Hannah bathed the baby and attended to Florence. "Only peasant women have babies with such speed," muttered Mrs Hoskins. "It's not decent."

"Babies take their own time," said Adam as he packed away the instruments that he'd not needed.

"Fat lot of good all that washing did," Mrs Hoskins said as she tidied the room.

"My husband…," said Florence who was now suckling the baby.

"I'll go and find him," said Hannah.

It was still early in the day with white mist rising from the fields around the church. Most of the leaves had fallen from the trees and they rose stark and ghostly from the whiteness. Hannah went out of the back door, along the driveway from the house and along the pathway that led to the church. She went through the lych gate and down between the avenue of yews that dripped onto the flagstones. Behind the yews, rows of gravestones stood sentinel. Hannah shivered at the eerie atmosphere, glad when she reached the shelter of the church porch.

She turned the iron ring on the door and it creaked open. The inside of the church felt chilly and smelled of musty hymn books and incense.

The vicar was kneeling by the high altar, his eyes closed in prayer. Hannah walked towards him, feeling awkward. Her footsteps echoed in the silent church.

The vicar crossed himself and stood up. He looked at Hannah, his face pale.

"You have news?"

"A fine boy, sir, and your wife is asking for you."

"She has survived?"

Hannah nodded. "She appears well, sir."

"Praise be to God." The vicar knelt down again. "I will be with her as soon as I have given thanks for her safe delivery."

Hannah left the church as quietly as she could and made her way back towards the vicarage. She shivered as she walked along the avenue of yew trees and had an uncomfortable feeling that someone was watching her. The mist was thicker now and made ghostly shapes around the gravestones.

She stood still, detecting a movement near a grave that had the statue of an angel on it. A man in untidy dark clothes was watching her. His intense gaze burned a hole through the mist. As soon as he realised he'd been noticed, he was gone leaving no trace. Hannah hurried out of the churchyard, not sure if she'd seen a living person or a ghost.

*

Matilda Marshall was disgruntled to find that she had been left to fetch the water that day. She usually avoided the gathering of women at the village pump.

However, today was a little more interesting than usual. A man was offering money for answers to questions about a runaway bride.

"I don't want no time-wasters, mind," he was saying. "If you're thinking of pulling tricks like that then I'll slit you from your gizzard to your clack and not think twice about it."

The other women melted away when they heard this invective, but Matilda Marshall was made of sterner stuff. She had, after all, gained the respect of many in the village for the way she'd handled her errant husband. He'd been well-known for taking his fists to her after a drinking session but she'd turned the tables on him and thrown him out of the cottage.

"I might know something," she said to Twister.

He turned to her, weighing her up with eyes as cold as the moon. Matilda shivered under the force of his gaze.

"What do you know?"

"I've got two women staying with me. One says she's my daughter-in-law – it's the other one I think you're looking for."

He stared at her with his strange quick-silver eyes.

"She's got blue eyes and dark hair, the one you're looking for."

Twister handed over a small number of coins.

"Oi, that's not what you said to the other women!"

"Half now and half when you deliver. That's the deal."

"How do I know you'll be honest once you've got what you want?"

"You'll just have to trust me, won't you?" Twister gave a grim smile showing teeth like yellow tombstones. He gave his instructions for the day in question. "Make sure you tell nobody – because if you do…" He made a movement with his hands that mimed a chicken's neck being wrung.

Matilda tucked the coins into her bodice and headed home, her legs feeling weak.

Chapter 30

A week of torrential rain followed the making of the arrangement with Twister. Dim memories surfaced in Matilda Marshall's mind of tales of Divine intervention and eternal damnation for doing wrong to others.

She pushed the memories to the back of her mind, but they intruded into her dreams. Work on the land was impossible, food was short and the children drooped listlessly around the overcrowded cottage. The water level grew dangerously high and, as the chosen day approached, Matilda became anxious that Twister would be unable to reach them. Anxiety made her short-tempered and unpredictable.

*

Lucinda, prevented by the rain from going to Bridgeton to sell her ring, didn't know whether to feel glad or sorry that she had her precious possession with her for a little longer.

On the first day that there was a pause in the endless torrent of rain, Lucinda set out early for Bridgeton before she had a chance to change her mind. White mist rose from the river meadows as she entered the town and her footsteps echoed eerily.

She passed over the bridge, noticing the sound of the rushing water and how it was the colour of strong tea, boiling and churning through the arches of the bridge. The river level lapped over the banks and a woman Lucinda met shook her head and said it could rise much higher yet. Lucinda remembered Matilda's story about being unable to get home and she hoped this wouldn't be the case today.

"Three days it was before it went down. I had to stay in the town until it did. You wouldn't even know there was a bridge…,"

The river reminded Lucinda of a voracious animal poised to devour anything in its path. She'd never liked water and remembered how she'd hung back from joining John when he got too close to the river on some of their evening adventures. He always wanted to go low down onto the bank in order to draw the reflection of the moon and trees and Lucinda had been frightened that he would fall in and be swept away. The swirling water reminded her of the nightmares she'd had lately about falling into the water and being pulled out by someone she couldn't see because of the mist that surrounded them. Then the mist cleared and she could see it was Adam Lennox… except that when she reached towards him he changed to his cousin Giles.

Lucinda shivered and hurried over the bridge. The trees that overshadowed the road that led into town dripped steadily and she was feeling damp and chilled by the time she passed the tollhouse. She made her way up the main street, past the big houses where maids had scrubbed the front steps to whiteness earlier that day. She hesitated, aware that she was probably being viewed with suspicion from behind the twitching curtains.

She noticed shady figures disappearing down alleyways that led to and from the main street. One of them turned and stared at her with piercing grey eyes and Lucinda remembered the man Hannah said she'd seen in the graveyard.

It began to drizzle and Lucinda hurried towards the apothecary's shop and pushed open the door.

She was immediately engulfed in the warmth of a crackling fire and the smell of pungent spices.

"My dear lady," said the apothecary. "I trust this does not mean that your friend is worse?"

"No, thank you. She is well. I have come about another matter."

"You appear distressed, mistress. Come and sit by the fire. My sister will bring you some tea."

As Lucinda sat in a chair by the fire a black cat emerged from the shadows and eyed her curiously through half-closed amber-coloured eyes. Steam rose from her boots and outdoor clothes as they dried in the heat from the fire. Lucinda sipped the tea she was given and sat gazing at the pictures in the flames as if she'd find a solution to her problems there."

The apothecary pulled up a wooden chair opposite Lucinda's. "What is it that troubles you, mistress?"

"I am in great need of money and must sadly sell something very precious to me," said Lucinda. "I need your help as to the best course of action to take."

"I will do my best to help you."

"I must needs sell something of great value to me in order that my friend and I can move to a place of greater safety," said Lucinda. "She is near her time now and I fear that if we don't go now, before the worst of the winter, she and her child may die."

"What is it you wish to sell and I will do my best to advise you."

Lucinda drew the ring on its chain from her bodice. The gems flashed in the light of the fire.

The apothecary gazed at it. "It is indeed a fine ring. You must be careful who you approach because some in this town may not treat you fairly."

"Do you know of a jeweller who will not cheat me?"

"All men have their price where honesty is concerned," said the apothecary, "but Amos Jennings in Bridge Street has a better reputation than most."

The rain had stopped and the mist returned to that end of town as Lucinda made her way through the quiet streets feeling as if she were part of a dream world. The mist swirled around her and she thought she could see faces in the whiteness.

She chided herself. Her agitation was making her lose common sense. She almost missed Amos Jennings' shop. It was tiny and had a door that was even lower than the apothecary's shop. She stepped inside and the small room smelled of leather and stale tobacco. The only light was from a candle that rested on the counter where an old man with a face that looked as if it was carved from wood was polishing a silver locket.

Lucinda picked her way through the narrow space between wood and glass cabinets that held what looked like a king's ransom of jewels. Rubies, diamonds and emeralds flashed from black silk cushions creating fiery rainbows as she stared at them.

"What d'you want? State your business," said a harsh voice.

Lucinda paused, startled. The jeweller had not spoken, being intent on his task. It was a moment or two before she saw the bird in the cage in the dark space behind the counter. It was glaring at her over the jeweller's shoulder with malevolent dark eyes.

The jeweller looked up as if he had only just become aware of her presence, although she was certain he'd missed nothing.

"Jericho has deterred many a would-be thief," he said. "Not that I'm implying for one moment that you are anything but honest, mistress." His glance swept her from top to toe as if assessing her wealth and what she might want from him. His voice was so similar to that of the bird that Lucinda couldn't help smiling despite her nervous feelings.

"What manner of bird is he, sir?" she asked.

"He's a mynah bird – I believe from somewhere in Africa. I had him from a sailor in lieu of a debt and he has proved to be better than any guard dog. Now what can I do for you, mistress?"

Lucinda unclasped the chain round her neck and took her mother's ring from it. She held the ring for several minutes, remembering the day of her mother's funeral when her father had called her into his study and handed it to her. Since that day, she had not been parted from it.

The jeweller cleared his throat and Lucinda reluctantly handed the ring to him.

He gave a gasp of surprise when he took it from her and held it to the light by the window. "How did you come by this?" he asked, his voice husky.

"It was my mother's ring, sir. She has recently died, leaving me with younger brothers and sisters to clothe and feed."

"Indeed." The jeweller looked at her. "And your name, mistress?"

"My name is Mary Taylor, sir."

"Taylor…," the jeweller sat looking at her through half closed eyes for so long that Lucinda wondered if he was still awake. The mynah bird also watched her with its elderberry bright eyes so that she began to feel hot and uncomfortable and as if he didn't believe her.

"Know you the history of this ring?"

Lucinda shook her head. "No, sir," she said, crossing her fingers behind her back to acknowledge the lie.

The jeweller picked up the ring again and examined it. He laid it on a black velvet cushion and stared at it as if seeing a long-lost friend.

"Diamonds and rubies," said the mynah bird, sidling up and down its perch. "Thieves and murderers," it said, peering down at Lucinda.

"You will excuse me one moment, mistress, while I confer with my son in order that I may give you a fair price." The jeweller stood, gave her a curt bow and headed through a dark red curtain to a room beyond.

Lucinda lost no time in snatching up the ring, pushing it into her reticule and hurrying out of the shop. Something in the way the jeweller looked at her made her feel alarmed – as if he was about to summon a magistrate and accuse her of theft.

She drew her cloak over her head and hurried down the street, careful not to slip on the rain-slicked cobbles. She was afraid that at any moment she would feel a hand on her shoulder and be dragged back to the jeweller's shop. She tried to blend in with the tide of people heading down the street towards *The Three Tuns* where the Mail Coach had just arrived and would be setting off soon for London.

She could hear the jeweller shouting from his doorway "Stop that young woman."

Lucinda focused on the cobbled street ahead of her and edged towards the safety of the inn yard. She'd almost gained the security of a doorway when her path was blocked by a tall figure.

"Well, what have we here?" said a voice she recognised.

Lucinda tried to move in a different direction but Farmer Braithwaite blocked her path. She could tell from the smell of his breath that he'd had his fair share of ale and was on the verge of becoming belligerent.

"Out on your own are you, Miss Taylor?" His eyes were bloodshot and he stood closer to her than was decent. "I expect you wish you'd taken up employment with me? I'd see you were a lot more comfortable than you are with Matilda Marshall – and I'll warrant you're a more luscious armful than she is." He flashed her a lascivious smile and Lucinda remembered the night a few weeks before when she'd heard a strange sound during the night and had gone to the window to see what was happening.

She'd been surprised to see Matilda Marshall locked in an embrace with a man in the passageway that went past the back of the cottages. She'd been unable to see who it was, but as the memory re-formed itself, Lucinda was sure it was Farmer Braithwaite.

She tried to get away from the farmer, but he caught her in a firm embrace. "I'll warrant that Old Matilda won't let the likes of you downstairs when I'm about because she fears for loss of income."

He stroked Lucinda's cheek and touched his lips to hers.

Lucinda twisted away from him and a group of men began catcalling in appreciation.

With a sick feeling inside, Lucinda understood how it was that Matilda Marshall could afford jugs of ale despite doing so little work – and why Farmer Braithwaite thought she would provide the same service.

"You'll not get away from me so easily next time," said the farmer. "If you don't make up your mind to be nice to me, then I'll make sure that Matilda and her brats are evicted from that cottage. Winter's coming. So is your friend's baby. Think about it…You be nice to me and I'll look after all of you. Maybe you could give me a bit on account…,"

"Never," she spat, wrenching herself free from his grasp.

"You're going nowhere Ned Braithwaite, with or without your doxy, until you settle your bill," said a loud voice. The man Lucinda recognised previously as the landlord was striding towards them from the inn yard.

*

In the confusion and raised voices that followed, Lucinda hurried away down Bridge Street and past the toll-house. The river level had risen and brown water was lapping the edges of the road. The rain was heavier and her clothes were soaked already and sticking to her skin. A pony and trap pulled up next to her. A market woman's offer of a ride part of the way back to Lower Warren was like an answer to Lucinda's prayers.

"There's no telling whether you'll get as far as Lower Warren the way the water's travelling," said the woman gloomily, clicking her tongue to the slow piebald horse.

*

The market woman dropped Lucinda at the crossroads that led to Lower Warren.

After she'd gone Lucinda had slipped her mother's ring back onto the chain round her neck, feeling glad to have it resting back in her bodice like a good luck talisman.

The trees were dancing wildly to the wind's tune again and the sky was black as ink. Torrents of water poured across the lane and every low point was filled with brown water.

She shuddered at the memory of Farmer Braithwaite's touch and the things he'd said to her.

As she walked past the vicarage, she was aware of a commotion by the front gate. The vicar, looking dishevelled, was sending the stable boy off on his horse with a letter.

"Be sure you give it to Doctor Lennox himself," he said, "and take the long way round. The lower road is sure to be flooded by now. I pray Heaven that you'll be back in time to save Nathaniel's life."

He hurried back inside the vicarage without noticing Lucinda.

Chapter 31

On her way back to Matilda's cottage from fetching water from the well earlier that day, Hannah had met Sal Bishop, one of the nosier village women who had been quick to regale her with tales of the man who had arrived in the village a few days ago.

"Didn't take to 'im," said Sal, wiping her nose on her shawl. "He'd got strange eyes."

Hannah was reminded of the arrival of Giles Milburn in Marchington and how frightened Tilly had been when she'd encountered him on Longdon Hill. She felt anxious for Lucinda, who had not yet returned home.

"Offering us money, he was," Sal went on, "wanted information about a lady who'd run away from a posh gent she was s'posed to marry. Wanted to talk to each of us individual like. I didn't like the sound of that. He looked like he'd slit yer throat for a farthing."

"What did he look like?"

"Ugly – sort of twisted looking and with eyes cold as the moon."

Hannah knew it was the man she'd seen in the graveyard.

"Where did he go?"

Sal shrugged. "Dunno. Last I saw your ma-in-law was talking to 'im. Lookin' mighty smug she was when she turned away. Mind you – I wouldn't want to be in her shoes if she crossed him!"

Hannah headed back to Matilda Marshall's cottage, relieved to find her sitting in her chair by the smouldering fire as usual.

"About time you was back. Where's Mary? Isn't she with you?"

"I don't know where she's gone," said Hannah. "She didn't say."

"It's not right, the pair of you taking off where and when you please without a by your leave."

"We pay you our rent on time," said Hannah, thinking it odd that Matilda should be so anxious for their presence when she usually didn't care if they were there or not.

Matilda fidgeted like a cat on hot bricks and grumbled at the younger children who were playing five-stones on the dirty floor.

*

The light was fading when Lucinda arrived home. She was soaking wet and looked exhausted.

"Where have you been?" asked Hannah, when they were both safely upstairs. "I've been worried that the man I saw by the graveyard had got you."

"I tried to sell my ring," said Lucinda, "but then I got scared in case the jeweller might think I'd stolen it. He came to the door and shouted '*stop that young woman*.'"

"Did they catch you? What happened?"

"I was stopped by Farmer Braithwaite...."

"What are you two whispering about up there?" demanded Matilda Marshall from the bottom of the stairs.

"Farmer Braithwaite and your mother-in-law…," began Lucinda.

"What of them? You're not making any sense Lucinda."

"That's how she gets her money – and manages to spend all day drinking ale. Hannah – we can't stay here any longer. He thinks – Farmer Braithwaite thinks we're the same as her. He's threatening to evict Matilda and the children if I don't go and work for him."

"You might be safer there than in the clutches of the man who's been seen in the village," said Hannah.

"What are you talking about?" asked Lucinda.

"He was offering money for information about you, Lucinda – and Sal Bishop saw Matilda talking to him and pocketing some coins.

"Giles!" said Lucinda. "He's behind it."

"From the way Matilda's acting, something's afoot. I've not known her be so concerned about our whereabouts before."

"We need to go now," said Lucinda, cramming her belongings into a bundle. "Before the flood waters rise and we get trapped here."

Hannah nodded, gathering her things together.

"Stop that whispering and come down," shouted Matilda.

The two women hesitated at the top of the stairs, clutching their bundles. Escape seemed impossible.

Then there was the sound of rushing feet from the direction of the scullery. "Ma, there's water pouring through the ceiling out there," shouted one of the children.

"With any luck it'll drown the lot of you," grumbled Matilda.

Lucinda and Hannah heard her get to her feet and head towards the scullery. The gaggle of children followed her.

Lucinda and Hannah hurried down the stairs, out of the cottage door, down the path and into the darkness beyond.

Chapter 32

The storm was raging as they made their way along the lane towards the vicarage. Thunder crashed and lightning flashed across the ink-dark sky in jagged forks. The air crackled with tension.

They hurried along the lane with their bundles but hadn't gone very far when Hannah stopped, doubling over in agony.

"Hannah, what is it?"

"It's the baby. I've been having pains all afternoon but I thought it was the gruel Matilda gave us.

The water from the brook was pouring in a torrent down the sides of the lane, making it even narrower than usual. There was still at least half a mile to walk until they reached the vicarage and every minute they delayed put Lucinda in more danger.

Below the noise of the storm, they heard the sound of carriage wheels. Lucinda looked around frantically for somewhere to hide.

"Quick, Hannah." She dragged her round behind a large oak tree and into a field sown with turnips. Giles Milburn passed them, sitting on the box of a black carriage pulled by two bay horses. If Lucinda had reached out a hand, she could have touched him.

Hannah bit down on her fist, clearly in pain now. She leaned heavily on Lucinda and they tottered the rest of the way to the vicarage. But when they reached the vicarage, it was to see the place in darkness and a wreath on the door. Lucinda remembered the scene she'd witnessed with the dishevelled vicar despatching the stable boy for Doctor Lennox.

"Poor Florence," said Hannah. "I should go to her."

"Hannah, you're in no fit state!"

Trying not to show how worried she was, Lucinda edged Hannah along the driveway that led to the back of the vicarage in the hope there would be an outbuilding or stables that would provide refuge. She knew she wouldn't be totally safe here. Giles, on discovering that she was missing from the cottage would know they hadn't gone very far. Finding them would be an easy matter, especially with Hannah in her present condition. Hannah was a dead weight now against Lucinda's arm – her face slicked with perspiration despite the coolness of the rain, and her eyes were half closed.

It was pitch dark now the storm had abated, although rain still fell in a torrent like water being poured from a bucket. Lucinda sensed rather than saw a movement in the shadows.

*

Adam had come immediately to see young Nathaniel but it was already too late. When the vicar's stable boy found him, he was trying to help some of his patients move their belongings to higher ground away from the flood water that threatened to sweep away homes and livestock. He was using the flat cart owned by Rose Dennett's husband Matthew and he'd headed straight for the vicarage to find the child lying still as a marble effigy surrounded by the rising tide of his mother's sorrow.

There had been little he could do other than to offer his sincere condolences.

When Adam had let himself out of the kitchen door, the last people he'd expected to see were Lucinda Beckford and her friend out in such weather and in such a state.

"Miss Beckford, I see you and Mrs Marshall need my help," he said.

He noticed that Lucinda Beckford opened her mouth to protest, as he had expected she would.

"I don't see you have any option other than to accept my help, Miss Beckford, "unless you wish Mrs Marshall to give birth to her child in a ditch."

*

Everything had gone quiet upstairs when Matilda came back into the living room having blocked the leak with rags and an old tin cup. She called to Lucinda and

Hannah: "When you've got yourselves dry, come down and I'll make some tea."

The words sounded false even to her ears.

The storm rattled and crashed overhead. There was no response from upstairs.

Matilda hurried to the scullery door, hoping that Twister or whatever his name was would keep his word and bring her the rest of the money. Once she had that, she'd be able to take a break from Farmer Braithwaite on Saturday nights. A holiday. Matilda smiled grimly at the thought.

The narrow lane between them and the back of the next row of cottages was empty apart from the continuous curtain of rain.

She came back indoors, shivering with cold and excitement. She swung the heavy black kettle onto the fire and added a screw of tea to the big brown pot.

She sent one of the boys, busy playing marbles in a corner of the room, to fetch Lucinda and Hannah.

"They ain't there, Ma," he said.

"Whatcha mean, not there?" Matilda gathered her skirts and hurried upstairs.

The straw mattress Lucinda and Hannah had shared was stripped of their belongings, and not so much as a shred of lace gave any clue that they had ever been there at all.

Matilda squawked with alarm and hurried back down the stairs. She was about to head towards the door again when Twister appeared before her looking like a vengeful goblin from a children's story.

"Lost something, have you?" His cold-as-the-moon eyes stared into hers. He was carrying a rope and a gag.

She shook her head, hoping he couldn't see her knees trembling.

"Where are they?" His voice sliced through the air like a knife.

"Gone to the ...doings. Where's the money you promised me?"

"Both together?" Twister laughed. It wasn't a pleasant sound. "I think you've been having a game – and I've told you what happens to people who play false with me – I slits them from their gizzard to their clack."

Matilda caught a look at the children sitting in a frozen huddle in the corner.

"Let's not be hasty," she said, "we'll have a cup of tea, shall we? They'll be back by then." She went to lift the heavy kettle from the fire.

"Tea be damned," said Twister, moving towards her, a thin silver blade in his hand.

Matilda gave a squawk of alarm as Twister lunged for her. He lost his footing on the marbles abandoned by the children and the knife flashed through the air and clattered on the flagstones. One of the boys picked it up.

Matilda snatched up the kettle of boiling water and flung it at Twister's face. He yelled in agony, tearing at his skin as he ran towards the scullery and out of the door.

Matilda and the children followed in time to see him run into the path of a sinister looking black coach and horses approaching at speed along the narrow entry.

An unearthly scream became part of the lightning and the storm as one of the horses reared up and kicked Twister in the head, spilling his brains onto the flooded road.

With a feeling of relief, Matilda watched as the black coach carried on past, leaving Twister's body on the ground. She checked his pockets for money, being well satisfied to find more than she expected. She waited until nightfall and then she went out and dragged Twister's lifeless body to the flooded brook and pushed it in.

Chapter 33

Giles cursed himself for a fool for panicking – but he hadn't expected Twister to run out of the cottage like that. Something had obviously gone very wrong with their plans – and now it was possible that he could be charged with murder.

Fear of the magistrate being called had made him keep the horses going until he reached a place further along the lane where a raging torrent that was once the river was swallowing land like a wild animal. It swirled around the carriage wheels and made the horses agitated.

He stopped. The wind and rain had chilled him, calmed his fevered imagination, and made him see things differently. He considered the possibilities. It was unlikely that anyone in Lower Warren would want a magistrate within fifty miles of them. They were all likely to be thieves and poachers. He laughed at his own stupidity and panic. Who was a magistrate likely to believe – a gentleman like him – or one of the villagers?

He needed to go back to the cottage and find out for himself what had happened. For all he knew, the occupants could have pocketed the money – his money - with Lucinda Beckford congratulating herself for eluding him once more.

Giles swung the carriage around, sending up a fountain of muddy water that soaked him from head to foot, and headed back the way he'd come. It was dark now and the only creature he saw was a man, or maybe a woman, huddled under an old sack, scuttling along the lane like a hedgehog.

When he reached the cottage, approaching from the other side this time to avoid the dead body of Twister, he got down from the carriage and looped the reins over the gate post. More muddy water sloshed over his highly polished boots and spattered his buff coloured breeches. He let himself into the cottage, almost gagging at the foul smell of what looked like gristly stew bubbling over the smoky fire.

"Ma ain't here. Be you a magistrate?" asked a boy with spiky fair hair and blue eyes who was staring up at him.

Giles tensed with fear. His anxiety about lawless mobs resurfaced. What if the whole village was prepared to testify against him?

"I'm here to collect my fiancée," he said, crouching down in what was meant to be a friendly manner and offering the boy a coin. "Will you tell me where I find her?"

The boy took the coin and pocketed it. "Dunno," he said, rubbing a grubby sleeve across his snotty nose. "If she be one of the ladies what used to be here, I dunno where she be now."

Giles let out an expletive and stamped his foot so hard it woke the cat dozing by the fire. "What do you mean? Used to be here? Explain!"

"Be you a magistrate?" asked the boy again, tracing a pattern on the filthy floor with a scabby bare foot.

There was no sense to be had from these people. Giles raced upstairs but it was obvious that nothing but fleas and lice lived in the two upstairs rooms that boasted only straw mattresses on the floors. The scullery was empty, as was the foul-smelling necessary house.

Giles stormed back to the carriage and headed off into the darkness, anxious to escape the swiftly rising flood water.

Chapter 34

Lucinda watched as Adam Lennox maintained a course between caution and speed. She was torn between wanting to be with Hannah, who now appeared to have gone into a world of her own, punctuated with animal-like howls of pain, and wishing she could run until she ran out of breath in order to be away from all danger of Giles Milburn. She was certain that Adam was in league with his cousin and would hand her over to him before much more time had passed.

*

"Some of the roads are in danger of being washed away," Adam said. "God willing, we'll reach my house safely.

The rain was easing by the time they reached the crossroads where the market woman had dropped Lucinda earlier. Lucinda was shocked to see how much higher the water level was – over half way up the cart-wheels now. The wind was still raging and the water filling the fields rippled like an inland sea. They turned right this time, away from Bridgeton, and before long reached a square white-washed house. It stirred a memory for Lucinda but she couldn't think what it was.

Adam guided the horse and cart round the back of the house to the stables. A tall man, his head and shoulders covered by a sack, hurried out of the house to take care of the horse.

"Many thanks, Matthew," said Adam. "Where is Rose? I may need her help."

"She's gone to Old Agatha Dixon at Trench Cottage," said the man. "The old lady was vexed on account of the rain and the storm. She'd gone looking for her lost boy again, convinced that this time the floods would bring him back to her. My Rose was afeared she'd drown herself."

Adam lifted Hannah into his arms and carried her into the house. Candles had been lit and the house smelled of fresh bread and beeswax polish. Lucinda followed

Adam's damp trail of footprints up the wooden staircase and into a bedroom.

Adam went downstairs and came back with more candles, a voluminous nightgown that evidently belonged to the housekeeper, and a change of clothes for Lucinda.

He brought towels and hot water.

Lucinda helped Hannah to change into the nightgown, piling their wet things on the floor ready to take downstairs. She was glad of dry clothes and relished the smell of clean cotton and lavender.

Hannah paced about restlessly between the pains, gripping onto the bedpost until her knuckles whitened when one overtook her. Her face glistened with sweat and her hair, loosened from its pins, hung lank around her shoulders.

Lucinda was relieved to see Rose Dennett – a dark haired, motherly looking woman who came straight to Hannah and took her hands and promised to bring her some honey cordial "to give you strength."

She took Lucinda downstairs and sat her by the kitchen fire where a tabby cat sat purring and looking into the flames. She wrapped her in a woollen shawl and gave her a cup of pale liquid flavoured with ginger and honey.

*

Adam came to the top of the stairs and called to Rose. She went to him.

Lucinda sat watching the shadows dance and the pictures in the fire. There was one that looked like a mother and child but as she watched it disappeared and Lucinda shivered thinking of baby Nathaniel who had lived for such a short time.

Rose hurried down the stairs. "Where did I put that goose fat?" she said.

"What can you want that for?" asked Lucinda.

"Best not to ask," said Matthew, coming in from the stables.

Lucinda listed to the footsteps and muffled cries upstairs. Then there was a silence, as if the house was holding its breath, followed by the thin high wail of a new-born child.

"Thank God," whispered Lucinda as she hurried upstairs.

Hannah was lying with her eyes closed, her face nearly as white as the pillows. The air was warm and stuffy and there was a metallic smell. Lucinda touched Hannah's hand and she opened her eyes.

Rose Dennett was bathing the tiny girl in a basin of warm water and Adam Lennox, looking grey with exhaustion, was tidying away his instruments. The baby thrashed her arms and legs and yelled, her whole body red with indignation. Rose cooed to her as she dried her on a soft towel and wrapped her in a shawl and carried her over to Hannah. Hannah tried to reach out her arms to take the baby, but she was too weak.

Rose tucked her into the bed. "Charlotte, I'll call her Charlotte," said Hannah, her eyes closing again.

"She should try to feed the child," said Adam. The words 'or it will not survive' hung on the stuffy air.

Rose helped to prop Hannah onto the pillows so that the baby could feed. It was at that point that Lucinda noticed some of the paraphernalia of the birth – blood-stained towels and newspaper and a bowl of carmined water. The room seemed to tilt and sway. She got unsteadily to her feet and headed towards the stairs, thinking that some fresh air would help her. She got as far as the hallway when black specks floated in front of her tired eyes and she crumpled in a heap.

She was aware of footsteps hurrying down the stairs, someone calling her name, and then being lifted by arms she recognised and a heartbeat that felt as familiar as her own.

*

When she awoke, she was lying in a camp bed of the type that she'd heard soldiers used, that had been squeezed into Hannah's room. In between the beds was a chair and Rose Dennett was dozing in it, wrapped in another eiderdown.

She woke as soon as Lucinda stirred.

"You gave us a fright there, Miss Lucinda," she said. "Still, they say shock does funny things to people."

"Hannah…,"

"She is well," said Rose, "and has fed baby Charlotte." She indicated the baby who was asleep in a drawer padded with a blanket that was doing service as a cot. "I'll go and rouse Doctor Lennox now. He was most concerned about you. The flood waters are still rising and I must see that Agatha Dixon hasn't woken and gone wandering again."

*

Adam Lennox sat watching the sky lighten from indigo to ice blue, feeling relieved that Hannah Marshall's child had arrived safely. There had been one point during the long night that he'd felt certain that both mother and daughter would die. The first few days after the birth were the most hazardous for mother and child, and only time would tell if they would survive.

He looked at Lucinda Beckford, sleeping now with her cheek pillowed on her hand. She looked better than a few hours earlier when she'd fainted at the bottom of the stairs. He'd been alarmed at the greyish pallor of her skin and was aware that Rose Dennett, following closely behind him, had looked at him curiously when he called her name. "Lucinda!"

Chapter 35

The week following Charlotte's birth was one of more settled weather, although Court Green was almost surrounded by water like a castle. Adam fretted about not being able to reach his patients and Rose fretted about not being able to get her washing dry.

Lucinda was thankful for the flood water because it meant that Giles was unlikely to be able to reach her. However, she felt unsettled by being so close to Adam. Apart from the night of Charlotte's birth when she'd fainted, he'd not touched her, so why did her heart race when she was close to him and she perversely wished he would take her pulse or check her temperature?

During the long evenings they'd either sat upstairs with Hannah and baby Charlotte or downstairs in the dining room with Rose as a chaperone. They'd talked about books they'd read and places they'd visited. They'd laughed easily together and Lucinda caught herself feeling sad at the thought of leaving Court Green.

"You're being ridiculous," she chided herself. "You and Hannah cannot stay here forever. If it wasn't for the birth of baby Charlotte, you wouldn't be here at all."

*

"Now that the flood waters are going down," she told Adam over breakfast a week later, "I must try to make contact with my Great Aunt. I am hopeful that she may permit us to stay with her. I did write to her before but am wondering if the letter reached her."

"I was hoping you'd reconsider…," Adam began. He flushed and cleared his throat and seemed to have trouble getting his breath.

Then Rose returned with tea and buttered toast and the moment was lost. Adam departed soon afterwards to see the patients he could reach and Lucinda was left wondering what he wanted to say.

*

"I'm enjoying having the company of another woman," Rose told Lucinda later as they prepared the dinner together. Adam had gone out to visit some of his patients. "Although if Doctor Adam marries Miss Dorothea Kenning, I fear she won't be as much help as you in the kitchen." Rose beat the pudding mixture with a wooden spoon to give emphasis to the words.

"Who is she?" Lucinda was surprised at the shaft of jealousy she felt.

"She's a patient of his from Overbury and has fair set her cap at him. She has a reputation for getting what she wants."

"Is she pretty?"

A loud thumping at the front door interrupted Rose's answer to the question.

"Now who's that trying to wake baby Charlotte?" grumbled Rose, wiping her hands on a damp rag as she clumped along the hall to answer the door.

Lucinda shrank in fear when she heard Giles' voice.

"I insist that you let me in, Rose."

"You know I cannot do that, Mr Giles."

Lucinda's skin erupted into goose-pimples and she huddled as close as she could get to the chimney corner, well away from the windows.

Lucinda was sure she'd been right not to trust Adam Lennox. She was certain he hadn't gone visiting patients this morning – he'd gone to meet his cousin Giles and inform him of her whereabouts.

Any minute now, Rose would let Giles into the house and Lucinda would have no hope of getting away from him. Every muscle in her body felt tense as she listened to the heated exchange on the doorstep.

"Stand aside woman, and let me in."

"I will not, sir. You know what happened last time when I did so. It took a week to get the house back to its rightful state."

There was the sound of the door being bolted and barred.

Rose Dennett returned to the kitchen dusting her hands on her apron. Her face was flushed and her hands shook. "I swear he's no better now than when he was a child –

and why he thinks his fiancée may be here is beyond me."

Lucinda remained huddled by the chimney corner.

"What on earth is the matter with you, Miss? There's surely no reason for you to be in such a state." Rose picked up her wooden spoon and resumed the task of preparing the pudding.

"He arranged for this to happen – Doctor Lennox arranged this. That's why he left so early this morning." Lucinda spat the words in a surge of anger.

The housekeeper rounded on her – clearly surprised at Lucinda's furious outburst.

"I'll have you know, Miss, there's no love lost at all between my Doctor Adam and his cousin Giles. Apart from what happened when they was children, it's the great wrong he did him by stealing away the lady he wanted to marry."

"What do you mean?" Lucinda's lips felt stiff and dry. She didn't move from her place by the chimney corner.

"It was a few years ago. Doctor Adam was away tending to a sick friend. In the weeks he was gone, Mr Giles took to calling on Doctor Adam's intended, Miss Amelia Reynolds. It was obvious from the first that he intended to have her. He enticed her father into a card game or two and ruined him – and promised that all would be kept quiet if she agreed to marry him."

"What happened to her?" Lucinda's stomach felt queasy.

"He married her, abused her, and when she showed some spirit and tried to fight back he had her committed to an asylum where she died. He bribed a doctor to sign the papers and then forged Doctor Adam's signature on them."

Lucinda shivered despite the crackling heat of the fire.

"When Doctor Adam found out what had happened to his beloved Amelia he nearly lost his mind. He went straight to the asylum and insisted on seeing her – but he knew as soon as he saw her that she was near death. He stayed with her, comforting her till the end – and then he left England to be with Wellington's army. I think he hoped a bullet would release him from his torment." Rose sat in the chair opposite Lucinda and wiped the tears from her eyes with trembling fingers. "Have you nothing to say, Miss?"

Lucinda was about to tell Rose Dennett how Giles Milburn had tricked her father, and how determined he was to marry her when there was a wail from baby Charlotte, the sound of Hannah getting herself out of bed, and then a loud thump.

"The poor lamb, she's not strong enough yet." Rose got out of her chair and hurried towards the stairs with Lucinda not far behind her, the opportunity to ask further questions lost for the moment.

Chapter 36

Giles Milburn was more determined than ever to find Lucinda. A return visit to Marchington and Orchard House to check on the progress of his 'investment' had revealed a number of problems.

Nobody answered his knock at the door. He stood fuming on the doorstep for several minutes before turning the handle and walking in. The hall table and coat stand were covered in a layer of dust and there were muddy footprints on the flagstones.

"Georgiana," he roared, "where are you?"

There was no answer.

Hearing movement in the kitchen, he went there in search of refreshment after his long journey. Mrs Parsons was there alone, chopping leeks and turnips. The look she gave him left no doubt of how she felt about him.

"Where is my sister?" he asked.

"Gone, sir."

"Gone where?"

"A travelling tinker called at the door wanting to know if there were any pots or pans that needed mending." Mrs Parsons smiled gleefully. "Before you could say 'knife' she was in his arms. 'Oliver' she said over and over again. Then without more ado she'd packed a bag and gone with him. I'll warrant before nightfall he'd have been fixing more than her pots and pans…Three weeks she's been gone now."

"Enough," thundered Giles. "Why is the house in such a disgusting state – and why is there nothing but pigswill to eat?" He'd routed in the cupboards and lifted the lids on the pans bubbling on the stove, crashing them back down with an expression of disgust.

"Miss Georgiana took the housekeeping money with her," said Mrs Parsons. "I've done my best with the little bit she left us. Tilly's left – got a new situation over in Stourton – you can't expect folks to work for no pay.

I'm only staying out of loyalty to Mr Josiah – and Miss Lucinda, wherever she may be."

"That's exactly what I'd like to know," said an imperious voice. An elderly lady dressed in purple and wearing a bonnet shaped like a coal scuttle stood in the hallway leaning on the arm of a liveried footman. She peered at Giles through a lorgnette. "Who are you?"

"My name is Giles Milburn and Lucinda Beckford is my fiancée."

"Indeed?" The lady's eyebrows shot up in surprise. "Nobody consulted me about such an engagement! And where is my great niece? I would like to speak with her."

Giles said nothing.

"Well – I asked a question. Will none of you dolts answer it?" The old lady rapped her cane on the floor in annoyance. "And is nobody going to offer me a dish of tea or a glass of Madeira wine?"

"Miss Lucinda ran away on the night Mr Giles proposed to her," said Mrs Parsons, earning a hostile glare from Giles.

"I'm not surprised," said the lady, sweeping Giles the sort of look she'd give to something the cat brought in. "I must speak to Josiah and find out the truth of the matter." She marched back down the hall and barged into Josiah's study without knocking.

✦

Giles fidgeted and fumed in the kitchen doorway, blustering at Mrs Parsons in frustration. "I could have you turned out without a reference for speaking so freely."

"If you did so, I would have something to say. Mrs Parsons has served this family a long time," said a cool voice.

Giles turned sharply to see the tall figure of Ambrose Leitch appear from the direction of the necessary house.

"God's teeth," he exclaimed. "Does nobody believe in minding their own business in this town?"

"I am concerned with honesty," said Ambrose, "and I suspect there has been foul play in your dealings with this family."

"Lucinda Beckford has been promised to me," said Giles.

"One would hope she had some choice in the matter." The lawyer's cold gaze swept like a moonbeam over Giles.

Giles turned on his heel and left. He intended to find Lucinda Beckford and marry her by special licence as soon as possible.

Giles was now certain that his cousin Adam was sheltering Lucinda Beckford. He'd re-started his search at Lower Warren – the place where Twister had told him the women were. The nervous villagers he spoke to reported that they knew the two women he was talking about, but they had not been seen since the night of the storm.

When Giles thought about his last visit to Court Green when Rose Dennett had barred the door, he was sure he heard the wail of an infant, quickly silenced. Lucinda's companion was expecting a child. Well, let Rose Dennett think she'd seen the last of him. He'd find another way of gaining entry to the house. He wouldn't be satisfied until he'd looked over every stick and stone of the place and assured himself that Lucinda Beckford wasn't there.

He moved as quietly as he could, approaching the village from a different direction. He made sure he couldn't be seen from any of the windows in Adam's house. He was also desperate to avoid the derelict cottage where the mad woman lived who seemed to think he was a long-lost son. Giles shuddered at the memory of her bony hands clutching at his clothes. He tied Black Boy's reins to a tree, before making his way on silent feet towards his cousin's house.

When he got there, he edged round the back of the house until he reached the back door. It was locked and he bit back a cry of frustration.

He resisted the urge to go to the front door and hammer on it until it was opened and then force his way in. "*More haste less speed*," he told himself. "*This time you need to take them all by surprise.*" He carried on round the building checking doors and windows, looking for a place where he might gain entry. His patience was rewarded when he noticed the door that led into the wash-house was open. Some items of clothing hung on the washing line in the adjacent yard.

It was an easy matter to go from the wash-house and along the stone-flagged passageway that led to the kitchen. Giles' nerves were as taut as piano wires and he forced himself to go slowly. The smell of yeast and fresh bread made his stomach growl with hunger. He discovered the pantry in a little alcove off the kitchen and memories stirred of the one from his childhood where he and Georgiana used to steal jam tarts. A plate of honey cakes stood invitingly next to a joint of pork on a stone slab covered with a fly net.

Everything looked so much more inviting than the chaos he'd left behind at Orchard House that Giles felt a stab of jealousy over his cousin's easy existence.

He crammed a honey cake into his mouth just as he heard light footsteps coming down the stairs and heading towards him. He shrank back into the shadows by the scullery door, his heart hammering with excitement and anticipation as he saw Lucinda framed in a sudden shaft of sunlight pouring in through the window behind her.

*

Lucinda had been upstairs helping Hannah to bath baby Charlotte. Hannah's recovery from the birth had been slow and she suffered from frequent bouts of dizziness. Many physicians would have insisted on blood-letting as a cure but Adam said that rest and good food was the best remedy.

"I made tea a few moments ago," said Rose coming upstairs with clean linen. "Now that baby Charlotte's asleep, we could have a little tea party up here with you and try some of my honey cakes."

The baby lay in the drawer lined with a soft blanket that made a make-shift crib, tiny fists curled, and her fair hair like a halo.

"I should be up and about by now," said Hannah. "I cannot imagine my mother-in-law looking after me as well as this had I remained at Lower Warren." The mention of Lower Warren reminded her of her friend Florence Temple and her sad loss.

"Let me fetch it," said Lucinda, noticing how Hannah's eyes had filled with tears. "There is nothing like honey cake for lifting the spirits."

"The tea is in the kitchen and the honey cakes are in the pantry," said Rose turning to admire baby Charlotte again.

*

Lucinda hurried down the stairs. Since her last conversation with Adam, she'd sent a letter to her Great Aunt informing her of her current situation and asking for help. Despite what Rose had said about Giles' previous treatment of Adam, Lucinda still didn't know for certain whether or not she could trust him.

She headed towards the pantry, pausing on the stairs as she did so with a feeling that something was wrong. From the hall window she could see the familiar figure of Agatha Dixon scuttling along the road with her crab-like gait, her ragged layers of clothing fluttering around her like black moths. She would tell Rose when she went upstairs that Agatha had again eluded the long-suffering granddaughter who had returned to look after her. In all likelihood Rose would inform Adam so he could administer a few drops of laudanum to give the old woman some relief from her constant feelings of loss.

Lucinda turned back towards the pantry, stopping when her nostrils detected the smell of cologne that reminded her of being in a crowded dining room with food she was unable to swallow and the unwelcome touch of someone's hands on her body. Her feeling of panic made her feel sick and giddy. She paused for a moment, trying to breathe slowly and deeply, telling herself she was safe here.

When Giles stepped out in front of her as she reached the pantry door, it was as if she'd conjured him with her nightmare thoughts.

She was too scared to utter more than a squeak. She knew she must look like a rabbit she once saw caught in the light of a fox's gaze. Giles stepped forward, breaking the moment, and Lucinda spiralled away from him into the hall, making for the stairs. Her cry for help was stifled as Giles leapt forward clasping one arm round her waist and the other over her mouth. The feel of his hands was hot and clammy and her flesh shrank with distaste.

"You've led me a merry dance," he hissed. His breath smelled of sour wine and tobacco. "You'll not escape this time."

He half carried, half dragged her along the hallway to the drawing room and shut the door, swinging her round so that Lucinda's back was against it. He released his hand from her mouth and fastened his lips against hers, his hands sweeping down her body with frenzied excitement.

Lucinda struggled to be free of him but this only served to excite him more. He picked her up and carried her to the sofa and laid her down on it, pressing his body on top of hers, almost driving the breath out of her lungs.

She felt his hand fumbling with her gown and at last found the strength to retaliate – pushing at him and screaming as loud as she could. Giles swore and hit her across the face, knocking her head against the wooden arm of the sofa.

Lucinda felt his hands on her skin under her petticoats, cold and clammy as the touch of a frog. He fumbled with his breeches and she felt his hardness pressing against her.

"I'll teach you to welcome my advances."

"Never." Lucinda spat at him and raked at his face with her nails.

"You'll not defy me." Giles took her left wrist in a bone-crushing grip that made her scream with pain. He fastened his lips on hers again, bruising them.

As soon as Adam saw Giles' horse tethered in the clearing a short distance from his house, he knew Lucinda was in great danger. He proceeded at a walking pace, even though his stomach churned with impatience to reach home as soon as possible. He dismounted, led his horse round to the stables, and then headed towards the back door.

It was then that he noticed the open door of the wash house and the door beyond swinging loosely on its hinges. He noticed muddy footprints and followed them into the house.

His senses on alert, he noticed the smell of roasting meat and fresh bread, the crackle of the kitchen fire and the scent of apple-wood. These were familiar sounds and smells. He paused. He could hear the wail of baby Charlotte upstairs and the sound of someone talking to her. Then, from behind the closed door of the parlour the sound of a scuffle, a woman's scream.

*

Adam flung open the door. The room was in chaos – small tables turned over, a glass broken and Lucinda lying crushed under Giles on the pale blue velvet sofa, a bruise spreading around a cut on her left cheek. She was fighting to get away and the distraction of Adam opening the door enabled her to summon the strength to push him away, clawing at his face as she did so.

"You little vixen," Giles said.

Adam crossed the room in a couple of strides and grabbed Giles by his collar, pulling him off Lucinda.

"Trust you to turn up when you're not wanted," Giles spat.

Lucinda scrambled away to the furthest corner of the room, wrapping herself in a shawl to cover her torn gown.

Giles aimed a punch at Adam. "It's a pity you weren't killed on the Peninsula."

"The only thing you excel at is mistreating women."

"I'm entitled to do as I wish with my bride-to-be."

"She is not your bride-to-be."

"Fancy her yourself, do you? Let me tell you, she'll be better sport when she's broken in than Amelia ever was."

Adam's punch met its mark with a satisfying crack and Giles lay still on the carpet, a purple bruise spreading along his jaw.

Rose Dennett burst into the room. "Mercy me, what's been going on here?"

"Help me move him outside, please Rose."

Giles was beginning to rouse himself and stagger to his feet.

Rose opened the front door and she and Adam hauled Giles through it and deposited him on the cobbles.

Giles limped along the road towards the place where he'd left Black Boy.

"I been waiting for you," said a familiar voice that sounded like a rusty key in a lock.

To Giles's horror, the old woman grabbed his arm in a vice-like grip. "I knowed them floods would bring you back to me. Folks said they wouldn't but I knowed that what the Lord takes with one hand he gives back with the other."

Giles struggled to get away.

"You've come back to me looking such a fine young man." She peered up at him through a thatch of unruly white hair, maintaining her grip on his arm. "Come indoors now. There's no need for you to go away again."

Giles cast around for a way out. He was thankful to see a black carriage with silver livery pulled by four bay horses approaching and he signalled for the coachman to stop.

It was only when it was too late, he recognised the coachman from his last visit to Orchard House.

As soon as the carriage stopped, the window was abruptly pulled down and a lady's head appeared, adorned with an ornate purple feathered bonnet.

"What is it, Jenkins?"

"Begging pardon my lady, I've just spotted something that didn't agree with me when we were at Marchington."

Giles felt himself the subject of intense scrutiny through a lorgnette. He was aware of his dishevelled appearance and scratched face and the foul-smelling, ragged old woman hanging onto his arm.

"If you have done anything to importune my great niece or any other young woman, then you will be severely dealt with. Jenkins – take me on to Court Green so I can find out the truth in this unsavoury tale. Pascoe, wait here and guard our prisoner."

Pascoe the footman got down from his perch at the back of the carriage and stood where his mistress indicated.

"He's mine," said the old woman, still holding Giles with a vice-like grip. "He's coming with me. Thirty years I been waiting for him to come home."

"You're welcome to him," said Pascoe, ignoring Giles' pleas for help.

*

Lucinda was holding an iron poker, poised ready to strike, when Adam came back into the room. She set it down in the hearth when she saw he was alone and moved closer to him.

"You're hurt," she said. Adam had a cut on his hand and there was blood on his shirt.

"So are you." Adam traced the bruise on Lucinda's cheek with a gentle forefinger.

She swayed and would have fallen if he hadn't caught her in his arms. To Adam's surprise, Lucinda clung onto him as if she would never let go.

"I am so glad you're safe," she said.

"If he'd hurt you, so help me I would have killed him."

Lucinda was surprised to see tears in Adam's eyes as he held her close.

There was the sound of footsteps in the hall and the door burst open. Adam and Lucinda sprang apart.

"Doctor Lennox – what on earth are you doing with my great niece? When I offered to be your benefactress I believed you to be a man of honour and integrity. Lucinda – cover yourself immediately and behave with a little more modesty."

There was the sound of baby Charlotte crying upstairs and Rose hurrying to soothe her.

"What sort of establishment are you running here, Doctor Lennox?" asked the lady. "It sounds more like a menagerie than a respectable household. The sooner I remove my great niece from here, the better as far as I can see. Lucinda, you are to pack your things and come away with me immediately. With luck, we may be able to avoid a scandal."

"I do not wish to leave here," said Lucinda. "Doctor Lennox has proposed and I have accepted."

She saw Adam's eyes sparkle with amusement and his lips curve in a smile.

"Indeed – this is highly irregular, when you already appear to have a man who claims to be your fiancé – even if he is undesirable."

"I never agreed to that marriage," said Lucinda. "My father…,"

"I might have known he'd have something to do with it," said Great Aunt Sophia.

At that moment, Pascoe the footman arrived in the hallway, out of breath and flushed in the face. His livery was spattered with mud and he looked as if he'd been in a fight.

"What is the meaning of this intrusion?" spluttered Great Aunt Sophia. "I do not know what the world is coming to."

"Begging your pardon," said Pascoe, but the prisoner tried to escape and I think he's in trouble, your ladyship."

"What sort of trouble?" Adam was on his feet with Lucinda not far behind him.

Following her ladyship, who was like a schooner in full sail, they went outside. They could hear Giles' cries for help as he tried to mount the restless Black Boy and escape the clutches of an increasingly agitated Agatha Dixon.

He managed to get one foot into the stirrup, but was prevented from mounting properly because Agatha was still hanging onto him with all her strength. She believed her long-lost son had returned safe and well and had no intention of letting go of him.

Black Boy was spooked by the clamour of voices and took off in the direction of Bridgeton, dragging Giles and Agatha in an unlikely embrace through the remains of the flood water.

By the time Adam and Rose's husband Matthew managed to catch up with them and calm the volatile Black Boy, Giles was dead, having hit his head on a rock. They were in time to hear Agatha's last words of happiness that she was dying in the arms of the man she believed to be her beloved son.

Adam returned to Lucinda and took her hands in his.

"It is over now," he said. "You are safe and do not need to marry me if you do not wish to."

"But I do wish to marry you," she said, smiling up at him and returning his gentle kiss.

Epilogue

June 1814

Lucinda and Adam's wedding took place in the little church at Marchington on a golden June afternoon. Great Aunt Sophia, as guest of honour, wore a new gown of lilac shot silk with matching bonnet and acted as if the whole enterprise was her idea.

"I knew you'd make a better match than your mother," she told Lucinda on the morning of the wedding, "although I do believe your father truly loved her."

Lucinda wore a gown of pale pink silk and carried a bouquet of her mother's favourite damask roses. Her dark hair was entwined with pearls and Hannah, as matron of honour, declared her the prettiest bride she'd ever seen.

"Not even your mother was as beautiful," said Josiah, tucking her arm through his as they entered the cool, musty-smelling church.

Adam and Lucinda had eyes only for each other as they exchanged their vows.

They stepped out of the church hand in hand and then ran through the double row of well-wishers throwing rice and rose petals. The afternoon was splashed with golden sunshine and the nearby fields were gilded with buttercups.

"It won't be long afore you're nursing a babe of your own," said Betsy, making sheep's eyes at Adam as she cradled Charlotte in her arms.

Lucinda and Adam exchanged a smile.

Then Hannah, looking down at the pathway below the churchyard, gave a cry and turned pale. She took off at a run towards a man in tattered uniform who was hurrying up the pathway towards them.

"Charlie," she said as she threw herself into the soldier's arms.

The soldier kissed her soundly and swung her round. Then Hannah whispered something in his ear and they hurried hand in hand back towards the bridal party.

There were tears in Charlie's eyes when he held his little daughter for the first time, marvelling at the tight grip she had on his finger. "She's beautiful," he said. "Just like her mother."

Baby Charlotte gazed up at him with big blue eyes.

"Where's John? Is he with you?" asked Lucinda, feeling a tremor of fear that the happiness of the day was about to be spoiled by unspoken news.

"The officers kept asking him for more pictures," said Charlie. "He'd draw anything while we were moving from place to place – cartwheels, birds, houses and people. He's found himself a patron in London just like he always wanted - and a pretty young wife to boot. He'll be paying you a visit as soon as he's finished his latest commissions."

"I've prayed for this every day since Giles played his nasty trick on you," said Hannah holding onto Charlie as if she'd never let him go.

Charlie scowled. "That reminds me – we've got a score to settle with him. Where is he? John and I would've bet money that we'd come home to find you married to him."

"My cousin is dead and it's a long story," said Adam, "but not one that has any place here today."

He and Lucinda gazed at each other as if fearing they were about to wake from a dream. "Today is a time for thinking of the future, not the past – and I'm sure I'm not the only one who would like a glass of cider."

He took Lucinda's hand and together they ran across the golden field.

The End

Thank you for reading

'Fortune's Promise.'

For details of my other publications,

writing courses, talks

and critique service

please see www.writers-toolkit.co.uk

Follow me on Twitter @SueJohnson9

Printed in Poland
by Amazon Fulfillment
Poland Sp. z o.o., Wrocław